Praise for the novels of USA TODAY bestselling author Victoria Dahl

"A delightful romance between two people who struggle to discover their own self-worth."
—*RT Book Reviews* on *Bad Boys Do*

"This is one hot romance."
—*RT Book Reviews* on *Good Girls Don't*

"A hot and funny story about a woman many of us can relate to."
—*Salon.com* on *Crazy for Love*

"*Lead Me On* will have you begging for a reread even as the story ends."
—*Romance Junkies*

"[A] hands-down winner, a sensual story filled with memorable characters."
—*Booklist* on *Start Me Up*

"Dahl has spun a scorching tale about what can happen in the blink of an eye and what we can do to change our lives."
—*RT Book Reviews* on *Start Me Up*

"Dahl smartly wraps up a winning tale full of endearing oddballs, light mystery and plenty of innuendo and passion."
—*Publishers Weekly* on *Talk Me Down*

"Sassy and smokingly sexy, *Talk Me Down* is one delicious joyride of a book."
—*New York Times* bestselling author Connie Brockway

"Sparkling, special and oh so sexy— Victoria Dahl is a special treat!"
—*New York Times* bestselling author Carly Phillips on *Talk Me Down*

**Also available from
Victoria Dahl
and Harlequin HQN**

*Real Men Will
Bad Boys Do
Good Girls Don't
Crazy for Love
Lead Me On
Start Me Up*

And coming soon

Close Enough to Touch

This book is dedicated to Jennifer, who convinced me I could—and should—write this story. I honestly couldn't have done it without you, Jif. Thank you.

ACKNOWLEDGMENTS

Considering the support I've received for this book,
I have a lot of people to thank. First a huge thank-you to
my agent, Amy Moore-Benson, who asked me to write this
story. You were right. I've never had so much fun
writing a book. Thanks for giving me the excuse
and opportunity to spread my wings.

And to Jennifer Echols...thank you for holding my hand
through the first three hundred pages or so. You're an
outstanding writer and a wonderful friend, even if you
don't like my monkey jokes. More important, you always
come up with the perfect book titles. Priceless.

I wouldn't be writing these acknowledgments
if it weren't for my editor, Tara Parsons.
Thank you for taking my characters (and me) under your
wing. You clearly go above and beyond the call of duty.
Your enthusiasm rocks my world!

As always, my family has supported me every single day
of my writing life. Thank you, Bill, for laughing
in the right places, even if you don't do it out loud.
You're my strong, steady hero, and you'd make
a great police chief. Or sheriff.

And thanks to Adam and Ethan
for understanding why I can't play Star Wars
every time you ask. You make me proud. I love you.

Lastly, I want to thank the incredibly generous romance
community. Romance writers are the most supportive
colleagues anyone could hope for. Thank you, specifically,
to Connie Brockway for reading another of my unedited
manuscripts. And thank you to all my online writing
friends for creating such a great community.

Romance readers are, of course, the most generous
readers in the world. You've welcomed this writer
with open arms, and I can't tell you how good that feels.
I hope you enjoy this story!

Talk Me
Down

Dear Reader,

Welcome to Tumble Creek, Colorado!

Tumble Creek is a lot like any other town nestled between the peaks of the Rocky Mountains. The winters are cold, the streets are steep and the scenery is unbelievably beautiful. But there is something a little different about Tumble Creek....

My first idea for this story came years ago, when I was visiting Aspen, Colorado. A road sign pointed the way toward a mountain pass, but warned that the road was "closed in winter." And "winter" lasts at least a good seven months at those altitudes! I wondered what it would be like to spend part of the year only a few minutes from all the amenities and luxuries of Aspen and then spend months completely isolated by the snow. And what would it be like to spend that cozy winter with a really hot man keeping you warm?

The pieces of Tumble Creek began assembling themselves in my mind at that moment years ago. First the little hometown bar appeared, where all the residents—even the respectable ones—hang out on frigid winter nights. Then came the sweet Victorian gingerbread houses, painted blue and pink and yellow, marching up the steep hills. Then that sexy policeman I mentioned above. Everything in Tumble Creek was set up perfectly—a quaint and quiet little mountain hamlet...until I decided to let Molly Jennings return.

I can't tell you how much fun I had watching Molly wreak havoc on her old town and on her old crush, Ben Lawson. Molly might be the girl next door, but she's not the innocent girl Ben remembers. She's something even better.

I hope you love Tumble Creek and its inhabitants as much as I do.

Happy reading!

Victoria Dahl

CHAPTER ONE

MOLLY JENNINGS STOOD frozen in dismay, staring over the tiny coffee section of the tiny Tumble Creek Market. Folgers, Sanka and a few brands she'd never heard of. And not a dark espresso roast in sight.

Instant coffee mixed with the smell of laundry detergent when she drew in a deep, sad breath. She'd forgotten all about small town markets. They didn't carry whole beans or special roasts, though a lonely can of French Vanilla Kreemer lurked at the back of the shelf. Molly shuddered.

Thank God for the Internet or she'd never have a homemade latte again. Or a Hostess Fruit Pie. Molly threw a scornful look at the so-called snack section near the registers. She was holding out hope for the gas station across the street, because she was pretty sure they were legally required to carry All Things Hostess. And CornNut.

"Ooo, CornNuts," Molly murmured, suddenly perking up. She hadn't had those since high school. She hoped they still made the barbecue flavor.

Grabbing a can of Folgers before she could think too much about it, Molly tossed it in her cart and pushed toward the frozen food section.

The teenager stocking baby formula barely looked up as Molly passed. Clearly, Moe Franklin no longer managed the store. He'd ruled with an iron fist and a frighteningly loud voice, and had hated teenagers with a passion. Thieves and punks, every one of them, according to good old Moe.

So things had changed around Tumble Creek, but that was fine. The past ten years had changed Molly, too. She'd left behind a gorgeous loft in Denver, along with a lively social life and, hopefully, a bad case of writer's block. Not to mention the cause of that writer's block: the bastard burning all the happiness from her life, otherwise known as Cameron Kasten, stalker ex-boyfriend.

Cameron was now a four-hour drive away on a good day, and Molly was starting fresh. No need to look over her shoulder or scan a store before walking into it. No need to skip a party at a friend's place because *he* would be there. Funny how a simple thing like that could cheer you up.

Another thing cheering her up...the possibility that she might have sex again sometime in her young life. Not that moving to a town of fifteen-hundred people would normally offer outstanding sex prospects, but she did have a specific person in mind....

She hadn't seen him in ten years, but Ben Lawson had been kind enough to make an appearance in her imagination almost every day, usually buck naked and looking for a good time, bless his heart.

She smiled at her reflection in the freezer door, but her smile chilled to ice when she saw the selection. Not exactly a Wal-Mart Supercenter spread, another drawback for a woman like Molly. Tumble Creek had only one diner and she couldn't very well eat there every day. Probably.

Man, she was already missing her favorite Thai restaurant. Mouth watering at the thought of spicy noodles, Molly reached into the freezer and pretended she wasn't buying frozen mac and cheese.

"That all, Chief?" a girl's voice asked, sounding barely awake. Despite the bored tone, those words sprang Molly's shoulders straight. She pushed her cart quickly toward the high-pitched beep of the register and stopped at the end of the aisle, frozen solid by an arresting sight.

A startling, terrifyingly *gorgeous,* arresting sight.

Him. And not in her imagination this time.

Ben Lawson had been her very first thought when she'd heard about her aunt's will and known she might be moving back to Tumble Creek. But she hadn't honestly realized what the sight of him would do to her.

He was perfect. Still. Harder and more muscular than the last time she'd seen him, which suited her grown-up tastes just fine. Also, he was clothed, a stark change from their last meeting. But the clothes were just fine, too. Faded, broken-in jeans and a deep brown uniform shirt. The sleeves were rolled up to reveal strong forearms that glinted with golden hair.

He nodded at the clerk, handing her some cash. His serious eyes were the same dark chocolate she'd pictured in so many late-night fantasies. His eyes were almost the same shade as his hair, which she supposed should have been boring, but the combination had always fascinated her. Those eyes crinkled a little in Ben's version of a smile. And then they rose and locked with hers.

They were separated by twenty feet, but Molly was sure she felt his shock reach out and hit her. His eyes widened. His hands froze on his wallet, a dollar bill pushed halfway in. The clerk glanced over her shoulder toward Molly, and that snapped him out of his shock. Molly watched him say "Thank you" as he grabbed a small plastic sack and stepped away from the counter. Away from the entrance. Toward her.

He remembered her, of course he did, and Molly was horrified that she found that so gratifying. *You are not seventeen anymore,* she chastised herself as his body grew larger in her vision, making her feel small in a very good way.

"Molly?" That tentative word rumbled from his chest and gave her goose bumps.

"Ben! Hi! It's been a long time, huh?"

Uh-oh. Wrong thing to say. He looked stunned again, and a dull flush crept over his face.

Yes, it had been a long time—ten years—and there was a reason for that. He was thinking of the last time she'd seen him, and now *she* was thinking of the last time she'd seen him. Hoo boy. She felt her own face heat in response.

Ben cleared his throat. "I, uh…" His mouth thinned and he nodded, perhaps chastising himself as Molly had done moments before. *You are the chief of police now.*

Pull it together. "I'm sorry about your aunt Gertie. She was a lively woman."

Lively indeed. Violently opinionated was more like it. "My mom always said Gertie was too stubborn to die, but all the same, it wasn't unexpected."

He tipped his head. "I'd heard she left you the house, but no one expected you'd move from Denver. Are you here to put it on the market?"

"Nope."

Wariness crept into his eyes. "Closing it up for winter?"

"Nope, sorry. I'm actually moving in."

The wariness shut down to a cold blankness that Molly imagined served him well as chief of police. "Moving in," he repeated.

"Yep. My stuff should be here in about an hour."

"You're moving back to town?" His eyes swept down her body before they jerked back to her face, and Molly was reminded that she wasn't exactly dressed to impress.

She had on a pair of loose khakis and a T-shirt that was almost as old as her beat-up Keds. Her dark blond hair was pulled back into a messy ponytail. Thank God she wasn't wearing shorts. She hadn't shaved her legs in a week, theorizing that October in the mountains was pretty darn cold and she might need the extra layer of insulation.

Molly swept a look over his body just as he'd done hers. Cold or not, she was going to shave.

"But you work down in Denver, don't you?" he finally managed.

His face had gone impassive with innocence, but Molly wasn't fooled. Ben was her brother's best friend. No way was he unfamiliar with The Molly Jennings Question.

She smiled up into his deep-brown eyes and winked. "Nice try, Chief." He raised both eyebrows, silently protesting confusion, but she was unmoved. "Speaking of work, congratulations on making it to chief so quickly."

His head tilted in acknowledgement. "Nobody else wanted the job."

"Wow, such modesty." Oops.

Ben blushed again, and then she blushed, knowing exactly what he was thinking about, picturing it until the heat spread from her face to her whole body.

"Well…" Ben stuck out his hand and when she took it, he gave her a curt, professional shake. "Welcome back to town, Molly. I'll see you around." Before she could respond, he was gone, the door of the market closing behind him and cutting off an excellent view.

Molly Jennings. Good Lord.

Ben changed out of his uniform and into his running clothes, suddenly wishing he was a smoker. He needed a cigarette. Or a drink. But a run was going to have to do since he was back on duty in a few hours. Frank was on vacation for the next couple days, and with a police force of four and a half, that meant overtime for everyone else, including the chief.

He gathered his phone and keys, then stopped on his way out the door to grab a lead-weighted stick. He'd seen too many cougar and bear attacks in his lifetime not to be cautious. Spring was far more dangerous than fall, but there was no reason to be careless.

Careless. Like he'd been when he'd seen Molly standing there in the grocery store like some vision from his most embarrassing dream. Ben grimaced and pushed his body into a fast run without bothering with any warm-up. Hell, he was warm enough already. He'd blushed like a damn schoolgirl at the sight of her. Another mortifying moment with Molly Jennings.

But he wasn't some twenty-two-year-old kid anymore. And she definitely wasn't seventeen. She'd looked fresh and natural and fully mature, standing there with her dark-gold ponytail swaying and her belly just peeking out between ratty cargo pants and a tight baby-blue T-shirt.

God, he loved cargo pants. Strange, probably, but they always seemed to hug a woman's ass just right. Thankfully he hadn't been treated to the sight of Molly's ass, because the rest of her had been more than enough.

Ben pushed his body up the steep incline where the road ended, then turned left onto a worn trail. The trail just happened to follow the ridge that ran behind Molly's house, but it was his favorite route and he wasn't going to change it just to avoid her. And if he happened to glance down into her back windows as he passed, that was only natural. Of course he was curious. They'd been friends, or at least he'd been around her all the time in their youth. And sure, he'd thought her utterly cute as a teenager, but she'd also been his best friend's underage little sister. Completely off-limits. Now she was twenty-seven…and still completely off-limits.

He didn't date women who lived in Tumble Creek. Too much talk, too many complications. If there was anything worse than being lovers in a very small town, it was being ex-lovers. The definition of messy. So Ben pretty much confined himself to women outside the town, and since half the roads were closed in winter, whatever affairs he did have were seasonal.

Molly would be here year-round. Or maybe not. Maybe she was just here for the winter. Maybe she'd stay for a few months and then leave for another ten years.

That decade in Denver had been good to her. She was slim without being skinny, curvy and firm in just the right places. And her sparkling green eyes were livelier than he'd remembered. More confident. Knowledgeable even.

Ben shook off the dangerous thought and ran higher up the path. The trail forked here, one path cutting back to the street, the other toward a ridgeline that eventually curved out to look over the wide valley west of town. The sun shone bright and warm, the air just crisp enough to cool his sweat but not nearly cold enough to numb his roiling emotions.

Breathing in the scent of turning aspen, he headed toward the ridge and did his best to breathe out the memories of Molly that insisted on flitting through his mind.

He was still in the thick of the trees when his phone beeped. "Lawson," he said into the phone.

"Chief," the voice of his secretary/receptionist/dispatcher answered. "It's Brenda. Are you home?"

"Not quite, why?"

"Oh, we've got a small problem. Andrew's over to the Blackmound place, helping round up some cattle that broke through the fence. Now there's a big moving truck taking up half of Main Street and it can't get through. Jess Germaine's car is in the way and he's not answering his door."

Ben grunted and slowed his pace. The situation would probably resolve itself by the time he got back down the ridge, but then again, if Jess was sleeping off a few drinks...

"All right. Give me twenty minutes. Call if Jess shows up."

"Right. Say, what's a moving truck doing here?"

He felt his jaw jump with tension. Thank God no one knew about his brief, inadvertent history with Molly or there'd be delighted whispering all around town. "Molly Jennings is back," he made himself say calmly.

And damned if she wasn't causing him trouble already. It was going to be a hell of a long winter.

EVEN AFTER WEEKS of vacancy, Aunt Gertie's house still looked spotless. Only the faintest sheen of dust dared to disturb the wood floors. No dust bunnies skittered when she moved.

And it'd likely never be this clean again. Molly took a good look around before she unpacked the computer and set it up on a desk in the dining room.

She didn't have a big table and chairs; though her loft in Denver had been everything she'd wanted, it had also been small. So Aunt Gertie's dining room was no more. It was now Molly's office. Wouldn't the old woman have been horrified?

I leave my home to my grandniece, Molly Jennings, in the hope that she will abandon her unsavory city life and move back to the bosom of God's country where she belongs.

Molly grinned and shook her head. Oh, she'd moved back all right, but she'd brought her unsavory life right along with her.

One push of a button and the computer hummed to life, prompting her grin to widen. Her work had ground to a halt in Denver thanks to the stress of living with constant anxiety, but here…here she was already finding inspiration.

The mystery of what she did for a living would take on a whole new life here in Tumble Creek, but she'd braced herself for that. And all the gossip and speculation would be worth it if Ben Lawson proved as wonderful a muse as he had been ten years before. Yes, indeedy.

She moved a few things around her desktop, and even opened a new, blank document. The tingly feeling that started in her stomach reminded her of the joy she'd taken in her work up until six months ago. Not as good as sex, but very close to being turned on.

Her blossoming good mood popped like a bubble when a familiar tune sang from her purse. Molly dug around until she found her phone, then groaned at the sight of the caller ID. "Wonderful."

She could just ignore it, but he'd call back. And then another one would call. Then the big kahuna himself. Cameron.

Not bothering to hide her impatience, Molly answered the call. "What?"

"Hey, Molly! It's Pete!"

"I know."

"How are you?"

She clicked around on her computer screen, opening random documents, wondering how many CornNuts were left in the bag in her purse. "Great."

"Are you really living in the mountains? I hope you're not planning on staying there. That's dangerous driving during the winter."

"I've moved here, Pete. It's done."

"We'll see what you think after a long, cold winter."

Molly groaned. "I know I'm a helpless, stupid female, but I did grow up here. Some knowledge of my surroundings managed to sink in over those eighteen years."

"Hey, you inherited a house, and that's exciting! I'm sure you want to try it out. But your condo hasn't sold yet. There's no need to make any decisions—"

"Did Cameron ask you to call?" she finally snapped.

"What? No. We're all concerned about you, Molly—"

"Who? Cameron and his band of merry men?"

"Molly, come on. We're friends. I just—"

"No, Pete," she interrupted. "No, we are not friends. If we were friends I would have made you a bracelet and painted your toenails. We would have laughed about how small my first boyfriend's penis was. We would have flirted with men over appletinis. We are not friends, we were *dating,* Pete. Until someone else swooped in and stole your little heart away."

"Huh?" She could almost hear him crinkling his forehead. "No one stole my heart. We both decided it wasn't working out."

"By 'both,' I assume you mean you and Cameron?"

"Hey, what are you implying?"

"I'm implying that Cameron seduced you away from me. Just like he's seduced every man I've dated since he and I broke up."

"That's sick!" Pete yelped.

"Yes, it is sick. Not that you or Michael or Devon seems to mind. You're all so eager to hang out with Mr. Wonderful Personality! *Jesus.*"

"Cameron's right," Pete muttered. "You've got problems."

"Yes! Yes, I have problems!" she screamed into the phone just before it went dead in her hand. Molly stared at it, panting in rage. They'd followed her to Tumble Creek. Cameron and his boy band of Molly's former potential sex partners.

She really couldn't allow that. She'd have to ditch the cell phone. She'd keep her aunt's local number. Her brother had it. Her editor had it. Plus her parents, and they'd finally gotten over their addiction to Cameron.

Cameron Kasten—*Supervising Sergeant* Cameron Kasten—was the star hostage negotiator for the Denver Police Department. His job was to manipulate, coerce, seduce and negotiate. And he was damn good at it. Everybody loved him. His friends, *her* friends, the whole darn police department. Paramedics, firefighters, district attorneys and any damn male of the species that Molly dared to date.

No one believed that he was ruining her life. He hadn't been able to talk Molly into staying with him, so he'd talked every man since out of her life. It was creepy. Not to mention frustrating. Cameron was a giant whirlpool sucking all the sex out of her world.

Or maybe not *all* of it.

She thought again of Ben Lawson, of his familiar brown eyes and big hands and…oh, so much more. He would make a glorious end to this dry spell. She just had to keep Cameron as far away from Tumble Creek as possible.

"Satan, be gone," she said to the phone as she purposefully turned it off.

Molly was back in Tumble Creek, Colorado, and she was ready to pick up just where she'd left off…with Ben Lawson naked and at her mercy.

Only this time she'd actually know what to do with him.

CHAPTER TWO

"CHIEF?"

Ben snapped awake from a quick doze in front of the computer. "Yeah?"

Brenda's bangs brushed her thick eyebrows when she shook her head. "It's 8:00 a.m. You need to go home and get some rest. You've got a whole twenty-four hours off."

"Right." He looked over the schedule for December once more before closing it. It was fairly straightforward. Winter made for slow work in Tumble Creek. No mountain biking, no rafting, and the pass to Aspen was snowed in until May. After the craziness of spring, summer and fall, it was a much-needed break.

And speaking of Aspen... Ben rubbed his eyes and glanced toward the ancient clock hanging in the hallway. Quinn Jennings had to be in his office by now. The man was obsessive when it came to his work.

A woman answered on the first ring. "Jennings Architecture."

"Is Quinn available?"

"Good morning, Chief Lawson. Yes, he's in. Please hold."

Ben nodded as the phone clicked to silence. He'd

tried friendly conversation with Quinn's receptionist, but the woman was having none of it.

"Ben," Quinn grumbled when he came on the line, absorbed as he always was in some design.

"Put the pen down and back away slowly."

"Huh?"

Ben rolled his eyes. "I learned the last time I called not to have a conversation with you while you're drawing. I sat in that damned hoity-toity bar until nine o'clock."

"Right. Did I mention I was sorry about that? I honestly had no memory of the conversation."

"That's my point," Ben grunted in answer. "So you never mentioned that your sister was moving back to town."

"Oh, yeah. She seemed to make up her mind real quick about it. I only found out last week."

"You sure about that?"

"Well, she claims to have mentioned it in September, but I'd swear she's lying."

"Uh-huh."

"So is she there? Would you check on her for me? Mom's worried."

Ben shifted in his seat and ran a hand through his hair. "You want me to stop by her place?"

"Yeah, you know. Check out the security. Single woman with an obsessive mother."

"She lived by herself in the big, bad city. I think she'll be fine here."

"Tell that to my mom. She's convinced Molly will

fire up the woodstove without opening the flue and die from smoke inhalation. Or was it carbon monoxide?"

Ben looked at the clock again. Eight-fifteen. Was she up yet? Dressed? Half-naked and heavy-eyed? "Okay, I'll drop by."

"Thanks."

"Mmm-hmm." Just a favor for a friend. "Hey, you guys must have found out what Molly does for a living by now, right?"

"Nope. All I know is she swears it's legal."

"So why won't she say?" His mind began to churn through all sorts of unsavory possibilities.

"Who knows? I think she's just stuck with the mystery of it now. It'd be damn anticlimactic to own up to being an IRS agent at this point. She's fine and she's healthy and I've finally convinced Mom to leave it at that."

Shit. He'd already used Google to search her name and had come up with nothing. He didn't like mysteries. Not many cops did.

Ben promised one more time to check on Molly— did she sleep in pajamas? Nothing at all?—said a quick goodbye to Quinn and grabbed his hat and coat.

Just a favor for a friend. It had nothing to do with Molly's tight blue T-shirt or the glimpse he'd caught of her moving through her kitchen when he'd come back down the path yesterday. It had nothing to do with the wicked sparkle in her eyes when she'd smiled up at him at the store. It certainly didn't matter that he'd spent a good part of his shift wondering if her ass was as perky as it had been ten years ago.

Damn, she'd driven him crazy that summer, always dropping by in little shorts and tank tops that he wasn't supposed to notice on a sweet, innocent girl like Molly. So he'd forced himself not to notice. He'd known her since she was a baby. Her smooth, tanned legs didn't exist for him. Neither did her firm breasts or round bottom. Nope. Nothing there.

And they didn't exist now, either. She was just another citizen. A responsibility. A favor for a friend. One who was surely awake and fully dressed.

Ben had assumed his strictest police mien by the time he pulled his black SUV up to her house on Pine Road. Then he saw the car in her driveway and his jaw dropped.

His fist hit her door a little harder than he meant, but after two minutes there was still no answer. He knocked again, then made himself take a deep breath and count slowly to twenty. The door opened on nineteen.

"Tell me that is not your car."

She hid her mouth behind a hand and yawned. "Hey, Ben."

"You've got another vehicle in the garage, right?"

"The garage is full of boxes."

"You can't drive that up here in the winter."

She leaned out a little to look past him toward the blue Mini Cooper. "I put snow tires on before I left Denver. It's fine."

"No. No, it's not fine. First of all, I'm almost entirely certain they don't make twelve-inch snow tires. Second, you're going to get high-centered on the first rut of snow you drive over. Third, you will then be crushed by one of the three-hundred SUVs driven by the saner citizens of this town."

She leaned against the door jamb and nodded sagely. "Mmm. Fascinating. Did my mother call you?"

"No, but she will call. And I don't have the manpower to drive by your place every time it snows just to reassure her. And I definitely don't have the manpower to rescue you from your own driveway twice a week."

"I've already arranged with Love's Garage to have it plowed."

"Okay, I don't have the manpower to rescue you from the grocery store parking lot every Saturday."

She crossed her arms and smiled up at him. "You're kind of sexy when you're in charge. Has anyone ever told you that?"

That was when he noticed her shirt. Her long, worn-out, practically translucent white T-shirt. Her naked legs. The bare feet tipped by painted pink toes. She yawned again, then shivered, clearing up any mystery about whether she was wearing a bra.

"I apologize," Ben said, his tone carefully formal. "Did I wake you?"

"Yes, but I'll have to keep some sort of civilized schedule here or I'll get awfully lonely. No one else stays up till three around here. Actually, maybe you do. It'd be just you and me…and the snowplows."

Just you and me…

"I really, really like your hat," she added with that twinkle in her eye again. "Really."

Ben found himself reaching up self-consciously to touch the brim and made his hand jerk back to his side.

It was the same kind of Stetson most law enforcement wore in the Rockies. Nothing special enough to make her look so…naughty.

"Back to the car," he growled. "If it can be called that."

Molly opened the door wider and a breeze swept in, molding the shirt to her chest. Ben almost swallowed his tongue at the sight of hard nipples outlined so lovingly by thin white cotton.

"You want some coffee?"

She turned, leaving the door open for him, and Ben stepped inside in self-defense. He had to close the door before another gust of wind caught her shirt, because he did *not* need to get that well acquainted with the curve of her ass. Even if his brain was giving a little victory whoop.

"Jesus," he muttered, and stayed next to the door. It was time to go. He couldn't remember why he'd come in the first place. She still needed waking up about that toy car, but now was the time for a strategic retreat.

"You want cream and sugar?" she called from the kitchen.

"No, I—"

The jangle of an old-fashioned phone interrupted him.

"Hold on!" Molly called.

Ben heard her answer cheerfully, then her voice dropped to an ominous note that brought all his cop instincts to life.

"Where did you get this number?" she growled.

Ben headed straight for the kitchen.

"Yes, I turned my cell off. Take the hint, Cameron."

He slowed as he came to the white molding that outlined the kitchen archway, but she'd stopped talking.
She stood with her hand pressed to her forehead, mur-
muring "Mmm-hmm," every once in a while.

She squeezed her eyes shut, then opened them to
catch Ben staring at her. Eyebrows flying high with
alarm, she whipped around to face the sink, but he could
still hear her side of the conversation.

"No. Is that clear enough? *No.* Now goodbye."

Her smile was bright and cheerful when she spun
back around, still clutching the phone. "The coffee's
almost done!"

"Who was that?"

"Who?"

"On the phone."

The wide smile didn't budge as she shook her head
in patently false confusion.

"'Cameron,' I think you said."

"Oh, *Cameron!* He's just a guy from Denver."

"An ex kind of guy?"

"Huh?" She raised her hands, palms up, and frowned
as if he'd just asked if Cameron were a superhero. "Of
course not. No. Why?"

"No reason." More secrets. Perfect.

"So, cream and sugar?" She moved through the small
kitchen with easy grace, completely comfortable wearing almost nothing in front of him. Who *was* this girl
he'd known his whole life? This girl with secrets and…
and…*nipples?*

"Yes," he heard himself answering. "Cream and sugar."

She flashed a smile over her shoulder as she poured. "A real man's man, huh? Confident enough to drink girly coffee? I'm impressed."

"*Girly* coffee? Wow. Thanks, Molly."

"I said I was impressed."

"Right."

She handed him a cup, then leaned against the counter with her own mug clasped between two hands. Ben was very aware of her eyes taking him in, pausing on his chest and his mouth. He was very aware of her thighs, golden and rounded and *totally off-limits* and what the *hell* was he still doing here?

He closed his eyes and raised the cup to his mouth.

"So…" she said. "About that night…"

Coffee exploded into his windpipe, burning and choking him. He wheezed and coughed until he could breathe again, then opened his eyes to her stunned laughter.

"Are you okay?" she gasped.

"You did that on purpose."

"Did what?"

Ben set his cup down with a thunk. "I'd better go."

"It's been ten years, Ben. I just wanted to apologize. I should never have walked in like that. And I certainly shouldn't have watched."

He froze in the act of turning away. His muscles seized up as prickly heat spread over his skin and horror turned his stomach. "Excuse me?"

"I didn't know you had, um, company. And then I was just…"

"What the hell do you mean, you *watched?*"

"Oh…well…"

"No. I looked up and you were standing there in the doorway. You'd just walked in."

"Yeah, um…there may have been a few seconds between my walking in and you noticing me. You were a little distracted by that blonde. She was—"

"*I know what she was doing.* Jesus, Molly."

"Right. Anyhoo… I just wanted to say I'm sorry if I caused you any embarrassment."

Embarrassment? More like abject torture. Mortification. Guilt. The knowledge that he'd corrupted a young girl. The utter shock in her eyes when Ben had looked up to see her there, both hands pressed to her mouth. The endless moment when his muscles had refused to react, when he'd tried to stop his date's avid attentions. Ben hadn't been able to fully enjoy a blow job for two years afterwards.

And now Molly was confessing that she'd been standing there for…how long?

"Oh, Jesus." He pressed a sweaty hand to his forehead. "You were just a kid."

"Ah… Yeah, not really. I lost my virginity that night, and I turned eighteen a week later. And then there was college."

"Stop it!" Ben slammed both hands over his ears. "Oh, my *God!*"

Her muffled laugh echoed through his head. "Ben, what is wrong with you?"

A picture of himself suddenly flashed before his eyes. He was standing in Molly Jennings's kitchen with his eyes clenched shut and his hands over his ears. Ben forced his heart to slow and lowered his hands. *A little dignity here, Chief.*

He let out a long breath. "You were like a little sister to me. It was very disturbing."

"Oh, it disturbed me as well. But if it makes you feel any better…" She leaned closer as if to confess a secret. One corner of her soft mouth quirked up. "You were never like a brother to me, Ben Lawson."

"I…"

She leaned closer still, just six inches away. Ben could smell coffee and something soft and sweet. Her shampoo or lotion or some other feminine thing. Her lips flushed a dusky pink that drew his eyes like a magnet as they smiled at him.

"And you *definitely* weren't like a brother to me after that night."

"Molly…" Good God. "I don't suppose you're just staying for the winter, are you?"

She pulled back and frowned. "No, why?"

"No reason. I've gotta go. Get a real car and check the flue before you fire up the woodstove. Bye."

"Thank you, Officer!" she called as he rushed for the door.

The cold air slapped him back to reality as soon as he stepped outside. Ben slammed the door behind him and made himself stop rushing. He rolled his shoulders and set his jaw.

Yes, Molly had grown up into a hot woman, but she was still off-limits. Nothing had changed. *Nada.*

He was almost to his truck when a white pickup approached from the west. It slowed, coming nearly to a stop before it rolled by Ben's truck. Through the window, Ben spied the gawking, wrinkled face of Miles Webster, proprietor of the town's biweekly newspaper, if one could call it that.

"Shit," Ben whispered.

He met Miles's eyes, careful not to show trepidation or guilt. *You've got nothing on me, old man,* he transmitted through his gaze. Then the man's eyes shifted, and Ben followed, turning to look toward Molly's house.

There she stood, waving, framed like a picture in the doorway, the early morning light glowing off her bare legs.

"Oh, *shit,*" Ben groaned.

Miles offered a smug grin when Ben turned back, then he sped off in a cloud of diesel fumes.

Ben had managed to stay out of the paper's gossip section for thirty-two years. Come Thursday that was going to change.

And if there was anything he hated more than secrets, it was scandal.

HER COMPUTER SEEMED to be purring at her when Molly sat down to work that morning. Or maybe that was just her body. She'd gotten her groove back and she could feel it. Hoo-yeah.

She knew what her next story would be. Months had passed with not a flicker of an idea, but now she knew.

A serious, hard-jawed cowboy. No, wait. *A sheriff.* Not in a mountain town, though. She'd made that mistake before. She would use Ben Lawson again, but only for inspiration this time, not as the flesh-and-blood man made into fantasy.

Her first story, the one that had made her into a star, the one that still sold better than any of her other books…that had been far too close for comfort. She'd written about Ben, about *that* night. She'd even identified him as the best friend of the heroine's older brother. In a small mountain town. In Colorado. Then suddenly her first attempt at erotic fiction had been sold, published, and read by thousands…and it was far too personal. She couldn't tell anyone what she'd done.

The big secret of her life had been entirely accidental, but she supposed it was for the best. She had a wonderful career that she loved, a decent income, and a little mystery to go along with her boring life. And now she had her muse back.

That first book had been her most inspired, but she had a feeling she could make this one even hotter. She was older and wiser and she had a few good ideas of what she'd like to do with a certain hard-jawed police chief.

"Sheriff," she corrected herself. "A sheriff in a Wild West town with dark brown eyes and a heart of steel. And maybe some kinky needs he just can't satisfy with the God-fearing women of the county."

Molly giggled in guilty delight. Oh, yeah. *The sheriff is a lonely man until a mysterious widow moves in next door. A widow who leaves her curtains open at*

*night, lamps blazing. Even an angel would be tempted
to watch the show, and the sheriff is far from angelic.
But indecent exposure is a crime, and the lawman is
determined to make her pay with his own special kind
of private discipline.*

She pictured Ben in his jeans—unbuttoned—and
his black cowboy hat tilted low over his face, and nothing else.

"This," Molly murmured as she typed the first few
words, "is going to be good."

CHAPTER THREE

STRIPPER.

Ben wrote the word in his notebook in black ink and underlined it. Then he crossed it off.

That couldn't be right. Sure, she'd started some mystery career during college, and plenty of good, nice, college girls had been sucked into dancing for money, but it still couldn't be right. There were no strip clubs up here. Whatever she was doing, she had to be able to do it from home. Stripping was good money, but she couldn't have saved enough to retire at twenty-seven.

Unless she was one of those headliners who traveled the country and got paid big bucks to dance at the best clubs. Maybe he shouldn't have crossed it off so quickly.

Or maybe he'd seen too many HBO specials in his life.

Ben threw the pen onto the flimsy newspaper open on his desk and turned back to the computer to search for her on Google one last time. His name was there in black and white in the weekly rag, right next to hers. He wanted to find out her secret before Miles Webster did.

Good old Miles had ruined Ben's high school years. Or more accurately, Ben's father had ruined those years, and Miles Webster had gleefully magnified each painful moment, drawing out the scandal until every last detail—true or not—had been reported.

Ben had hated Miles for years, perhaps because it had been so hard to hate his own father. Hard, but not necessarily impossible. Not for a teenager anyway.

Still, he'd worked through all that, or thought he had, but seeing his name in Miles's gossip column was burning a hole in his gut.

> And our dedicated Chief Lawson added a new duty to his job description this week. He played welcoming committee to Tumble Creek's newest citizen, visiting her in the early morning hours to offer a friendly and thorough hello. And who is this new citizen? Our very own Molly Jennings, returning to a hometown that welcomes her with open arms. Check back next week for more information on what Molly's been up to for the past decade!

"More information," Ben snarled. Miles was going to love this.

What a fiasco. He was going to have to avoid her like the plague, at least until he figured out her secret. What if she'd been a prostitute, for God's sake?

"You've lost your mind," he muttered to himself. He was not going to let Miles drive him crazy again. He was an adult now, not some tortured kid.

"Chief?" Brenda asked from the doorway. "You're not upset about that column, are you?"

"No." Ben closed the Google screen and reopened the report he was supposed to be working on.

"He's got no right to gossip about you when you're doing your job."

"It's nothing, Brenda. I was just doing a favor for a friend. No big deal."

She nodded, but her eyebrows fit together like two puzzle pieces. "How's Molly Jennings holding up?"

"Fine."

"I suppose she's…" Brenda tapped her fingernails together and shrugged. "She must be real different after living in the city so long."

Different. Ben frowned at his computer. Yeah, she was different.

"Chief?"

"What?" He glanced up just in time to catch Brenda shaking her head as she headed back toward her desk by the front door.

Disgusted with himself, Ben forced his mind back to his Monday duties. He reviewed the report he'd finally finished, then sent it off to the Creek County Sheriff's office. They kept in close coordination so Sheriff Mc-Teague didn't have to waste time patrolling this part of the county. If anything needed his attention, Ben got in touch. If Ben needed something—rescue equipment or a search party—the sheriff volunteered it.

A few minutes later, the sheriff's own report popped up on the screen and Ben took a half hour to go over the whole thing. Nothing out of the ordinary. A few accidents. One dead moose in the middle of the highway. Two DUIs. Domestic incidents.

Ben memorized the names involved and printed out the document to add to his files. Done.

A weather alert popped to life on his screen and Ben scanned it quickly, then breathed a sigh of relief. The first big snowstorm of the season, but it looked like they'd only catch the edge of it. Good thing, since it was supposed to hit on Halloween night. The poor kids around here had a hard enough time with the steep streets, sloped lawns and ancient, icy steps leading to every door. And the teenagers would have the inevitable party—the same Halloween party every generation had had in this town for forty years—and Ben didn't want them driving home in a whiteout.

With a reluctant smile, Ben thought of the costume party he'd been to when he was sixteen, the last one they'd managed to throw in one of the old mines. Damn, that had been a good one, complete with strip poker and smuggled tequila. And he was darn glad it'd been the last. The idea of a party in an abandoned silver mine had been exciting as hell as a kid, but it scared the shit out of him now.

Ben made a mental note to go check the locks on all the mine gates sometime in the next four days. A drunk kid falling down a mine shaft would haunt him for the rest of his life.

"Chief, I'm heading out to lunch," Brenda interrupted.

"I'll walk you out. It's time for my patrol." He grabbed his hat and, with a glance out his small window, reached for his quilted uniform coat as well. Snow or not, a cold front had moved in with a vengeance. "You haven't heard anything about the old mines, have you? I thought I'd better check the gates before Halloween. Remember that last bash when we were kids?"

Brenda's face blossomed into a rare smile that made her pale-blue eyes sparkle. "Well, I don't know what you remember, but my night ended when Jess Germaine threw up all over my new boots."

"That's right. I had to take both of you home, then go wash out my dad's truck."

"You always were a gentleman."

Ben opened the door and gestured her through with a wink. Brenda was laughing as she passed him, but when he tried to follow he walked right into her back.

"Sorry. Is something—"

"Hi!" Molly said to both of them from the bottom of the steps.

Ben nudged Brenda to get her to move out of the doorway and down the three steps to the sidewalk. Molly grinned up at them, a pink, fuzzy hat pulled low over her ears. Her wool coat was feminine and way too white to be practical, but at least it was warm.

"Hey, lovah," she said to Ben. "I hear we're a hot item. You move fast for a big man."

He stumbled on the last step—the cement must have buckled this summer—and had to lock his knees to keep from falling.

"That's not funny," Brenda said. "Chief Lawson hates gossip."

"Oh, I'm— Oh." Molly grimaced. "I totally forgot about that. Sorry."

Ben shook his head. "No big deal. Brenda, I'll see you when I get back."

Brenda hurried off, glancing back to scowl in Molly's direction more than once.

Molly watched her go. "*Brenda?* Oh my God, is that Brenda White? She looks just like her…um, never mind. Wasn't she in your class?"

"Yes." Ben scanned the block, looking for Miles's old pickup.

"Ben, I'm sorry. I forgot about that thing with your dad. I didn't mean to get you into Miles's column."

"Not your fault." Great, now she was feeling sorry for him. "It's really no big deal. That was a long time ago."

Her face brightened, eyes sparkling once more, and Ben was shocked again at how different she was. The same, almost, but more. No longer hesitant or self-conscious, she practically oozed assurance, as if the constant flow of people in the city had burnished her to a lovely glow.

She'd braided her hair into two little pigtails that followed the line of her long neck. She looked soft there… really soft.

"Sooo…" she said. "I was just coming over to tease you about the paper, but now I want to see the station." She looked behind him toward the double doors.

"It looks the same as it did ten years ago."

"Well, I don't know what you were doing with *your* youth, Ben, but I never saw the inside of the police station. I was a good girl."

Jesus. He successfully fought off the blush this time,

which was a great relief. She seemed to take joy in embarrassing him.

Ben opened his mouth to explain that he was leaving and couldn't give her a tour, but then he noticed that her nose was beginning to resemble the color of her hat. She clasped her pink-mittened hands together and blew against them.

"All right. Come in." He waved her up and followed behind her. Yes, her ass looked perfectly perky in tight jeans. Round and succulent. Two little globes of—

"Off-limits," he whispered. When Molly looked back at him, he just shook his head.

HE WAS FROWNING AT HER, clearly not having a good time, and Molly felt a twinge of guilt.

She'd forgotten about his issues with his father when she'd walked over here to laugh about the column. It had all happened when she was twelve and not quite tuned into the scandal of Mr. Lawson having an affair with a teenager. Mr. Lawson, *the high school principal,* having an affair with a teenage *student.* What a nightmare.

Ben gestured toward the oversize front desk. "During the summer, the station's always manned. But in the winter, it's just us locals. Everyone knows where to find Brenda at lunchtime."

"Do you guys only work half-time during winter?"

"No, we have an Aspen officer who works here during the summer. It works out perfectly because they need her for their busy season, then when the pass opens in spring, she commutes here for a few months, and the rest of us get to work full-time during the slow season."

"Quinn said there's a lot more traffic through here than there used to be."

Ben nodded. "The mountain biking has really taken off. The rafting companies expanded to include biking and bought more buses. They take the riders and their bikes up to the top of the trail, then meet them back at the bottom to do it again. Helluva way to break your neck, if you ask me."

"Professor Logic as always."

"God, no one's called me that since your parents moved away." He led the way back, giving cursory explanations. "My office." He waved into a small, plain room with a neat desk. "The other offices." A larger room with three desks crammed into it. "Holding cell."

"Whoa, *this* is your jail?" She walked up to the big metal door to look through the thick glass window. Nothing very interesting, just a toilet and sink and cot.

"It's just a holding cell. Anyone we place under arrest gets put over in the county lockup."

"So who's this for?"

"Minor violators."

She glanced back to find him watching her closely.

He raised an eyebrow. "Girls who block snowy streets with their tiny, useless, stranded cars even after they've been warned by the police."

"Ha!" She turned and stepped closer to him, happy when he backed up into the wall. "I'll be nimble as a little bunny. You'll see."

"I do have experience in this kind of—"

"Oh, I know you have experience, Chief. But I'm no beginner, either."

Clearing his throat, Ben pushed off the wall and headed back toward the front. Unfortunately his coat hid most of his butt, but she could still appreciate the movement of his hard thighs and the tempting sight of the nape of his neck beneath his hat. "Thanks for wearing the cowboy hat for me, Ben."

The neck turned pink. "It's part of my uniform, Molly," he growled.

She was almost positive he was more than a little interested in her, but she suddenly had the fear that his blushes were more the "just leave me alone" kind than the "you're hot, don't tease me" variation. He'd always been quiet and almost shy, until he loosened up and got funny. So was this shyness or interest? How to find out?

Well, she'd always believed in the shortest route. "My brother says you're single."

Ben stopped so quickly that Molly reached out to stop herself from bumping into him. Her hand connected with a rock-solid back. When he turned, she felt muscles shifting even under the heavy coat, and then, instead of her hand resting on his back, her arm was actually curled around his waist, her hip touching his. Even Molly was startled at how she'd just made herself at home.

He raised a meaningful eyebrow at her arm until she removed it.

"Accident. Sorry. I swear I'm not a hussy." The word *hussy* made her laugh until she snorted, and Ben's eyes crinkled a little in amusement.

"Look, Molly. I think you're cute. And I am single. But it's a small town, you know? Too complicated."

"Too complicated? Really? Jeez, you're a real live wire, Professor."

"Come on. You know how it is."

"I was only trying to finagle a date. *A date.* I promise not to chain you to the basement stairs."

"I don't date women in Tumble Creek."

"Seriously?" Yes, he was probably being serious. He'd always been too logical for his own good. "Come on, Ben. What do you do, fly north when the days get longer? Do you have a set migration route or do you have a different set of stops each year?"

"I… It's complicated."

"Huh. I'll say." She brushed past him, making sure to inhale his scent when she got close. Mmm. Cold air and forests. Nothing complicated about that. He reached past to open the door and his chest brushed her back. Nice. She wasn't giving up that easy.

Grinning, she walked down the uneven steps and waited for him at the bottom. "It's not complicated," she finally said. "I promise you I'm a simple girl."

He didn't look as if he believed her. It probably didn't help that a man across the street started shouting her name. *Please don't let it be one of Cameron's boys,* she prayed as she turned toward the sound of a car door slamming.

"Molly Jennings, is that you? I was just on my way to your house." Mr. Randolph was heading for his trunk.

"Hi there, Mr. Randolph."

He popped the trunk, then reappeared with a big vase of roses. "These are for you."

"Oh, good God," she groaned, though she did manage to paste a smile on her face.

The flowers bounced jauntily in the man's arms as he jogged across the street. "Two dozen roses. This young man must think real highly of you." Mr. Randolph shifted the flowers to one hand, fumbling for the note. "Was it Devlin or Evan?" He patted around for his reading glasses.

"Devon," Molly snapped, reaching for the damn flowers. She caught the smirk on Ben's mouth and sent him a glare.

"Simple, huh?" he muttered. "Just another Denver guy, Molly?"

"Yes. He's a friend. From Denver."

Mr. Randolph exploded with laughter, totally overdoing it in Molly's opinion. "A friend! Ha! Those are long stems. Forty dollars a dozen. What've you been up to down in Denver, Ms. Jennings?"

"Nothing."

"You one of them rich business women?"

"No." She tried to leave it at that, but Mr. Randolph just waited, his rheumy blue eyes staring hard. Molly sighed. She'd been through this before. She knew the easy way out. "I do some sensitive work for a tech company. Nothing exciting though."

"A techie, huh? Well, congratulations on the flowers. I'll be seeing you around. Good to have you back."

"Thank you, Mr. Randolph."

She watched him go, ignoring the burning sensation at the back of her neck. The older man waved and disappeared into his flower, gift and fly-fishing shop, leaving Molly with no choice but to turn around and meet Ben's hard eyes.

"So you work for a tech company."

"No."

"Then you're a liar."

"Yes. I've found it's a lot easier than the truth."

"The truth being?"

"That I don't discuss my work with anyone."

He rocked back on his heels a little, looking her up and down with a suspicious glare. "And why is that, Molly?"

"That's none of your business. Plus it's complicated, and I know how you hate complications."

Ben didn't look any friendlier at that. In fact, Molly felt an undignified urge to squirm under his examination and blurt out a false confession. When he put his hands on his hips, she could see his big gun, and not the big gun she was interested in, either. She clutched the flowers hard to her chest.

"I won't have anything illegal going on here."

"I'm not—"

"Is that clear?"

"Jeez Louise, Ben!" She threw up one hand and waved it in frustration. "Who do you think I am?"

He looked her up and down one more time, sweeping her body with little tingles. "I have no idea anymore."

"I'm just Molly Jennings, all grown up. And hopefully charming as hell."

"It shouldn't be any mystery to you why I don't appreciate the excitement of a secret life. I wouldn't date a woman who kept half her life hidden, even if I wanted to."

"Do you want to?"

He only gave her a frown, so with a little groan of defeat, Molly gave up. "All right, I'm leaving. Bye." She turned up the sidewalk and headed toward her house, but she couldn't resist one last attempt. "But I will be at The Bar tonight," she called back. "Maybe I'll see you there."

A blast of cold wind kicked up and drowned out his reply. If he'd made one.

The breeze carried the scent of snow and pine and crisp, gold aspen leaves. Molly smiled despite Ben Lawson and his ridiculousness. Fall had always been her favorite season, and nothing was better than fall in the mountains. Dry leaves tumbled down the narrow street, scraping and tapping the blacktop. Clumps of red berries clung to leafless bushes, bobbing in time to the gusts. On the steep hill above town, groves of bright yellow leaves quaked against a backdrop of green pines so dark they were nearly black.

She couldn't believe it had been ten years since she'd come home. But when she'd left for college—after hiding out from Ben for the last three weeks of summer—her parents had sold the feed store, packed up the family home, and moved to St. George, Utah ("Just like Santa Fe! Only less crowded and snooty").

Her brother lived mostly in Aspen, and she visited him a couple times a year, but other than that... Her world had been in Denver. But not anymore. Unless she needed new clothes.

Tumble Creek was her home again, and if Ben Lawson wanted nothing to do with her that was fine. There was no history between them; she certainly wasn't in love with the man. Okay, maybe she'd had a crush on him for a few years. And maybe she'd spent more than a few years fantasizing about his lean, strong body and big, sure hands. But she would take care of that the same way she always did.

Molly picked up the pace and hurried toward home.

HE WAS STANDING in the dim light of her bedroom, waiting in the doorway for some signal from her. Molly let him wait. She wanted to take him in first, explore his body with just her eyes. And what a body it was.

His wide shoulders curved down into arms that looked carved from stone. Dark hair dusted his chest and danced a thin line over his sculpted abdomen. Oh, she wanted to feel his bronzed skin just there, where his belly was ridged with strength. She wanted those firm muscles to jump under her touch.

His cock grew harder as she watched, and she ceased to care about his abs. He was long and thick, the skin stretched tight until it glowed like silk.

Itching for something naughty to do, Molly's fingers drifted over her hip and pressed against her damp panties. A moan crawled from her throat as she pictured Ben watching her, getting harder, his cock throbbing with need. She wanted him desperate, delirious. She wanted him to watch until he snapped, until he took her rough and hard.

Molly's free hand reached blindly for the knob on the nightstand drawer as her other slipped beneath pink cotton and stroked.

"Oh," she whispered, encouraged by her own slickness and heat. God, she wanted him there, sliding in, stretching her until she begged for more or for mercy or for anything he'd give her.

Her other hand closed around her favorite toy. Not Ben, but it had been her best friend for months now.

Molly slipped off her panties and clicked the switch. The familiar buzzing made her smile, and then it made her arch her back and moan in approval. *Oh, yeah.* Oh, yes, yes, yes.

She began floating up into pleasure and turned back to her fantasy of Ben. He was eyeing her with hot anger, furious that she hadn't let him near yet.

Molly stroked one of her nipples, imagining the way he—

A sudden metallic screech interrupted, terrifying her into a scream. She sprang up, flinging the vibrator across the room. It landed with a thud and writhed itself into a dim corner. "Jesus! What the—?"

The ancient phone next to her bed rang again, nearly jangling itself off the table.

"Oh. My. *God.*" She thought she'd electrocuted herself with a defective sex toy. Her heart was still trying its best to escape from her chest, jumping ship at the first sign of danger. She pressed her hand to it, panting to catch some air.

Brrrrrrr-ring.

It had better be Ben. Maybe the two of them had some sort of psychosexual connection. If they did, she'd been giving him a hell of a ride for the past ten years.

Molly snatched up the phone and attempted to answer with some dignity. *"What?"*

"Hey, beautiful."

Unfortunately, she knew exactly who it was. Cameron, that *bastard.* "Go away!"

Molly slammed down the phone, hoping she broke the ancient menace in the process, but of course they didn't make 'em like they used to. No, this phone wasn't slapped together in China. The damn thing was probably made of pure American steel.

It jangled alive again. Loudly. Her aunt had clearly been hard of hearing.

Molly was nearly weeping with frustration when she answered. "Please, Cameron, for the love of God, leave me alone!"

Cameron just chuckled. "Pete said you were in a bad mood. I don't think mountain living suits you."

"I'm not coming back to Denver. Now, *goodbye.*"

When she hung up this time, Molly turned the phone over, searching for an off switch. But apparently Ringer Off switches hadn't been invented forty years ago, so she just unplugged it.

Un-fricking-believable. Cameron Kasten was now officially ruining even her solo sex life. Had he *known* she was masturbating? Molly glanced at the windows, just to be sure, then shook her head to clear the shocked buzzing away.

The buzzing stayed. Frowning, she tugged the sheets up over her chest and glanced around the room. But of course it was nothing menacing, just her favorite toy, shaking its little blue self half to death against the baseboards. Despair slapped Molly full in the face.

She didn't even want her favorite blue toy. She wanted Ben Lawson, and he didn't want her.

Legs weak and heavy, Molly forced herself to get up and retrieve the vibrator. She stared down at it for a moment, but she wasn't even close to being in the mood now. She just switched it off and headed for the shower.

Thank God she hadn't adjusted to the altitude yet. She was going out tonight and she needed those drinks to hit her hard. It was all the hard she'd be getting for a while.

CHAPTER FOUR

PROSTITUTE.

Ben cringed even as he wrote it.

No way was Molly Jennings a hooker. She was sweet and smart and had always been a good student and daughter.

But then who were all these male "friends" she seemed to have acquired? Sure, she'd claimed she was doing nothing illegal, but she'd already lied about a half dozen other things, why not that?

He glanced at his computer, tempted to do a background check. It'd be easy enough to find out if she had any arrests on record. But it felt unethical; he didn't really have a good reason to pry into her life.

Even if she had been a hooker in Denver, it was nothing to him. He wasn't going to date her. She certainly wasn't going to be turning tricks up here; she'd have moved to Aspen for that. So he just couldn't convince himself he had a reason to look her up.

"Plus, she's not a prostitute," he muttered. There was no way in the world she'd be so cute and shiny if she'd been living that lifestyle. She had a sharp wit, but that was the only thing hard about her. Molly Jennings was all softness and light. And heat.

Ben crossed the offensive word off his list and let his body fall back in his chair. He cracked his neck, ran his hands over his face.

It was almost seven. He was exhausted and frustrated and jumpy. He needed a damn drink.

Leaning as far to the left as he could, Ben craned his neck to catch a glimpse of The Bar outside his office window. The *h* on the sign had burned out long ago; half the locals called it T-Bar now. The place was worn-out and small, and it was the only place in town to get a drink.

And she'd be there.

He couldn't avoid the woman; there was only one gas station, one grocery store, one bar. Still, maybe seeing her tonight wasn't a good idea. He'd been picturing her in her fuzzy pink hat and white coat and high-heeled boots…and nothing else. In his mind, she looked all wrapped up and proper, bundled against the cold. But then she untied the belt on the thigh-length coat and tossed it open and there she was in all the natural pink and white glory of her naked body.

"Jesus, I need to get laid," he groaned, rubbing his face again. Except that he immediately thought of Molly and his body began to cast its own vote on the subject.

No, he wouldn't date her. But drinking wasn't dating, after all. Neither was flirting.

Ben shut down the computer and headed for home. A shower and then…bed. Probably.

MOLLY PRACTICALLY hopped down her front steps as she left to meet Lori Love at The Bar. It had been a good evening, despite her disastrous afternoon. All that sexual desperation had served her work well. She'd channeled her lust into the new story and managed to bang out twelve pages. Twelve awesomely good pages, if she did say so herself.

Hips swaying over her heeled boots, Molly hurried down the hill toward Main Street, her grin widening as she walked. Even the new e-mail from that nasty Mrs. Gibson hadn't ruined her mood. The woman wrote to Molly and her colleagues on a regular basis to call them whores and smut-peddlers, but she was strangely well-versed in the stories. In fact, it seemed clear that she read every one. Sometimes Mrs. Gibson even provided statistics about which dirty words were used and how many times. This new book was really going to set her off.

Molly had never written anything quite so wicked before, and Mrs. Gibson wouldn't be the only one shocked by it. Molly expected her editor to be very pleasantly surprised. Though Molly wasn't into bondage herself, there was a huge market for that kind of story.

And heck, even if she wasn't into being tied up, she just might change her mind after this book. That sheriff was one hot hero. Almost as hot as Ben himself.

Ben. If he didn't show up at The Bar tonight, Molly had promised herself she'd leave the poor guy alone. If he *did* show up...well that was another beast altogether. She didn't want to add complication to her life any more than he did, but there was nothing complicated about gettin' it on.

She was giggling at her own thoughts when the night

darkened around her. She'd passed all the houses on her street and walked right out of their friendly porch lights and into the small strip of forest that divided her neighborhood from Main. Her neck prickled in warning. She stopped.

She wasn't scared. This was Tumble Creek, after all. But she did turn in a slow circle all the same, searching every shadow for signs of movement. Nothing except her city-girl imagination.

The full moon shone on the street a dozen yards ahead of her, illuminating the back lot of the feed store. The apartment above the store was where Ben and Quinn had lived together during college summers. The rent had been cheap—really cheap—and the summer jobs plentiful. And Molly had hung around as much as she could manage.

She'd made herself at home there, even to the point of bursting in without knocking.

Oh, her little heart had broken that night, even if her sex drive had roared awake at the sight of Ben naked and impressively aroused. That girl—definitely not a local—had…

Molly's familiar thoughts froze when dry leaves crackled behind her. Her steps stuttered as she shot a look over her shoulder. That wasn't the sound of the wind tossing dead leaves around. A twig snapped. All her muscles jumped.

"Who's there?" No answer.

She hurried toward the lights ahead. She'd had this feeling before of being watched and followed. But that had been in Denver, where Cameron had shown up in odd places—at restaurants, at her local Starbucks, even a women's clothing store. A complaint to his supervisor had resulted in nothing but a lecture about how she was clearly sending mixed signals.

Was he here now? Trying to scare her? Chase her back to Denver where he could control her life?

Molly rushed down the sidewalk, almost to the light, and the corner of Main Street was only a little farther. She broke free from the shadows, gasping, and dared a look back.

Dark shifted against dark, then deepened to nothing. But she was sure that shadow had been movement, and not just her imagination.

It took only seconds for her to reach the corner and dash around it. Leaning against the brick wall of the feed store, Molly drew freezing air into her lungs and watched it rush out in clouds as she exhaled.

This is Tumble Creek, she told herself. *You're in the wilderness. It was a raccoon or a possum, maybe even an elk.*

Her heart seemed to believe her. It slowed to an almost normal pace, and Molly risked a glance around the corner. She saw nothing. Was it possible that cheap coffee had more caffeine in it than the good stuff? She'd been jumpy all day. Her vibrator hadn't tried to kill her and neither had that raccoon or whatever the hell it was.

Willing herself into a shaky laugh, she pushed off the wall. The Bar was just across the street, less than a block away. As if on queue, she heard the door of the place open and tinny music spilled out. Someone pulled out of the grocery store parking lot and drove toward her. Life resumed its normal pace. Everything was fine.

Forcing a smile, she headed for The Bar.

"Molly Jennings!" the barkeep called as soon as the door swooshed shut behind her.

Molly tilted her head, studied his face, and then grinned. "Juan! You look great." A bit of an exaggeration, but he smiled and shrugged. Juan was two years older than her. He'd been a star football player at Creek County High, but his bulky muscles had softened to something that looked suspiciously like fat. His smile was just as wide and genuine, though. Molly grabbed a seat at the bar.

"Lori called," Juan said right away. "She'll be a little late. Had to go pull a car out of a ditch."

"Thanks, Juan."

"What can I get you? Some kind of wimpy drink? Cosmo? Appletini? Pomegranate Twist?"

"Oh, um, really? You've got pomegranate juice?"

"Nah, not really. But I do have cranberry juice and apple sour. What's your poison?"

Molly glanced around. Most of the booths were full and every single person had a beer or shot glass in front of them. But, damn, she wanted a cosmo.

Her sigh ruffled the little napkin Juan had set in front of her. "I've got to build up some street cred here, Juan. I'd better have a Coors."

Juan glanced up and down the bar, then leaned a little closer. "How about if I make you a lemon-drop martini and put it in a highball glass with ice? Think you could pull it off as a vodka tonic?"

Molly sat straighter and laughed. "Hell, yeah. Bring it on." This night was gonna be all right after all.

While Juan turned his back on the bar to mix the secret drink, Molly strolled over to the jukebox to check out the selections. Apparently they hadn't been updated since the eighties; all the selections were still classic country or guitar rock. She chose George Strait and made a beeline back to her drink.

When the door opened, she turned to say hi to Lori. The sight of Ben walking through the door froze her tongue to her front teeth. Oh, hell yeah, this night was gonna be all right.

He was looking down at the floor, but he shot a glance at her past his lashes. Warmth melted from the top her head to her toes. Her tongue relaxed.

"Hey, Ben," she drawled. "What're you doing here?"

He raised his face to her, wearing the policeman mask. "Just dropping by to check on things like I always do."

"Hey, Chief!" Juan yelled from the other end of the bar. "What're you doing here?"

Blood rushed to his cheeks, but one side of his mouth turned up. "I'll have a bottle of Bud," he answered.

Molly grinned, then she let her eyes drop and her smile faded. Ben wasn't in uniform tonight. He was wearing his jeans and boots and an old brown coat, but besides that he wore a faded green T-shirt that clung to his chest. When he took off his hat and shrugged out of the coat, she felt like she was seeing him naked. Her sex actually tingled.

Oh, God, his shoulders really had gotten wider, his arms more solid. His hair was slightly damp and it clung to his nape. Molly bit back a groan, trying to fight the urge to walk over and run her tongue down the back of his neck.

She'd never even kissed the man, but right now she wanted to eat him up, swallow him whole, ditch Lori Love and this bar and drag him home with her for mindless, sweaty, dirty sex. He looked young and hot and delicious. And he was here. With her.

Molly grabbed her drink and drained half of it in four swallows.

"Maybe I should start making you another," Juan guessed, and Molly confirmed his question with a hurry-up motion as Ben took the seat beside her.

She didn't look at him. Her panties were already wet, her nipples hard, and she was sure if she met his eyes his police instincts would pick up on her horniness right away.

Yes, she wanted to do him, but there was a difference between seduction and taping a big sign to your forehead: *You don't have to bother with small talk, mister. Just take me in the broom closet and use me like the cheap ho I am.* That kind of thing should really come later in a relationship.

"So, um…" Ben cleared his throat. "Did you have a nice day?"

"Yes."

When he shifted, his knee brushed hers, making Molly jump.

"Sorry," he offered and moved his leg a few inches away.

Molly slumped and sucked down the rest of her

drink. A pleasant warmth soaked into her muscles and relieved some of her concerns. So she was horny? It wasn't a crime even if she was thinking about molesting a policeman.

"You're mad, aren't you?" Ben said softly. "I didn't mean to offend you today. Asking questions is my job."

"It's fine."

Juan set the new drink down and Molly picked it up.

"I just can't understand what you're hiding and why. If you'd tell me…"

"Dream on, Chief." Buoyed by the lemon drops, Molly turned on her bar stool and let her knees press against his hip. "My secret is the most interesting thing about me. Why, look! You can't stay away! Don't deny that you came here to see me. You're not even on duty."

"Maybe." He arched a look down at her knees, bare except for the black tights she wore under her miniskirt. "Does this mean I'm forgiven?"

"Well, my legs have forgiven you, and isn't that all that matters?"

His eyes warmed by slow degrees, and when he met her gaze, alcohol or not, Molly plummeted right back into heady lust.

"I won't deny the importance of that," he murmured. Then he took his sexy eyes off her and raised his empty bottle to signal for another.

The door opened behind them and Molly prayed it wasn't Lori. *Let there have been an accident…. No injuries! Just a slow-speed pileup in the gas station parking lot that will keep her busy for another hour.* Ben's resolve was weakening, Molly could *see* it, like he was stripping his clothes off right in front of—

"Long time no see!" Lori said from behind her.

Ben tipped his head and stood. "I'll let you two catch up."

"You don't have to—" But he was already moving away. Molly watched him go with mournful eyes.

"Don't tell me Miles actually got it right?"

"What?" Molly asked, distracted. What a gorgeous ass that man had, all tight muscle and—

"Are you and Ben hooking up? Didn't you just move back to town—" Lori looked at her watch "—about seventy-two hours ago?"

"No." Molly laughed as Lori perched her petite little behind on the seat Ben had vacated. "It's been a full four days. Wait, how many hours is that? More than seventy-two?"

"I'll have whatever she's having," Lori said quickly. Juan raised an eyebrow at Molly.

"It's a lemon-drop martini," she confessed in a whisper.

"Perfect."

"And I've waited ten years to get in that man's pants, so don't begrudge me."

"Only ten?" Lori asked, green eyes sparkling like polished jade.

"Okay, more like twelve. I can't take it anymore. Something's gonna fall off if I don't use it soon."

"Oh, no, you can't have my sympathy on that, Molly. I've lived in this town my whole life and most of the eligible men think I'm gay. You got to go to Denver to spread your wings. And legs."

Molly nearly spit her drink out as she collapsed in laughter. Juan was blushing, so he must have overheard, but surely he'd heard worse than that before.

When she recovered, Molly looked over her old friend's tiny waist and narrow hips, then up to the big curls she wore in a chin-length bob. "Why does everyone think you're gay?"

Lori held her drink with just her thumb and pinky and raised the other three fingers above the rim. "One," she said and ticked it off, "I never put out in high school. Two, I refused to give Jess Germaine a blow job in his backseat when I finally did start dating. Three, I fix cars. Lesbian, all the way."

"Well, I'll try not to drop my keys near you, then."

"Oh, I'll be on you like white on rice, sista."

They both roared with laughter at that, drawing looks from the other patrons. "Sorry," Molly called. "Nothing to see here." The men turned back to their beers, all except Ben, who sat at the other end of the bar, watching them like a movie. He aimed a disapproving glance at her drink, so Molly ordered another.

"I noticed you painted all the Love's Garage trucks lavender."

"Aren't they pretty?"

"And your dad doesn't mind? How is he, by the way?"

"He died a few months ago, Moll."

"Oh! Oh, shit! I'm so sorry, Lori. No one told me."

"It's okay. You've been gone a long time."

"I just… Last I heard he was doing better. Oh, Lori, I'm sorry."

"No, it was time. He was ready—I could see it in his eyes."

Molly nodded. "So you own the garage now?"

"Yep, the garage, the tow truck, the snowplows, all the land. And the glory, of course."

There was a definite edge to her friend's voice. "That's great," Molly said carefully. "But…I thought you were only going to put off school for a couple of years."

"Yeah, so did I."

"Didn't you get an internship in Europe or something?"

Lori smiled, but there was no mistaking the sadness in her eyes. "Responsibility's a bitch sometimes, you know?" She shook her head, setting her curls rocking. "Enough about that. Let's talk about Ben. Did you two have a thing going before? I thought you were dating Ricky Nowell."

"Yeah, I— Jeez, he doesn't still live here, does he?"

"No, why?"

"Because I've told dozens of people how small his dick was, so that would be *totally* awkward."

Lori snorted citrus vodka up her nose and spent a full thirty seconds coughing and wiping her eyes. Everyone was staring again.

And it only got worse after that.

BEN NODDED AT THE giggling pair of tipsy women. "I think I'd better offer you ladies a ride home," he said as if he were just polite and not a police officer.

Molly waved him away. "Oh, I walked."

"Then I definitely insist."

"What, you think you'd find me ass-up in a snow-bank tomorrow morning?"

"Not enough snow yet," Ben answered and steered her out the door. To her credit, she managed to walk without weaving.

Lori followed behind, giggling. "I'm only two lots down, Ben. I'll be fine."

"I'll feel better if I drive you."

"Yeah," Molly added. "And it'll give everyone some-thing to talk about if we all leave together. Lori's totally hot for me, Ben. She's on me like…something. And we might let you watch if you ask real nice."

Jesus. Not the image *or* the gossip he needed.

"Deal," Ben said. "Let's go to my place." That shut her mouth quick. Lori collapsed against his back, shak-ing with laughter, and he couldn't help but smile. "All right, ladies. Let's see if we can get you home before you embarrass yourselves." That only sent them into an-other fit of laughter. "Nobody's gonna throw up, right?"

"I only had three drinks!" Molly protested, but when Ben stopped to open the passenger door of his truck, he shot her a quelling look.

"All right, four, but that was over two full hours."

"So you're just naturally hilarious?"

"Yes! Didn't you know that?"

He had, actually, and he'd also known she was cute

as hell before she'd shown up in her black boots and tights and tiny black miniskirt. Then there was the snug pink turtleneck. Pink, pink, pink. It was his new favorite color.

"Lori, you need help?"

"I've got it," she called as she crawled into the backseat. Ben didn't bother asking her to buckle. She really was only about a hundred feet from home.

Molly started to climb up, pulling herself in slow motion, so what could he do but wrap his hands around her waist to hoist her in? The sweater was thin, her skin hot beneath, and Ben had an almost irresistible urge to follow her up, stretch her out on the wide front seat and cover her up with his body.

Then again, all the computer equipment in the middle might put a damper on things. Not exactly satin sheets and feather pillows.

"Ben?" she breathed, as if she wouldn't mind having a keyboard pressed into her back at all.

"Mmm?"

Her eyes were wide in the dark, her face turned up to his. She licked her lips, calling all his attention to her mouth, his favorite shade of his new favorite color... and then she collapsed into laughter.

Right. The drunk-off-her-ass part had escaped his mind for a moment.

"Let's go, Chief," Lori called from the back, reminding him there was also a friend-in-the-backseat part of the evening. Then there was the possible-illegal-sex-trade complication.

"Okay," he breathed and stepped far out of the way

before he shut the door on Molly and her many shades of pink. He'd only had two beers tonight; he was fine to drive, but apparently not fine to press his hand into the hot curve of her waist.

Ben tried to convince himself he wasn't half-hard in the middle of Main Street as he rounded the truck and slid in behind the seat.

Lori waved her hand from the back as he started the engine and jacked up the heat. "Ben, do you think I'm a lesbian?"

"Um..." A glance in the mirror showed nothing but her upraised wrist and limp fingers. "No, I hadn't really... Why? Are you trying to, uh, find yourself or...?"

"I just want a decent date!" she wailed. "And not with some Ricky Nowell!"

"Mmm-hmm." He'd found over the years that it was best to simply feign understanding with drunk people.

"If the opportunity ever arises, would you send a nice guy my way? I just want to go out to a movie, you know? Maybe get a little some-some. Is that so wrong?"

"Of course not."

Molly was shaking her head in very serious sympathy. "I was just kidding about getting it on in front of you, Ben."

"Yeah, I got that."

"Lori's not really a lesbian."

"I'm getting that, too. And here we are!"

Lori popped up from the seat, and her forehead made a slow beeline for Ben's headrest.

"Ow."

That settled Ben's question about whether she needed

to be walked to her door. He ended up walking her all the way to the couch. By the time he returned to the truck, Molly was curled up with her cheek pressed against the seat back and her feet tucked beneath her.

"Hey, Ben," she breathed and opened her eyes in a slow, sleepy smile. Some malevolent force sat hard on his chest. It was the devil, or maybe just a random satyr, whispering that this was exactly how she'd look after a night of good, hard sex. This was exactly how she could look tomorrow.

Ben twisted the ignition with extra force and heard the outraged screech of the starter. Right. The truck was already running.

"What's wrong with your truck?"

"It's horny," he muttered.

"Mmm." Another sympathetic shake of her head. Apparently it all made perfect sense to her.

Though he was well-versed on every speed limit in town, Ben broke every one on the way to Molly's house. Professor Logic he might be during the daylight hours, but he was becoming acquainted with a whole new personality tonight. Captain Man-Slut, maybe. He didn't care about complications or questions or intoxication. He knew he'd care in the morning, and he didn't give a shit about that, either. He just wanted some Molly, bad.

The two hours in the bar had been pure pleasure for Ben. He'd recognized the old Molly he'd liked so well all those years ago. She'd been silly and immature, giggly and girly, but all of her still glowing with that sheen of comfort, of being at ease with herself.

She seemed to draw eyes without even noticing,

seemed comfortable with attention without needing it. And she laughed. A lot. Ben didn't laugh much, and he thought it would be a grace in his life, a blessing, to hear a woman laugh every day, every hour. To hear her laugh in his bed.

Something shivered inside his chest, scaring the hell out of him. Ben eased his foot off the accelerator and slowed down to twenty-five. He had to get it together, or he was going to make a serious mistake. He didn't know a damn thing about her, not anymore.

As soon as he pulled into her driveway, he put the truck in Park and turned to her. "Please tell me what you do for a living."

She arched an eyebrow. "Are you trying to take advantage of my blood alcohol level?"

"Absolutely. You know me, Molly. You know how much I hate secrets. You know I could never trust someone who wouldn't be honest and up-front."

"I am being honest and up-front." She didn't seem at all disturbed, just sad. She was still curled up and sleepy, unconcerned that his guts were tangled in knots.

"You must be doing something you're ashamed of or you wouldn't hide it."

"No, I'm not ashamed."

Instead of banging his head against the steering wheel, Ben made a calculated move. Calculated, but pleasurable all the same. He reached across the space of the truck and touched her, brushing her temple with the pad of his thumb. "Why won't you tell me?"

Her eyes closed. She made a tiny humming sound as he dragged his knuckles over her soft skin. His thumb brushed her bottom lip, a kiss of her pink temptation against his rougher texture.

"Why, Molly?" he whispered.

She opened eyes full of sorrow. "Lots of reasons. My parents... Quinn is so smart and successful. They're so proud of him, and they should be. He's amazing.

"But I've never been as smart, never as good in school. And my work isn't like his, either. It's easier this way. They understand that they'd probably be disappointed, but they don't *know*. They can't be sure. Maybe I'm a spy. Maybe I'm an artist. Whatever it is, they can't measure it against Quinn's accomplishments, because I won't let them."

"Jesus, Moll. I know they've always been gaga over Quinn's grades and awards, but they love you to death."

"Yeah, and I'd like to keep it that way."

"What does that *mean?* Just tell me, I promise not to say anything to Quinn. Tell me what you're doing."

She turned and looked out the windshield. "No. If you're going to think I'm a bad person, just go ahead." She made a wide gesture, nearly clocking him in the face. "Look, I know I said all that stuff about Ricky Nowell, and nice girls don't do that, but he was really horrible to me that night, and I just..." She turned a corkscrew with her left hand.

"Ricky Nowell? I don't... Wasn't he your boyfriend in high school?"

"Yes, unfortunately! So don't go judging me!"

"Molly, I have no idea what you're talking about."

"I'm not doing anything wrong, that's what I'm talking about! If you're not gonna like me, fine! Don't like me. You just sit over there and be cute and disapproving. And sexy. And… I don't have to—"

When he leaned in and kissed her, she drew a sharp, deep breath and then held it. Ben smiled against her mouth and took advantage of the quiet moment to explore the satin texture of her lips. She was just as soft as he'd fantasized, warm and yielding as he brushed his lips slowly over hers. But she didn't taste pink; she tasted shimmery yellow.

"Why do you taste like a Jolly Rancher?" he wondered aloud.

"Oh." She breathed citrus against his tongue. "Three lemon drops and an appletini."

Then he followed the sweetness into warmth and wet. She opened for him, pressed closer, and Ben forgot about lemons and apples. She let him explore slowly for a moment, gliding against the slickness of her mouth, but then she wanted more and so did he, and she moaned and coaxed him deeper.

His earlier lust exploded through him, dragging him into urgency as quick and wild as the creek in spring. He felt he'd waited forever for this, through countless youthful fantasies when his hormones had nearly driven him mad. Ben grasped her hips and lifted her over all the clutter that kept them separated.

"Oh, my God, did you just *pick me up?*" She wiggled against him, settling her knees on either side of his legs. "That is so *sexy.*"

That surprised a laugh out of him, but it turned to a groan as she finally got her skirt hiked high enough that she could settle her ass against his lap. He curled his hands around her thighs, because what else was he supposed to do? And the black fabric was like cashmere, it clearly demanded petting...stroking, even.

"Oh, yes, Ben," she whispered, pressing small kisses to his jaw. "Your hands are so hot. So hot and, and so... *big.*"

Jesus, was she talking dirty to him? No one had ever done that before, but he was damn sure he liked it. Ben kissed her hard and stroked up to cup her ass in his palms, and oh, what a perfect fit. All that firm, flexing muscle and, *damn it,* her mouth tasted like heaven.

Her encouraging noises weren't hurting anything, either. He pushed higher on her hips, slipping her skirt up until his fingers touched the bare skin waiting for him above her tights. Her skin was even softer than cashmere and scorching hot.

Molly arched back, pressing her sex down, and Ben, determined to oblige, lifted her and scooted down a little in his seat. When she rocked forward, she fit perfectly against the bulge in his jeans.

"Ah," they said in unison.

"Oh, Ben," she went on, while he was still trying to reconnect with the speech center of his brain. The hollow between her legs, the plump flesh there...it all seemed perfectly designed to cover him, torture him. Her thighs strained as she shifted herself against him.

"Oh, Ben, you feel so good."

Hell, yeah, he felt really good. She seemed to have everything under control as she rocked back and forth, so he let go of her hips and reached for the pink sweater instead. As he pushed the hem up, he made a mental note to remember the sight of her in that white lace bra later. Right now he just needed to get rid of it, and Molly seemed in agreement. She shrugged out of her coat, tangled her arms in the sweater and pulled up and then suddenly it was off, her hair falling around bare shoulders.

The delicate bra had a front clasp, thank the sweet Lord for genius inventions. All it took was one little flick of his clumsy fingers and it was falling away. Her breasts were white and small and perfect, begging for attention. He licked one rosy nipple, a slow circle around the hardening bud.

Her sigh filled the truck as she worked her fingers into his hair and rocked her hips faster.

"*Ben.* Yes. Oh, yes. I've wanted this for so long. Ever since that night. I saw you and I wanted to be *her.* I wanted to be on my knees for you, taking all of you into my mouth."

Holy *shit.* He knew his fingers were digging too hard into her waist, but he couldn't stop them, just as he couldn't stop his mouth from being too rough. He scraped his teeth over her pebble-hard nipple and Molly keened. When he reached up her back to ease one hand into her hair, to hold her tight to his lips, Molly moaned in eager approval.

He knew she was close to coming, the friction of her rubbing driving even him close to the edge, and Ben's mind was a writhing mess of conflicting ideas. He wanted to push her further, make her come screaming, and he wanted to lift her up and unzip his jeans and sink deep inside so they could come together. He wanted to gather her up and take her into her house and do this right, on a bed, in private, for hours.

And, Jesus, he wanted her talking to him the whole time.

"Ben," she panted.

"Yes."

"Please, I'm… Oh, God."

He moved to the other breast, licking more softly this time, knowing just what he wanted. And he got it.

Molly began to beg. "Ben, please. *Please*. I'm so close."

Her fingers wound tight into his hair, demanding and pleading. He refused to give in until she began sobbing his name over and over. Finally, he sucked hard and pressed her carefully between his teeth.

She drew in a long, rough breath and raised one hand to the ceiling to press her body harder against his cock. All her muscles tensed into long, shaking lines…and then Ben saw stars and she was screaming and the world exploded into color and…and sirens?

Caught at the very edge of an orgasm, Ben looked up and saw one of her clutching hands pressed high, right against the light controls of his truck. Sirens blared, blue and red beams danced and jumped off the front of her house. And the neighbors' houses.

"Oh, fuck."

She was still shuddering against him.

"Molly. Molly!" He tried to flick the switches, but her fingers wouldn't move. "Move your hand, Moll!" She moved the wrong one, letting go of his hair.

Finally, he was able to push her loosening hold away

from the box and turn off the light-and-sound show. But it was too late, of course. Porch lights were coming on as far as five houses up the block. He wondered if the loud speaker had been on.

Shit, shit, shit. One more second and this would have ended in a high-school-era orgasm for him, too, and now he had to think his way out of this? Ben snatched up her sweater and tugged it over her head. Her eyes blinked at him above the turtleneck.

"You'd better get dressed, sweetie. We're about to have company."

He saw the exact moment that awareness flashed to life in her clouded gaze. Her eyes got bigger, rounder, and then she forced her arms into the sleeves and yanked everything down over her unfastened bra.

"Oh, God, I'm sorry." Her voice shook. "I'm so sorry."

"It's all right, Molly. It's okay. Calm down."

"No, it's not!"

Several dark shadows huddled on stoops, stomping their feet and craning their necks. "I don't think anyone even noticed. Just get your coat on and I'll walk you to your door."

"No one noticed?" She started to look around, so Ben gathered up her white coat and handed it to her.

"Here. Your hat's under my foot, can you reach it?" That busied her long enough for most of the neighbors to give up on the winter show and go back inside to spy from the window.

He didn't know why he was trying to protect her. The Thursday edition of that pitiful ink-jet excuse for a paper would reveal all. But it didn't seem right that her pleasure should end like that, tripping over mortification and regret.

The thought made him cringe in memory, though it was just habit at this point. Molly was here now to replace that old incident with new, more spectacular disasters. He'd probably care more once his dick gave up hope and eased its monopoly on his blood flow. But right now everything seemed okay, because Molly was gorgeous and flushed and confused and still perched half on his lap.

"Molly?"

"Yeah?"

She looked up from tugging on her hat, and he caught her in a simple, soft kiss. "I had fun tonight."

"Oh," she sighed, eyes closed, lips turned up in a secret smile. "Oh, so did I."

There was nothing to be done, so Ben walked her to her door, gave her a quick lecture because she'd forgotten to lock it, declined her invitation to spend the night, then told her to sleep well. She assured him that she would.

Whatever his regrets, Ben walked back to his truck feeling glad that one of them was in for a peaceful, sated night.

UNBELIEVABLE. Molly Jennings was out of control.

An owl screeched from somewhere close by, probably irritated with the human hiding in the moon shade of the trees, scaring all the prey away. But the shadow watching Molly didn't budge.

The girl had just had sex in a truck, in public, with a man she barely knew. She'd been in Tumble Creek all of, what? Four days?

She didn't even look ashamed of herself as she closed her front door. Hell, she probably knew she'd been watched, and had enjoyed it all the more. It would be in keeping with her personality. Always drawing attention.

Perhaps she slept with strange men in public all the time. Perhaps she'd screwed all the patrons in the bar tonight before leaving with Chief Lawson.

Damn it.

She probably felt safe here, living a charmed life in these mountains, but the razor peaks and icy nights had broken thousands of men over the centuries. It would be easy enough to change her mind about returning to this town.

The lock-pick gun shifted in the black bag, heavy as a gold bar but so much more valuable. People—single women in particular—locked their doors at night and felt secure, but that was pure ignorance. Every locksmith owned one of these gadgets that could open any cheap lock. Every locksmith…and every police department.

Molly would sleep soundly tonight, satisfied with her evening's fun, and she'd have no idea of her vulnerability. No idea that someone could stalk through her house with no fear, even stand over her bed and watch her sleep.

But she would realize her ignorance soon enough. Her female instincts would try to warn her, niggling at the edges of her consciousness. Fear would worm its way into her head, but there'd be no proof of anything, no implication that her terror was well-founded.

She'd be afraid. She'd feel confused. Soon enough, paranoia would set in. And then she would move away from Tumble Creek and back to Denver where she belonged.

CHAPTER FIVE

ONLINE SEX PERFORMER.

"Jesus," Ben sighed into his hands.

It was a good possibility. Better than the first two had been. It wasn't illegal, she could work from home, and she could make a heck of a lot of money doing it. And how the hell was he supposed to rule it in or out?

The background report glowed on his computer screen, bathing him in its censuring light. Nothing. Not even a traffic violation. Molly Jennings *was* a good girl, at least as far as the system was concerned. As far as Ben was concerned, she was fascinatingly bad. But just how bad, he didn't yet know.

When she'd had the wi-fi antenna attached to her roof the day after she'd moved in, he hadn't thought much about it, but he was thinking now. Was it just about a city girl's love for speedy Internet connections or did she need to upload huge amounts of information?

A few days ago he wouldn't have been able to imagine her doing sex shows for money, but now he could picture it all too well. She was…*easy* to watch. Even easier to listen to, and holy hell, what if that was how she'd learned how to turn him on like a goddamn switch?

"Please, no," he whispered to the computer. The vast universe of online sex loomed on Ben's horizon, glittering and ominous and writhing with danger. He'd never find her in there, even if he searched for weeks. Which brought up the question of how he was supposed to search anyway. He was on dial-up at home, and he could just imagine trying to explain to the mayor why he'd visited hundreds of online sex sites on his office computer, stalking a female citizen who hadn't broken any laws.

Nice. Just the kind of behavior Ben had been aiming for his whole life.

He reached for his cold coffee that was sitting on top of the latest *Tumble Creek Tribune*. "*Tribune,* my ass," he growled into the mug. "More like the *Tattler.*"

He'd called Molly on Friday morning to apologize and warn her what was coming—she'd seemed fairly unconcerned—and his gut had been churning the rest of the weekend. But when he'd found the paper on his porch this morning, the column had been only slightly enraging.

I'm officially declaring our esteemed Chief Lawson a workaholic. You may remember that last week he greeted our newest citizen, Molly Jennings, with unexpected enthusiasm. This week he's become a one-man fire brigade, putting out fires at the Jennings home in the darkest night. It's all on the up and up, though. He even used a siren to announce his late-night arrival.

As for Ms. Jennings, she's presenting a bit of a

mystery. Her very own brother has confirmed that she keeps her work life a secret…even from her family! Check back on Thursday for more details.

So no one had seen Molly half-naked in his truck— or no one had reported it to Miles—but that bastard had finally sniffed out the really important question. Who *was* Molly Jennings? No doubt he'd hang on like a pit bull for months, trying to shake out the truth. Ben just had to be sure he found out before Miles did.

There was nothing scandalous about the chief of police dating a single young woman. People might smile as they read the details, they might talk it over with their friends, but it wasn't a scandal. Ben had seen a true scandal, and he knew the difference.

He'd seen people stop their errands to stare at his family. He'd watched friends' parents snatch their children back before they could approach. He'd seen hateful joy on faces he'd known his whole life. And pity. And disgust. Hostility. Mocking laughter. Superiority. Delight. Sorrow.

Everything he'd ever known about himself had cracked and crumbled when his father had slept with a girl only one year older than Ben. Lucky for all of them she'd been eighteen at the time. Unluckily, she'd still been in high school. There had been the initial denials, then the small irrefutable details, then admissions and confessions and apologies. There'd been police investigations, emergency school board meetings, dismissal, serious money problems. The townspeople's outrage, his mother's horror and grief, Ben's own confusion and anger. Tales of his father's sex life. Divorce. Bankruptcy. And all of it reported in loving detail in Miles's paper.

So, yes, Ben knew the difference between harmless gossip and true scandal. And true scandal would be Tumble Creek's chief of police dating a prostitute or a porn star. Miles would love it. And Ben would be a pitiful echo of his father.

He could not date Molly Jennings until he found out the truth, even if he had spent the past days thinking incessantly that he should have taken her into the house and done things right.

"Happy Halloween, Fire Chief!" his second in command called as he walked by. He waved the paper as he passed, just in case Ben failed to get the joke.

"Kiss my ass, Frank," Ben called back in a cheerful tone.

Brenda appeared almost immediately in his doorway, shooting a disapproving look at Frank's back. "I'm sorry, Chief. You shouldn't have to put up with this nonsense."

"It's fine, Brenda. Honestly."

"Miles Webster should be shot."

"He's just doing his job." The words stuck in his throat, but he got them out.

"Job," Brenda spat, her face turning red with anger.

"Did you have a message for me?" Ben asked quickly.

The blood began to fade from her cheeks. She shook her head, setting her graying hair bouncing. "No, but you wanted me to remind you to check the mine gates before tonight."

The chair squeaked as he leaned back with a sigh. "Right. I got to three of them yesterday, but I've still got to check the one up on the ridge. Everything looks fine so far."

"Be careful if you're going up there. You seem a little tired."

"Nah, I'm fine."

"Oh, I almost forgot." She held up a plastic bowl and stepped in to set it on his desk.

Ben couldn't help but smile as the aroma of spices and tomatoes filled the small room. His stomach growled. "Chili?"

"Yes, sir." Her eyes sparkled with satisfaction and her cheeks balled up into rosy globes when she smiled. She really did look just like her mother.

"Thanks, Brenda. This'll get me through a long evening."

"You work too hard," she sighed, shaking her head as she left. "And try to stay out of trouble, will you?"

Ben didn't answer. He couldn't. Because all he really wanted to do was get *into* trouble. Deep into it. As if he'd never learned anything from his father at all.

"LOVE'S GARAGE."

"Lori, it's Molly. Can I ask you a favor?"

"It doesn't involve martinis does it? I think I'm still hungover."

Molly laughed. "We need to get you out more often."

"I... Really? All right, I'm in. Training, right? Practice makes perfect."

"We'll start tomorrow. But first... Listen, we're supposed to get snow this weekend, and I need a favor. If I get stuck in the snow, will you pull me out and—here's the important part—not tell Ben about it?"

"Well, I rarely report back to him anyway, so no problem. But if you're that worried, why don't you get a truck?"

"I had one all picked out in Denver, but they wouldn't give me the deal I wanted. I'm just driving the Mini until I can wear them down. I think they're close to breaking."

"I think you're close to breaking your ass in that tiny car."

"Eh. I'll be fine. And I'm having fun scaring the hell out of Ben in the meantime."

They were both still laughing when Molly hung up, but her humor faded the longer she held her new cordless phone in her hand. She was going to have to call Cameron, because she was starting to get that feeling again. That feeling she'd had in Denver. Of being watched, of little things being out of place.

First, the noises on her walk down to The Bar, then afterwards, the front door had been unlocked. She'd thought she'd forgotten, but she'd woken the next morning with the thought still on her mind... *I could've sworn I'd locked it.* But maybe she hadn't, or maybe it was hard to lock. She didn't know this house yet, didn't know its quirks. And that was a problem, too, all the shifts and sighs of the house as it cooled at night.

In her paranoia, she'd even let Mrs. Gibson's latest nasty e-mail get to her. Maybe the old lady wasn't so harmless. Maybe she was more like Kathy Bates in *Mis-*

ery than an eccentric grandma. But when she'd done a Google search for Mrs. Gibson's name and address, all the hits had pointed directly to an eighty-year-old woman who lived in a Long Island nursing home and wrote frequent letters to the editor of the local newspaper. Mrs. Gibson wasn't only outraged by erotic fiction; she was equally upset by liberal school boards and unfair sales taxes.

All of that pretty much eliminated her as a stalking suspect, which left only Cameron.

It occurred to Molly that she should consider getting a gun, just so she could sleep soundly. Or a dog. "Probably a dog," she said to the phone.

When the doorbell rang, Molly jumped about a foot and her new phone arced through the air. It clattered against the countertop, slid two feet to the sink and dropped in with a hollow clunk. No harm done.

"Coming!" she yelled, grabbing her bowl of candy on the way. The kids here didn't have many houses to visit, so she'd filled the bowl with full-size candy bars and packs of bubble gum and had received squeals of approval from all her visitors so far.

"Trick or treat!" the little girl chirped from behind her scarf as her mom offered a wave from the bottom of the steps.

Molly grinned down at the girl in her bulky parka and white sweatpants. A pink tutu stuck out between the layers and a sparkly crown perched on top of her knit cap.

"What a beautiful, beautiful princess you are!" she gushed as she dropped a big chocolate bar in the girl's bag. The girl's eyes bulged. *Oh, yeah,* Molly thought, *I'm a rock star in this town.* "All princesses deserve chocolate."

The big eyes sparkled, warming Molly's heart. She loved this small-town thing—

"I'm not a princess!"

Oops. That didn't sound like delight. "Oh! Sorry, I'm…"

Big fat tears began to drop from her eyelashes to the scarf. Molly threw a desperate glance to the mother, but she just stood there cringing.

"I'm not a princess!" the girl screamed, waving a previously unnoticed wand. "I'm a fairy. *I'm a fairy!*"

The mom reached up. "Kaelin, let's just go, hon—"

"I don't wanna wear my stupid coat. No one can see my w-w-wings!" She crumpled into a little sobbing mound of down and waterproof nylon. "I told you no one would see my wings!"

"Oh, for God's sake," the mother muttered as she scooped up the broken child.

"I'm sorry," Molly whispered in horror.

The girl stirred to scream, "I'm a fairy!" one more time before her mother spirited her down the steps.

Molly was hardly surprised when Ben chose that moment to drive up. He stepped out of the truck while the mother lectured quietly and furiously on the front lawn, but he just strolled into the reach of the porch light and watched until the little girl blinked away her tears and looked at him.

"Happy Halloween, Chief Lawson," she said mournfully.

"Happy Halloween, Kaelin. I must say, I don't think I've ever seen such a beautiful fairy. You look like you just stepped out of a magic snow palace."

"Really?" she breathed. *"Really?"*

"Police officers can't lie." He dug a crumpled pack of candy corn from his pocket and dropped it in the girl's bag. She glowed as though he'd just given her diamonds.

"Thank you, Chief," the mother gushed before pulling her daughter on to the next house.

The half smile Ben offered Molly was chock-full of arrogance. "Making children cry on Halloween, Moll? That something they taught you down in the big city?"

"How the hell did you know she was a fairy?"

"Wand," was all he said, and Molly slumped.

"I didn't see the damn wand."

"Not your fault. I'm trained to notice the details."

"I think I liked you better when you were shy."

The half smile flashed briefly into a full grin that stole Molly's breath away. His next words knocked the breath back in on a rush of anxiety.

"Speaking of noticing the details, this package was on top of your mailbox. It's from a Cameron Kasten. That the guy who's *not* your ex-boyfriend?"

"Yes," she snapped, wondering what the hell this meant. Though he held the package out to her, Molly just stared at it.

Ben looked down at it and then up at her with a frown. "You wanna tell me what's going on?"

"Nope." Her composure firmly back in place, she snatched the box and moved back into the warmth of her house. Ben followed. Oh, sure, he was willing to come in *now*.

Molly tossed the box on a table and headed for the kitchen. "Do you want a piece of homemade apple pie?"

"Who made it?"

"I did."

"Pie? What's gotten into you?"

"Coffee!" Just the sound of the word cheered Molly up. "Coffee got into me! My beans came!" She gestured toward the ripped-open FedEx package.

"I see."

She followed Ben's gaze to the staggered trail of coffee beans that littered the floor and counter. "Sorry, I was pretty excited. You want a latte? I've got my fancy city-girl espresso machine up and running."

He cocked his head as if he was figuring something out. A few seconds later, his shoulders lost a little of their stiffness. "You've got coffee and pie. I've got a container of chili in the car. That sounds like dinner."

"Dinner? That's a date!"

But Ben was already shaking his head. "No. A real date would be a drive up to my cabin where we'd have dinner in front of the fireplace. Wine. Dessert. Then maybe we'd walk over to the hot springs at the edge of my property. I'd strip you naked and carry you in. And then, Molly, then we'd make love in the warmest part of the water while snowflakes melted on our skin. We wouldn't care about the cold. We wouldn't care about anything but getting more of each other. *That* would be a date."

Holy mother of God, it certainly would.

"But we're not dating because you refuse to tell me anything about yourself. So we're having chili and pie in the kitchen, and that's it."

"That's it?" she whispered.

He held up his hands in regret. "Is this Cameron Kasten someone you work with?"

Molly fought the urge to throw the whole pie at him. "Shut up and get the chili. And don't look so sure of yourself. You think I couldn't get into your pants if I wanted?"

He left without a word, though she thought he looked a little worried. Good. It would serve him right if she stripped down and laid herself out naked on the counter. She did have whipped cream.

Hmm. Maybe.

But then he was back, carrying a big Tupperware bowl.

"Why do you carry chili around in your truck?"

"Why do you have a big wi-fi antenna on top of your house?"

"What?" She shook off the question. "Listen, I'm really sorry about the paper. Again. I shouldn't have seduced you into...you know."

"I'd hardly call it seduction."

"Wait. What the hell does *that* mean?"

"It means you were drunk and slightly incoherent, and I should have been the one to know better."

"Slightly *incoherent?* Wow, you paint a beautiful picture." She'd been thinking pretty damn fondly of that night, but she was suddenly overwhelmed by a very different image. A scene in which she, sloppy drunk and cracking unfunny jokes, masturbated herself against an unwilling man's lap.

Oh, holy hell, she'd totally used Ben Lawson as a sex toy.

Molly put her hands over her eyes in horror, determined to talk herself down. That wasn't what had happened. Okay, yes, she'd used him as a sex toy, but he hadn't been unwilling. In fact, his mouth had been tremendously friendly.

Ben touched her hand and she peeked above her fingers.

"I told you I had a good time, Molly. And remember, policemen can't lie."

"But I think I used you."

"Oh, you used me. And I'm so traumatized I can barely keep my hands off you, even though I've given us both every reason not to get involved."

His eyes, normally so careful and guarded, sparked to life. They practically shimmered with heat. *Hot* heat. Hot, I-wanna-rip-off-your-clothes-and-do-you-outside-in-the-water heat. That fire reached out to her and shivered over her nerves, especially the most important nerves.

He'd done it again; made her wet with just a look. How was that possible?

Molly slowly dropped her hands and stared open-mouthed at this man who'd lost any semblance of familiarity. He wasn't Professor Logic anymore, he was just sex, pure and gorgeous.

And there was only one way she was going to get it.

"Okay, I'll tell—"

The doorbell cut off her sex-crazed confession. Ben's eyes narrowed; the super-seduction beam focused and strengthened. "Tell me what, Molly?"

Ding-dong.

Oh, God, she wanted to tell him, tell him everything so he'd take her to bed and let her fulfill all her fantasies.

Except he wouldn't. Because her fantasies were the problem.

An impatient fist knocked on the door. Molly shook her head in disgust at Ben and his powers. "Do they teach you that at the police academy?"

Before he could answer, she spun and stomped to the door. "Happy Halloween," she grumbled to the three teenage boys and stuffed half her candy into their bags.

They muttered things like, "Dude!" and "Awesome!" just like teenagers anywhere, and she knew they wouldn't give a damn when she closed the door in their faces. They had their loot; the crazed, flushed supplier meant nothing to them.

"What were you going to tell me?" Ben asked from close behind her.

She waved him off. "Nothing. Your evil spell is broken."

"What evil spell?"

"You know, with the eyes and the sexy."

"The *sexy?* Jesus, Moll." He burst into laughter, stunning her with the rich, husky sound. Oh, she hadn't heard him laugh like that since he was twenty-two. And drunk. She'd forgotten the way that sound worked through her insides.

"And none of that, either! Not unless you're putting out, mister."

He leaned his shoulder against the wall and grinned down at her. "I think I should call Quinn and find out about your pharmaceutical needs. Make sure you have all your meds for the winter. You've clearly lost it."

Molly sang a verse of "Sexual Healing" as she moved past him toward the kitchen. Ben just shook his head.

"Then make me some dinner at least," she said. "I haven't eaten anything but apple pie since noon. And a candy bar, but that goes without saying. It's Halloween."

He set to work with a nod and moved with ease between the microwave and the cabinets and the table, setting out bowls and spoons and paper towels. Molly knew she should help, but the show was so damn nice, she didn't budge. She just leaned against the counter and watched Ben move through her space.

His hips were that lovely narrow shape that did everything to set off a man's chest and shoulders. And ass. And all the rest that she really, really wanted to see again.

She could still picture him naked on that memorable night, totally aroused and...*impressive*. Thick and long, and slippery wet from that woman's mouth.

Even as she bit back a shiver, Molly told herself that it had happened a long time ago. She'd been supremely inexperienced, and she might have exaggerated his assets in her mind. Yes, he'd been bigger than Ricky, but who wasn't? Maybe the other night he'd been wearing really thick underwear and that was why he'd felt so big against her lap.

He's just a man. You're not missing out on that much. But her brain was trying to con her and she knew it. He was a damned work of art.

His voice broke into her thoughts. "Speaking of meds…"

She made herself raise her eyes to his. "Mmm?"

Ben gestured with her new phone. "Are you giving this a bath? I don't think it likes water. Lucky I didn't turn on the faucet."

"Oh, I, uh… I dropped it."

"I like being the one making you blush for a change. Was it the phone in the sink or staring at my ass that did it?"

Molly edged her jaw forward and glared. "I'm not flirting with you anymore. I won't participate. You don't deserve it. I'm not even interested."

"Mmm-hmm."

She waved him to the table. "You want a beer? A glass of wine?"

Ben glanced at his watch as he sat and started dishing out the steaming chili. "Better not. If anything goes wrong tonight, I'll be called."

Savory spice flash-filled the room with scent. "Oh, man, that smells good."

"Brenda made it."

"Well, please tell Brenda she's a goddess." Molly put on a CD and got herself a Coke.

They ate in silence but exchanged looks that quickly evolved from cautious to challenging.

"Aren't you going to open your package?" Ben finally asked, setting his spoon down with a clank.

She glanced toward the front room. "Nope."

"So you know what it is?"

Actually, she didn't. But it was from Cameron, which meant that it was perfect and meaningful and bound to make her throw up just a little. Either that or he'd gone over the edge and it was the head of a small animal.

"I'm not going to open it in front of you just because you're nosy."

"Cameron Kasten," Ben said thoughtfully, which was when a serious new problem occurred to Molly for the first time.

She managed to grind out, "Don't," past clenched teeth.

"Don't what?"

"I won't think it's cute if you go digging around for dirt on me."

He met her gaze and showed her absolutely nothing.

"You ran a check on me didn't you?"

His jaw ticked. "This isn't about me."

"Of course it is. You're the one with the problem. You don't see anyone else looking into my life around here."

"No? Because Miles called your brother to check into you and then ran the rather intriguing answer in the paper."

Well, he'd given her just what she needed to end this argument. Molly raised an eyebrow. "You comparing yourself to Miles, Ben?"

"Fuck no!"

A distant giggle drifted to Molly's ears, followed by a tentative knock. "Excuse me. Duty calls."

She got rid of the trick-or-treater fairly quickly; a

surprise considering it was Miles's granddaughter…
escorted by a smirking Miles who shot a meaningful
look at Ben's truck at the curb.

Molly closed the door with a snap and didn't say a
word to Ben. She just served him pie and coffee and
sent him on his way.

CHAPTER SIX

IT WAS FREEZING COLD and still dark. She really didn't want to get out of bed.

Molly squinted at the bedside clock—3:27 a.m. Ugh.

If she ignored her bladder, she might be able to get back to sleep. But if she went to the bathroom now, she'd be able to sleep late in the morning.

With a loud groan, she pulled the comforter tighter under her chin and tried to work up the courage to break out of her warm cocoon. She shifted one foot toward the edge and grimaced as cold snaked under the covers and wrapped around her ankle.

Her robe was lying on the floor within arm's reach, but there was really no point. The robe was as cold as everything else, and she hoped to be back in bed before it had time to heat up.

Molly clenched her eyes shut, tossed back the covers and jumped out. Awake enough to be sensible, she shifted the comforter back into place to hold as much warmth in the bed as she could, then ran for the hallway and the bathroom beyond. The white tile burned like ice on her bare feet until she reached the fuzzy rug she'd bought at Target before she moved.

"Thank God," she sighed as her feet sank into softness, then she sat down and her thankfulness disappeared on a little scream. She'd been wrong about the tile; it hadn't been ice, but the toilet seat was one solid cube of it.

Tomorrow, first thing, she was going to get online and see if the Japanese had invented a heated toilet seat yet. Maybe even buy some pajamas to replace the tank top and underwear she normally wore.

Less than sixty seconds later she was back in bed, shivering under the lukewarm sheets. Amazing how easy it was to go weeks, even months, without realizing that the greatest pleasure in life was being in a warm bed on a cold night.

Now that her eyes had adjusted, she saw that it wasn't really so dark. Beyond the row of bedroom windows the moon shone off heavy white clouds, setting the sky aglow. The hill behind her house was true black against the pale night, its crags and crevices silhouetted in a stark, jagged line.

Her body began to relax, warm now, as she stared out at the beautiful scene. She traced the silhouette of the ridge at the edge of her property, following it from one window to the next. A towering pine interrupted the line, a black rocket aiming for the stars. And just past that, a smaller shape…almost like a man.

Molly frowned and tried to remember what was up there. A twisted piñon tree maybe? But the harder she stared the more it looked exactly like a man, the black shadow of a head and shoulders, arms jutting out like Vs, fists against hips.

What the hell?

Her muscles froze, a slow explosion of icy fear that snuck from her belly to her limbs. But the tingling started at her toes and fingers and moved in the opposite direction, gaining strength until it reached her stomach as a white-hot ache.

The figure stood immobile. She felt connected to it, as if she could see the eyes locked onto hers. If she didn't move, he wouldn't move. If she held her breath, he wouldn't dare inhale, either.

Whatever warmth she'd managed to capture beneath the covers leached away. She began to shiver, trying to hold it back, but the harder she fought it the more startling the tremors became.

Who was it? Who would stand in the winter night and *watch her sleeping?*

"Oh, God," she whispered, finally taking a breath. That was too creepy. It'd be less scary if someone was scratching around the door. *Why was he just standing there?* Did he know she'd seen him?

Her fingernails bit into her palms. Her teeth chattered together. But she tried not to move in any perceptible way. If she didn't move he might just fade into the night. Disappear.

The figure cocked his head. Then he slowly raised a shadow hand in silent, menacing acknowledgment.

Terror snapped her free from her bounds. She dove for the ancient phone, and nearly knocked herself out with the ear piece as she slammed it to her ear. She thought for a brief moment that she'd really caused some damage, because she couldn't hear a damn thing. Then she remembered what she'd done in her fit of temper the other day.

The phone was unplugged.

"Oh, God. Oh, *God*." She glanced out the window and saw no one. The pine tree stood alone. Where had he gone?

Molly dropped off the bed and landed on her hands and knees to feel around for the disconnected line. It couldn't have gone far, for God's sake. It couldn't *move*.

Her fingers dragged over the carpet, finding an earring, then a Kleenex. She fought back tears.

Finally—*finally*—the little clip at the end of the phone line was in her hand. She pulled the phone down to the floor and plugged it in and dialed Ben's number before she even brought the receiver to her ear. Her fingers didn't need instructions from her brain. All the numbers in town started with the same three digits, and Ben lived in the home he'd grown up in.

"Lawson," he said, his voice so clear, like he was with her already.

"Ben, there's somebody behind my house."

"Molly?"

"There's somebody outside on the hill."

"Where are you?" He sounded sharp, as if she hadn't just woken him up.

"In my bedroom."

"He's on the hill? There's a trail there, you know. He could be—"

"No one hikes in the middle of the night! And he wasn't…he was just standing there, watching me *sleep*."

"Okay, but it's probably nothing. Are your curtains

open? You shouldn't leave your curtains open at night, Moll."

She'd begun to calm down, but now she felt panicky again, expecting to hear a downstairs window break at any moment. "That's *it?* You're just going to lecture me? Tell me to close my windows? He could be… Aren't you even going to come check it out?"

"Jesus, Molly, I'm already in my truck. I'll be there in two minutes. The phone's about to—"

And he was gone. Lost. She was alone, but only for two minutes. She could do that.

Despite having just used the bathroom, Molly felt an urgent need to pee. She'd written suspense stories before, but she realized now she hadn't really captured fear. Her heroines had never been close to pissing themselves, but here she was, curled on the floor, edging more and more fully under the bed, wondering if she might wet her pants.

There'd been something so innately threatening about that figure, despite that he'd only stood there. It was just so…*freaky.*

But he hadn't *done* anything. And Ben would be here in just a minute. She was fine. Everything would be fine.

Molly set the phone on the floor and slowly eased her head above the mattress. No one there. Unless he was crouched down in the shadow of the hill. Unless he was climbing down, heading for her back door.

It was locked. She was almost sure of it.

The fear was still strong, but it was subsiding into

something manageable. She needed to open the front door for Ben, and he'd be there any moment.

Refusing to crawl like some scurrying animal, Molly got her feet under her and pushed up to a crouch. Once she reached the hall, she turned on the light. No way was she creeping around in the dark; that was practically a guarantee that she'd run smack into the bad guy when she turned a corner. She hadn't watched all those scary movies for nothing.

Rule number one: turn on the lights.

Rule number two: don't check the cellar.

Rule number three: call the hunky policeman for help *immediately.*

"Right," she whispered, then peeked around the wall to check the stairs. All clear, but it was a little dim for her nerves down there at the bottom.

A shadow glided in front of the living room window, just a flit of motion, dark and sinuous.

"A tree branch. Please let it be a tree branch. *Please.*"

Then a flash of light. Red. Then blue, then red again.

"Ben," she gasped and raced for the stairs. "Ben, Ben, Ben." His name burst from her lips with every stair she touched.

A booming knock exploded through the house the moment her foot slapped the bare wood floor of the entry.

"Molly!" he shouted, and she was clawing at the lock, and then finally the door was open and his arm reached out and wrapped around her. "Are you okay?"

She nodded into his chest as he guided her backward and eased the door shut behind them. "I'm fine."

"You didn't…" The deep breath he drew whooshed against her ear. "I tried to call you…on my cell… You scared the shit out of me."

"I'm fine." He smelled warm and safe. Her fear seemed foolish now and far away.

"Frank's on his way. I need to make sure everything's secure in here, and then he and I will take a look around outside, just in case."

She tightened her hold on him. "It might not be safe."

"Molly…"

"Right. I know. You're a cop. I just…" She wanted him to stay, just stay. Maybe tuck her into bed, soothe her back to sleep.

"Let me check the doors and windows, then I want you to show me where you saw him."

Trying not to follow too closely, Molly trailed Ben to each room as he tested every single lock and latch. He even descended into the cellar, but she remembered rule number two and waited at the top of the steps, muscles vibrating with nervousness. She held her breath until he was halfway up and clearly whole.

A sharp voice snapped to life as he stepped past her. "I'm here, Chief."

"Wait for me," Ben replied into a little contraption, while Molly tried to force her heart back down to its appropriate place.

"Let's go upstairs." His hand rested briefly on her hip, and she felt a brief flare of grief as she led the way. What a different moment this would be if he weren't here on official business.

As soon as they were in the bedroom, Molly grabbed

her robe from its crumpled puddle on the floor and slipped it on. Ben reached past her to lift the phone from the floor and set it back on the cradle with a weary sigh.

"Okay, show me what you saw."

She explained everything as well as she could, feeling increasingly ridiculous as she spoke. But Ben was serious and attentive. And then he was gone. Back out into the night after a brief check of the upstairs rooms.

Molly watched flashlight beams dance and weave as he and his backup made their way around the yard and then farther away to find access to the trail.

Having Ben here had helped calm her, but her certainty didn't waiver. She'd seen someone. A man. And only one name sprang to mind.

She'd have to tell Ben about Cameron. Who he was and why she suspected him. But would Cameron really do that? It seemed a bit...*hidden* for him. No one was here to watch and pat him on the back. No one to give witness that his intentions had been totally innocent.

But who the hell else could it be?

Molly grabbed the phone and dialed his home number.

"Sergeant Kasten," he rasped, careful to include his title even in the middle of the night.

"Cameron, where are you?"

"What?"

"Where are you?" she demanded.

"Molly? It's 3:30 a.m. I'm asleep. In bed."

"Turn on your TV."

"Why?"

She wasn't going to be fooled by a technological

trick. It was a simple thing to forward calls to a different phone. "Turn on that giant TV hanging two feet from your bed. *Now*."

"Okay! Jeez, did something happen?"

Something clattered against the phone on the other end, and then the unmistakable sounds of ESPN screamed to life in Molly's ear. He was home.

"All right," she whispered, her blood churning with several different emotions, none of them identifiable.

"What the hell's going on? You okay?"

"Yes. I'm sorry. Bye, Cameron." She hung up and then thought better of it and picked up the receiver again to lay it on the table. When the beeping started, she shoved it under her pillow. Cameron would be calling all night if she didn't take precautions, and then she'd have some 'splaining to do to Ben.

Her feet were starting to get numb, so Molly dug her bunny slippers out from under the bed and flip-flopped down the stairs to turn up the heat. Then she got herself a fortifying cup of wine and sat down at the kitchen table to wait for Ben. There was really nothing else to do.

If it wasn't Cameron, she was at a loss. While he had started acting very creepy on occasion, he'd never dragged any of the other guys into physically stalking her. He wouldn't risk letting them see his true intentions.

And it definitely couldn't have been letter-writing Mrs. Gibson. Even if she had the means to ferret out Molly's true identity and fly halfway across the U.S. to stalk her, an eighty-year-old wouldn't have made it up that hill. So who the hell could it have been?

It felt as if the sun must have started rising by the time Ben knocked, but when she glanced at the clock it claimed that only fifteen minutes had passed. She raced to open the door, and he brought the scent of snow with him when he entered. Tiny crystals glittered on his shoulders and hair.

"Did you find him?" she demanded as he reached past her to re-lock the door.

"No, there was nothing up there. The trail's dry and it didn't start snowing until we were making our way down. You're absolutely sure you saw someone? You weren't dreaming?"

"I was awake. I'd just gone to the bathroom."

"Wearing what?" His eyes made a quick journey down to her slippers and back up.

She shook her head, not understanding.

"The King mine is less than a mile up. I checked it yesterday—the gate lock was broken and there were beer cans around. If teenagers have been hanging around there…" He shrugged and ran an impatient hand through his hair, dissolving the snowflakes. "I'll go check the mine again tomorrow. It was probably some kid coming down from there and he saw you walking around in your underwear and stopped to watch."

Molly started to deny it—surely it had been more threatening than that—but then she paused. Could it be that simple? A horny teenager drunk on a six-pack of cheap beer? She headed back toward the kitchen, aware of Ben following close behind.

"Unless," he continued, the tone of his voice dropping to a slight warning, "there's something you should tell me. Some reason you think someone would be watching you."

Since she'd tracked Cameron down, it was easy to shake her head. "No. It just felt so menacing. Do you really think it could have been accidental?"

"Were you in your underwear?"

"I was wearing a shirt!"

"*That* shirt?"

She glanced down to the neckline of her white tank peeking above the silk robe. "Yeah."

"I would've stopped to look at that when I was seventeen, too."

"Yeah, right. You would've spied on a girl through her bedroom windows in the middle of the night."

"He wasn't exactly climbing on hedges to peep through the curtains. Close your damn drapes, all right?"

"Fine," Molly snapped and slammed down her juice glass so hard that the last bit of wine sloshed out. "I just like to see the view when I wake up. I shouldn't have to worry about creeps wandering around on the trail at three in the morning!"

"Molly…"

When he pulled her into a tight hug, she realized she'd started crying, which really pissed her off. But he felt so good that she let him hold her, and the anger slowly eased away. "I'm okay, Ben," she insisted, pressing her face into the warm space between his chest and his jacket. She breathed in the scent of his skin and the dark leather of his coat. He smelled just like a man should, strong and clean.

She sniffled on another tear and heard him sigh.

"Frank went back to the station to fill out the reports. I'll take another look in the morning, I promise."

"I saw someone," she repeated, and felt his chin slide against her hair as he nodded.

"I know. Come on, I'll tuck you in if you think you can sleep."

Yowza! Was he kidding? Molly made very sure that her voice didn't hold a hint of excitement. "I suppose I could try," she said in a tiny, hopeless whisper.

"It's only 4:00 a.m." His big hand was on her waist again, curving over the top of her hip as he turned her and guided her toward the stairs. "You should try to sleep."

"If you think so, Ben." *Yes, take care of me, you big, strong hunk.* How far would he go to help her sleep, exactly? Now that any sign of true danger had passed, she'd regressed to her normal state of mind when Ben was near: abject horniness. But he didn't have to know that. Yet.

She swayed her hips as she ascended the stairs. Surely he couldn't help but notice. Her robe only came to midthigh. Maybe he could even see her panties.

But he was all business when they reached the door of her room. He brushed past her to close all the blinds tightly, then drew the curtains, too. "It's freezing in here. Why don't you fire up the woodstove?"

"Umm…because I'm not *exactly* sure which way the handle goes?"

"What handle?"

"The one that opens the flue. I don't know which way is open and which is closed."

Ben popped open the cast-iron door and stuck his hand in. "Well, there's cold air gusting in, so I'd guess it's open right now."

"Oh." She waited for him to say something sarcastic, but he just set about pulling wood from the big basket and stacking it inside the stove. She took the opportunity to ease the phone back onto the hook. Hopefully Cameron had gone back to sleep by now.

Ben had a big fire blazing within seconds, which was a helpful, if annoying, skill. Molly was sure it would've taken her a good half hour.

Before the warmth could gather and migrate over to her side of the room, she slipped off her robe. No point in wasting a good set of erect nipples when she had them.

Ben stood, dusting his hands, but he froze mid-motion when he saw her, gaze locked on her breasts. "I might've been willing to climb a hedge or two," he muttered. She noticed how rumpled he was then; the gray T-shirt he wore under his coat was wrinkled and not tucked in. His hair stuck up a little in back. He looked like a man who needed to get back to bed.

Heat from the stove began to creep closer and Molly shivered in response. His eyelids dropped to a sleepy, dangerous look. Encouraged, she started to move seductively toward him, but her bunny slippers slapped the floor and he blinked from his trance.

Muttering curses, she kicked the things under the bed. *Sexy and fun, my ass.*

"I'll let you know what I find in the morning," Ben said in a fast, too-loud voice as he edged toward the door.

"Thanks, Ben, but..."

He paused, one hand clutching the door frame.

"I'm sorry, I know it's dumb, but... Could you...?" She scooted up onto the high bed and pointed her toes toward the floor. "Could you check under the bed before you go?"

His gaze moved to the space beneath her toes before it climbed slowly back up to her feet, then her legs, and finally paused on the fingers she'd spread wide over her bare thighs. "Sure."

"Thanks." She pulled her feet up to the mattress and tucked them under her so she could lean slightly forward. Ben approached warily, moving in a careful, fluid motion as he knelt down and ducked his head.

"Nothing under here but some slippers and, hmm, three socks and a shirt."

Molly rocked forward on her hands and knees to watch. "Thank you."

He straightened and said, "No problem," but his body stuttered as he rose from his crouch.

Smiling up at him, she stayed on her hands and knees, confident that her gaping tank top would keep him still for a moment. Or maybe her hot-pink boy briefs. "Do you make it a habit to tuck your citizens in after a frightening incident? It's very sweet."

"Huh-uh."

"Well, thank you for taking care of *me*." She wiggled her ass a little and watched his eyes darken to melted chocolate in response. "I'm sorry I dragged you out of bed in the middle of the night."

"It's my job." His gaze trailed liquid heat over her hips and up her spine, then back down again. His hands clenched and unclenched at his sides, and Molly's belly echoed the pulse of that tension as she pushed up to her knees. She inched closer, her mouth almost even with his.

"You're not on duty," she reminded him as she eased her palms up to slide them beneath his coat. His chest rose in a deep breath as she pushed the coat off his shoulders and let it slide down his arms with a little whoosh. "And I'm not sleepy."

"Molly…"

Hot power licked through her as his breath came harder. Her breasts brushed his chest, and fire shot down her nerves, straight to her clit. God, she wanted this. Wanted him panting, unable to fight his need, all his logic swirling away like so many falling snowflakes.

Smoothing her palms down his T-shirt, she marveled at the impossible strength beneath the warm cotton. Greed swept through her, tangled with sharp lust. When her fingers reached the hem of his shirt, she didn't bother with subtleties, she simply pushed it high and tugged it off his head. Ben helped her by raising his arms, but he still didn't reach out to offer more.

Not that Molly cared. His bare chest was spread before her like a banquet of hot skin. And, God, he looked delicious. Just like she'd always pictured him. Tanned, muscled shoulders and big arms. A dusting of brown hair that led the way to his flat belly. The top button of his faded jeans was undone, likely due to his haste to get here, and they perched insecurely on his tight hips.

Hungry, starving, she licked her lips and squeezed her thighs tight against the hard pulse that pushed blood into every nerve between her legs. She wanted to be ravished. Wanted him to pick her up just like he'd done the night before. She wanted no choice in it, no control.

"Was this..." he said in a gruff voice she'd never heard from him. "Was this all a ruse to get me in your bedroom?"

Molly smiled at him through her lashes and pressed one hand just below his heart. She spread her fingers wide and brushed her thumb over and over his nipple. "Do you really believe you needed to be tricked here? You think I couldn't have had you earlier today?"

His laugh was humorless. "No," he grumbled, then sucked in one short, violent breath when she leaned in to swirl her tongue around the nipple she'd been teasing.

She kissed it again, then slid her lips lower, pressing tiny kisses to his chest. She was back on her hands and knees, supplicant to his body, and the idea turned her on so much that she couldn't help wiggling her ass as she pressed an openmouthed kiss just above his navel.

"Molly," he growled, and his fingers curled into her hair just hard enough to be forceful. He dragged her up so fast that her body slammed into his chest and his mouth was on hers, open and hot and demanding.

Boy, her body remembered that taste, and every nerve that hadn't been awake perked up as soon as his tongue rubbed hers. She moaned into him, then gasped with surprise when his hands took her elbows in a tight grasp to hold her still. He kissed her so hard she had to tilt her head back to take all he was giving, and, Jesus, it felt good.

His mouth left hers and she was breathing hard, gasping, as his teeth scraped her jaw. Then he leaned down, his hands still holding her still as he licked his way down her neck. The shadow of a beard scraped her chest, rasped against the cotton of her shirt, and he was on his knees on the floor.

"Ben," she panted, her fists curled into her own hips, because his hands still held her pinned. His lips closed over her nipple, then his teeth, scraping her through the wet fabric. Molly keened and pushed against his hands, but her arms didn't budge. She was helpless to stop his sucking, biting kisses, and the knowledge tightened everything inside her to a glorious tension. Her clit felt swollen. When she clenched her thighs, just that slight shift of her panties made her tremble.

"Oh, God. Oh, Ben. I need you to touch me."

"I am touching you." His words were ice against her wet nipple.

"No, I..."

He moved to the other nipple and lavished just as much attention there. She squirmed, arching into him, wishing he would just crawl inside her and ease this terrible pain.

"Please," she begged.

His lips left her with a tiny wet sound and he smiled up at her, eyes burning hot. The wet cotton against her nipples had faded to transparency and the sight of her pink flesh begging for more attention only ratcheted her need higher.

"Please touch me," she whispered. His thumbs skimmed over the inside of her elbows as a reminder that he already was. "Touch me…" She swallowed against the danger of what she really wanted to say. But his brown eyes glowed with demand. He wanted what she was afraid to give, afraid to admit.

"You like to talk," he said, a challenge.

Molly gasped. "I was drunk!"

"Yes, you were. And you like to talk. So talk to me."

She swallowed again and felt her heart quake in her chest. She'd always tried to control herself, tried to swallow back the embarrassing things she wanted to say. But Ben was looking up at her with a half smile that was secret, wicked and not the least bit sweet.

Her whisper hurt her throat. "I want… I want your fingers inside me. In my pussy. Fucking me."

Oh, yeah, that was what he wanted, what they both wanted. His smile widened to victory, and her knees began to shake against the mattress as he released her arms. When he reached for her top, he stood and whipped it over her head with as little hesitation as she'd shown with his shirt.

She thought he was going to pull her close again, but his hands—his big hands—tucked under her arms, fingers spreading over her rib cage, and he picked her up. Just picked her up as if she weighed *nothing,* and he set her on her feet right between his body and the bed.

"Man, I love it when you do that."

"I know," he answered with the distinctive sound of male pleasure rumbling low in his voice. And then he pushed her panties off, shoved them off, really, and lifted her up *again,* as if she wasn't horny enough. Her breasts pressed into the crisp hair of his chest and she wrapped her legs around his hips and pressed herself against his jeans.

"Mmm, déjà vu," she moaned as he lifted one knee to the mattress and hauled them both up. She hung on like a monkey on a tree. A big ol' hard, straight tree with a massive trunk.

"What—" Ben asked over her sudden laughter "—is going through that head of yours?"

"Phallic symbols," she giggled as he lowered her to the pillow.

"Phallic *symbols?* Really? Not any specific phallus?" His hand paused on the zipper of his jeans. "That's kind of an ego blow."

Molly watched his hand with pained interest. "Don't stop."

"Well, I don't know, Moll. I'm kinda—"

"Take those jeans off *now.*"

"Huh. That's not so much dirty talk as it is bossiness." His hand fell away from the zipper. "Now where were we?"

She opened her mouth to object, she really did, but he planted a hand on either side of her shoulders and lowered himself down for a kiss. One taste of him and Molly didn't care about his jeans; there were so many other good parts of him to enjoy. His back, for instance, a smooth expanse of muscles that rippled under her touch.

His tongue was slick velvet, his chin the slightest rasp of stubble against her skin, but his back was hot silk beneath her fingers. One more texture against her— warm denim—and she'd be golden.

Molly smoothed her hands down his back, snuck beneath the waistband of his jeans, and gripped his tight ass in her hands. They both grunted when she pulled his hips tight to hers and ground herself against him.

"Oh, hell yeah," Molly moaned, but Ben shook his head.

"Not this time, babe. This time we're doing it right."

She rolled her hips and little stars twinkled through her body. "Feels…pretty right."

Ben half groaned and half laughed, but he managed to slip from her clutches, sliding his body lower, rubbing his skin against her sensitive nipples until she arched up to get more, more, more.

Oh, yeah, there was the scrape of his beard again, drawing a swath of prickly pleasure down her chest, and over one happily startled nipple just before he sucked the tight peak deep into his mouth. Molly arched her head back so far that the room turned upside down. "Oh, yes. Yes, yes."

His laughter rumbled through her, trailing sizzles of pleasure. He followed the echo of nerves down, pausing to press a kiss or slow bite to a few different spots. And then he was licking the hollow of her hip, the tight tendon of her inner thigh. She dug her hands into the sheets to keep from grabbing his hair and tugging him to the right place. She'd already used his crotch as a sex toy; it probably wouldn't be right to use his face.

And he would get there eventually. He couldn't suck that one spot at the very top of her thigh forever. He'd get—

"Now!" she cried out. "Now, *please*. I need you. Oh, Ben, I want your tongue and your mouth and…sucking and…"

That chuckle again, only this time it was trembling through her sex, because his tongue was finally *right there*, pressed against her clit. He licked, curled his tongue around, sucked, and this was *so* much better than her little blue friend.

"Oh, God, oh God," she groaned, adding a few more words she tried not to hear herself say. But Ben seemed to take it as encouragement, because he repeated the little swirling motion with his tongue. "More, please. Pretty please?"

And just like that, Ben obliged. He didn't mess around with preliminaries, didn't ease in and let her adjust; instead, he sunk two fingers deep, forcing a wild scream from her mouth just as he withdrew and did it again. She didn't have time for dirty words, she was too busy coming her heart out.

Ben worked his fingers and his tongue until he wrung every last whimper from her, then finally let her push his head away. "Now," he growled from between her legs, "wasn't that better than dry humping?"

She shook her head, way too limp to nod, and hoped he'd take it as agreement.

"You sleepy enough now?"

Molly lolled her head far enough to the side to get a look at him peeking above her belly. His eyes were fire and joy and wicked desire. "No," she lied. "I'm not close to sleepy."

His eyes crinkled in a smile. "You sure?"

"Oh, I'm hella sure."

He rose up and knelt above her, like some kind of Greek god in unbuttoned Levi's, and Molly felt her knees weaken despite the fact that she was sprawled on her back.

Finally. Finally she was going to have Ben Lawson.

He seemed to be done teasing, because he backed off the bed and reached for his zipper without a word. And how was he going to unzip past that huge—surely it was huge—bulge? What if it got stuck? But disaster admitted defeat in the face of his gifted hands. The zipper slid down and so did his pants and his underwear and—

"Oh, sweet mother," Molly heard her lips saying.

Ben toed off his boots and glanced up at her through his lashes, neither proud nor self-conscious. Just…intent.

He slid back into bed, and Molly flipped to her stomach and stretched toward the night table. "Condom," she stammered as his hand closed over her ankle. She got the drawer open about the time his fingers grasped the back of her knee.

"I've got it," he murmured, his palm sliding higher. Molly froze, trying to act like she might be doing something, when in reality she was simply holding still. His palm pressed up her leg to the very bottom of her ass. She closed her eyes and sunk her teeth into the pillow.

"You…" His right hand joined in, cupping the other cheek. He kneaded her in a slow, sensual motion, sliding, testing the give of her flesh. "You've always had the most amazing ass."

She wiggled it again, trying to be subtle and probably failing, but he murmured appreciatively.

Molly grinned, high on her power. "I've got a very generous booty."

"Oh, yeah," he agreed, making her laugh.

"You like that, Professor?"

"Oh, yeah."

His teeth pressed gently against her left cheek and Molly yelped. He kissed it apologetically, then seemed to forget that he'd been apologizing and bit again. This time she was ready and she sighed in excitement that only increased when he kissed a slow circle up to her hip and back down. When his hand slipped between her legs and stroked, she moaned into the pillow and arched her ass higher.

My God, she was hot again, even hornier than she'd been a few minutes ago. And Ben…well, poor Ben hadn't had his turn yet and his breath was rushing across the rise of her ass in long, ragged bursts.

"I want…" he started to say and then growled as his wide hands closed over her hips. He pulled her up to her knees and she heard the crinkle of the condom wrapper. "I want this," he rasped, just before he steadied her hips and pushed the broad head of his dick into the wetness he'd inspired.

Molly pressed her forehead to the pillow and whimpered in sublime anticipation. He felt big already, only an inch in, and Jesus, it was good.

Her body resisted, so Ben eased just a tiny bit out and pushed forward again.

"Oh, Ben. Oh, God," she groaned, edging her knees farther apart. That provided just enough ease for him to press all the way in, inch by steady inch. Her sex squeezed hard against him, fighting the invasion, and she gloried in the way his breath caught with every inhalation.

Once his hips were pressed flush to hers and Molly was squirming with fullness, Ben stopped to catch his breath. His fingers dug into her skin as if he wouldn't let her go even if she begged. She reached blindly for the rails of her headboard and clutched them tightly, waiting, waiting.

Then, just as slowly as he'd entered, he pulled out again, almost all the way, before he paused. She thought he'd make her beg again and she fought it, bit her lip, tried to defy him, hoping he'd make it worse, but then he surged in and all her thoughts broke into glittering pieces.

"Ohmigod," she prayed into the pillow as he began to fuck her in long, hard strokes. "Ohmigod, ohmigod."

"I've wanted *this*," he ground out, taking her even harder.

"Yes," she panted. "Yes, yes, yes." And then she was saying too many things, yelling and whispering. Groaning and crying. Things like *harder* and *more* and *please*. Things that started with *F* and ended with "me."

And all Ben said was her name, over and over, and

she loved it. Just as he began to quicken his stroke, he paused, buried deep, and drew in a long, slow breath. Then he pulled back, his cock sliding out for an impossibly long time, and smoothed both hands from her hips to her thighs.

His hands pulled her legs back, lowering her to her stomach and twisting her at the same time. Molly swung one trembling leg over his ducking head, and he settled nicely between her legs. "And I want this," he said, just before his mouth caught hers and he slid back inside her.

She couldn't speak while they kissed, but she found it easy to encourage him in other ways. She dug her nails into his clenching ass, tilted her pelvis, up, up, up, wrapped her ankles around his thighs to pull him deeper.

Jesus, she was going to come again. She wrenched her mouth from his to tell him so. A few times. And Ben rose up on straining arms to thrust harder and higher.

"Come for me," he ordered her. *"Come."*

And she did. Long and loud, sobbing his name.

When he finally plummeted over the edge, Molly had recovered enough that she could watch and appreciate the beauty. The tense muscles of his shoulders, the straining tendons in his neck, and his pained mask of pleasure as he climaxed with a ragged groan.

A moment later, he collapsed in slow motion. First his forehead hit the pillow. He pulled out of her body as his shoulders tilted to the side, and then he fell like a big tree, twisting so he landed right beside her.

She wanted to tell him how good he was, how many of her fantasies he'd just managed to fulfill in the space of a few minutes, but Ben offered a tired smile and rolled out of bed before he'd even caught his breath. He headed for the bathroom, and Molly, rude sex hostess that she was, snuggled beneath the covers and fell asleep before the toilet had even flushed.

The warm weight of his chest pleased her enough to wake her for a bare moment when he returned, but then she was far gone, floating in a dream world of shirtless policemen with big guns.

To serve and protect, indeed.

CHAPTER SEVEN

PHONE SEX OPERATOR.

Ben cast one long last glance at Molly's sleeping form and closed the door softly behind him. With that voice and those words...she'd be a popular 1-900 worker.

Stomach churning with an acid urgency to find out who the hell she was, Ben took a detour to the kitchen. He didn't have time for coffee, a Coke would have to do, but when he opened the fridge all he saw was diet.

"Damn," he muttered as he shut the door, but as it swung past him, he caught sight of a glorious treasure and stuck his hand out to snatch it back open. There, on the bottom shelf, were three Mocha Frappucinos.

"She's a goddess." He popped open a bottle and headed for the door. Luckily there was a thumb lock he could turn before leaving, though he wasn't happy with the security of such a flimsy device. He'd have to talk to her about a dead bolt. While he was on the doorstep testing the knob, he heard the gravelly sound of a truck slowing behind him and glanced over his shoulder, grateful to see a dark blue SUV on the street instead of Miles's truck.

His gratefulness was short-lived. In the time it took

him to walk from the front door to the driveway, another truck passed. For God's sake, Molly's house was
on a dead-end street. What the hell was the whole town
doing out? He glared up the street as another car pulled
away from a house at the very end. Baffled, he watched
as it passed him, and noticed the woman driving and
the child seat in the back.

"Well, fuck me," Ben sighed as an important fact
tunneled out of his memory bank. Miss Amy's Daycare
was at the end of Pine Road, perfectly situated to pro-
vide him with the least amount of discretion possible.

He slammed his door way too hard, and then felt
guilty that he might have woken Molly. It wasn't quite
seven, and she'd had a long night.

The smile popped to his face even though he tried to
suppress it. Last night had been a big mistake. A mind-
shatteringly satisfying mistake, but still…

Forcing the smile into a scowl, Ben backed out of her
driveway and headed for home and a quick shower. By
the time he made it to the station for his split shift, any
urge to grin had faded. In fact, he was pretty sure he
looked damn grim as he typed in his only viable clue.

Cameron Kasten. Denver.

Wham. Nine hundred and fifty-two hits. And almost
all of them related to the Denver Police Department.

"Ho-ly crap."

Sergeant Cameron Kasten. Ben scanned the first
page for the word "vice" but it didn't appear. Instead
he saw "crisis management" and "negotiation team"
and, sprinkled throughout almost every hit, "lead hostage negotiator."

Who the hell was he sleeping with? A girl who worked with the Denver Police Department's hostage unit or—and this sent a cold finger down his back—someone who'd been involved in a hostage situation?

But her name hadn't appeared in any newspaper articles, and Ben suddenly remembered the phone call he'd overheard. *Take the hint, Cameron.* Not exactly a professional conversation.

Ben grabbed the phone, started to dial, than glanced at the clock. Still a little before eight. He hung up and dialed a different number.

"Quinn Jennings," Molly's brother muttered.

"Who the hell is Cameron Kasten?" Ben barked into the phone without preamble.

"Ben? What the…?" His voice dropped lower. "Why are you asking me that?"

"I—" Ben cut himself off. What was he supposed to say to that? *Well, I'm sleeping with your sister, and…*

"Are you sleeping with my sister?"

"What?" Ben felt sweat break out along his hairline in an instant tingle.

"Jesus, it's true! I saw the little hints Miles dropped in the *Tribune,* but I never thought you'd—"

"Don't tell me you get that rag *mailed* to you?"

Quinn gave an exasperated huff. "Of course not. I read it online."

"Online? No. You're fucking with me."

"Where the hell have you been? It's been online since August. And I saw the gossip about you and Molly, but, jeez, Ben. My little sister?"

Ben swiped the back of his hand across his forehead. "I... I don't..."

"Well, I guess she's all grown up." He didn't exactly sound convinced.

"It's not anything, you know..." Ben searched for the right word. "Sordid."

"No? So you're not jumping into her bed just a week after she moved to town?"

There was no good answer, and the seconds were passing by. Ben thought he heard crickets chirping and glanced out the window to confirm that it was light outside.

When the awkwardness finally stretched out too long, Quinn made a low noise. "I see."

Ben ran a hand through his hair and bit the bullet. "I've known Molly since she was a baby. I'm not using her or screwing around with her, okay? I like her. And I'm sorry she's being dragged through the paper like that. I didn't exactly intend for anything to happen, and I certainly didn't intend for it to be public."

"I know you're a good guy," Quinn said, though the words came slow and with no enthusiasm.

"Quinn, we've been friends since kindergarten. You know I don't fall into bed with women casually."

"Not during the winter, you don't."

"Ouch," Ben muttered, rubbing his forehead.

"All right, I'm sorry. That was a low blow. I've seen you hook up here during the summer, but not often. I apologize."

"Mmm. So about this Cameron Kasten."

"Sorry, man. Ask your girlfriend."

Ben's eye twitched at the word. "She's not forth-coming."

"Ha! You got that right. But I can't help you. I received a very disappointed phone call from Molly after that little gaffe in the *Trib*."

"Yeah, what the heck was that about, Quinn?"

"Miles caught me at a bad time. I was distracted and..."

"I get it."

"But I promised Molly I'd be more careful. And she specifically brought you up."

Ben sighed in disgust. "That's really flattering."

Quinn's chuckle irritated the heck out of Ben, but he wasn't in a position to protest.

"He's her ex-boyfriend, right?"

"Mum's the word."

Ben ground his teeth together. "Like I said, I'm interested in starting a real relationship here, which is going to be impossible if I don't know anything about her."

"Correct me if I'm wrong, but that's more of a trust issue than an information issue. I could tell you everything I know and you still won't be any closer to Molly."

The words were true enough to sting like hell, so Ben hurried Quinn off the phone and got back onto his computer. What in God's name was she hiding, and why was she hiding it from *him?*

As he glanced through one short article about Sergeant Kasten, Ben tried to ignore the department phone number listed at the end of the page. Nosy, he might be, but even he knew that would be over the line. His fingers were twitching though, so he closed the page in a hurry and picked up the phone to check in with Sheriff McTeague.

The receptionist was just asking him to hold when Brenda passed by Ben's door. He stopped her with an upraised hand and waved her in.

"Thanks again for dinner last night. Molly Jennings asked me to pass on her compliments to the chef. Best chili she's had in years."

"Molly?"

He smiled at her frown. "Don't worry, she said she'd wash your bowl today and bring it right over. Apparently some women are sensitive about their Tupperware? First I've heard of it."

"Oh. Yeah. I just… I didn't expect—"

Ben pointed at the phone as Sheriff McTeague answered with his usual gruff manner. "Hey, Sheriff, you ever planning to return that GPS tracker we lent you?"

"I didn't think you'd need it any time soon. Heard you're real busy with the new girl in town."

"Unbelievable," Ben muttered. Word had already spread through the whole damn county. When he realized Brenda was still standing in his doorway, he looked up in surprise, but she was turning away, hurrying toward her desk.

"Listen, Chief," the sheriff said, suddenly all business. "I've got a problem with Nick Larsen. He's not doing a damn thing about those rotting fences of his, and he's got two or three heifers breaking out every week. Can you keep an eye out since he's so close to Tumble Creek? Damn fool's gonna let those cattle stand on the road till someone gets hurt."

"Yeah, I'll do a drive by in the evenings."

"Stubborn old coot."

"I tell you what. The only thing Larsen cares about is money. I'll remind him he could lose the whole ranch if someone runs into one of those cows at night and ends up dead. See if that'll convince him to spend a few hundred on fencing."

"Thanks. Let me know."

A call beeped in before he'd even hung up the phone. A mule deer had got its head stuck in a wrought-iron fence, trying to nibble on the last of a flower garden. The doe's neck was scraped raw from trying to escape.

Ben grabbed his shotgun from the gun safe and headed for the door, knowing what the outcome could be. Surely the day had to get better after this.

MOLLY JENNINGS WAS having a wonderful day.

She snuggled deeper into the pillows she'd piled against her back and shifted the laptop higher on her knees. Her contract called for a two-hundred page book and she was already up to ninety-five. At the rate she was going, she'd be done in ten more days.

She glanced around the room, at the little hints that someone else had been there.

Maybe less than ten days.

With a sigh of happiness, she ran her hand over the wrinkled sheets that still smelled of Ben and sweat and sex. No point in working in her office when there was so much inspiration here.

The blankets were rumpled, the fire in the wood stove still burned, and the air shimmered with remembered pleasure. Not caring in the least that she felt like a teenager, Molly grinned at the little scrap of masking tape stuck to the front of the black stove. *Open,* it said, with a crooked arrow pointing to the right of the flue handle.

Jeez, he was cute. And sexy. And *hot.* "Soooo hot."

Molly thought of something Ben had done with his tongue and started typing. Not that she was foolish enough to use those personal details—not this time— but, boy oh boy, did that man give her good ideas.

Her dark sheriff was in the process of describing to the wicked widow just what he was planning to do to her that night when the phone rang. Molly's phone, that is. She hit Save and picked up the receiver. "Yello."

"Molly, you sound great!" a smooth male voice said.

She tried not to smile, but she was in a wonderful mood, and Michael *was* her favorite of all the almost-lovers. She didn't even mind that he'd gotten hold of her new number. "Hey, Michael."

"Are the mountains being good to you?"

"Oh, they definitely are. And how's the race for partner going?"

"Really well, actually. I was just telling Cameron that the senior partner invited me to sail the Bahamas with him over New Year's."

Though her mood dipped at the mention of Cameron—of course they'd just talked. Why else would Michael have called?—she offered congratulations on the vacation coup.

"Speaking of travel," Michael drawled, "I can't wait to see *you* this weekend."

Her heart stuttered over his words, a chill sneaking through the warm flesh beneath her skin. "What?" What did he mean, *see* her? She'd never have suspected Michael in a million years, but—

"The Policeman's Ball. We all bought tickets so we could see Cameron get his award, but mostly I wanted to see you. Don't tell Cameron." He laughed.

"But why would you see me?"

"Uh, because you're his date? I was hoping you'd wear that little red dress, the one with the—"

"I don't know what Cameron told you, but I am not his date. I live four hours away, not to mention that we broke up over six months ago."

"Yeah, but you two are kind of meant to be. This is just a little blip."

Spoken like a true automaton. "I've gotta go, Michael. Have fun on your trip to the Bahamas. I'm sorry I won't see you this weekend."

She hung up before he could spout any more of Cameron's lies. She was truly sorry she'd never see Michael again. He was handsome, smart and funny. She'd even trusted him enough to warn him about Cameron, yet he'd fallen faster than any of the other men. Sometimes smart guys were a little too confident in their intellect; his brain had sizzled like popping bacon in the face of Cameron's charisma.

And what exactly was Cameron up to now?

Molly reluctantly disentangled herself from her sex sheets and stepped into the bunny slippers. She slapped down the stairs and stopped at the table by the front door to glare at the box Ben had delivered.

Measuring the sides of the square box with her eyes, she tried to determine what it could possibly be. A tiny robot that would kidnap her and fly her back to Denver? Probably not, though Cameron might have access to those little rolling guys used by the bomb squad. Did it hold a gas capsule that would break open and knock her out for a few hours? Molly shuddered, then she grabbed her keys and sawed at the tape. He wasn't 007, for Pete's sake.

Will you wear this for me? the note on top said. Molly swept it aside and scrunched up her nose, anticipating some perverted underwear, but inside was a clear plastic box. At first, she thought it held a real flower, but when she drew the box out, she saw that the little bloom was made of delicate art glass in shimmering violet-blue.

As she'd predicted, a lovely gift, if only it hadn't come from a crazy. She set the flower aside, noticing that there was more beneath it. Ah, here were the underwear, consisting almost entirely of a string to chafe the crack of her ass and a little violet bow to accent her pubic hair. Nice. Cameron had always had a thing for thongs.

Another note was lying at the bottom of the package. *The flower is for Saturday evening. The other is for Saturday night.*

"You wish," Molly growled and stalked off to find the phone.

"Cameron, what the hell do you think you're doing?"

The noise of the Special Operations department clattered through the earpiece. "I was wondering when you'd call, babe. What was that drama about last night?"

"You mean the drama of you sending me underwear? We are not dating anymore. We will never date again. Why can't you get that through your head?"

He chuckled as if she'd just promised him kinky sex.

"Cameron, I'm serious. You can't keep this up."

"You forgot about this weekend, didn't you?"

"Wha— I— You were persistent before, but now you're delusional. The next time you call me, I'll be recording the conversation. Consider yourself notified."

"You called *me,* babe. And don't think there's not a record of that."

Molly made an obscene gesture at the phone. "So?"

"So, everyone knows you run hot and cold. Flirting one minute, pushing me away the next. I'm just trying to help you make up your mind."

"My mind is made up! I don't want you and I haven't wanted you for six months!"

"Not quite six months. Remember that night in the alley? *After* we'd broken up?"

Her jaw creaked in her ear as she bit back the raging curses she wanted to rain on his head. "That was a mistake."

"Well, it was quick and nasty, but I wouldn't say it was a mistake."

"Fuck you," she ground out.

"I'll pick you up Saturday morning."

"You're insane and I'm not going anywhere with you."

"Sorry, babe. You promised, and I'm the guest of honor."

"That was six months ago, and we are *through*. Over. Find another date."

Molly hung up and then just stood there, squeezing the phone and trying not to cry. He wouldn't come up here and ruin everything with Ben. Surely he wouldn't. And anyway, she'd already gotten Ben into her bed. There was no turning back from that. She'd broken the cycle.

Picking up the whole box, she went to the kitchen and dumped it in the trash, hardly even a bit tempted to keep the panties and wear them for Ben. She had other sexy underwear that weren't tainted by Cameron's psychosis. And anyway, Ben seemed perfectly content with *normal* panties. What a relief. It was much more fun to dress kinky for a man who didn't demand it.

She was wondering if she had a pair of black thighhighs to go with her new red-and-black bra when the phone rang. Molly glanced around for a moment, trying to track the sound.

"Oops." She plucked the phone out of the trash and answered it with trepidation. She really had to set up Caller ID.

"Hey, Moll," Ben said gruffly, his tone not the least bit smooth. In fact, he sounded pretty irritated. The genuine emotion was a nice change after talking to Cameron.

"Why, hello, Chief." She wondered if he blushed at her little purr of affection.

"Just…uh, just calling to let you know I walked all the way up to King Mine today. I'm sorry to say I found nothing. The lock's still on the gate."

"But it still could've been some kid going up there to party—he just wasn't successful."

"I see no reason to suspect anything more serious, but if you have any suspicions, any thoughts at all…"

"No, none." Cameron was crazy and starting to scare her, but he simply hadn't been in Tumble Creek.

Ben's voice dropped to a gentler rumble. "Are you okay?"

Molly smiled and leaned against the counter, letting liquid relaxation ooze back into her muscles. "I'd say I'm more than okay. How 'bout you, Chief?"

"Maybe."

She could definitely hear a smile in that one word.

He cleared his throat. "But you realize this means we're going to have to talk. Openly."

"About what?"

"Molly."

"Mmm?"

"We're dating now. You have to come clean with me."

She twirled a strand of hair around her finger and acted obtuse even though he wasn't there. "Dating? Did you take me to Grand Valley for dinner and a movie and I didn't even notice?"

"Excuse me?"

"Because I thought we were just having sex. Really good sex. Not a café or a corsage in sight."

"Goddamn it, Moll—"

"Look, dating you seems to come with lots of conditions, and I'm just not interested, Ben."

"That's ridiculous. You slept with me."

"And I truly hope to do so again. Soon. Tonight even. Are you gonna be at The Bar?"

"Don't push me, woman. I'm not—"

"Thanks for your help last night, Chief Lawson. You're a real doll." She hung up on his sputtering curses, then ignored the phone when it rang again. The answering machine picked up, but he declined to leave a message.

Ben didn't just want sex with her; he wanted more.

A grin spread so far over her face that her cheeks hurt. A serious relationship was impossible, unfortunately; he'd never accept the scandalous truth about her. She had to keep it light and casual, but it was a joy to know that he wasn't satisfied with that.

"Ah, well," she sighed, running her fingertips over her mouth. Light and casual it would be, and she would enjoy every minute of it because she deserved some damn fun.

Molly glanced at the calendar that hung next to the kitchen sink. If Cameron really did come, he'd be here Saturday morning, and he'd do everything in his power to edge Ben away from her. If she couldn't keep it from happening…at least she had four good days to work Ben into exhaustion. Better than nothing, which was exactly what she'd had up to now.

Maybe she could try calling Cameron's superior officer again, or sending a letter to… Who? Internal Affairs? But he was right about one thing. She had called him today. Not only that, but she'd called him in the middle of the night just a few hours before that.

"Shit." The phone records would not look good for

her. Plus, he really didn't call her that often, and the last time she'd tried the old "He has all my exes calling to spy on me" line, she'd been laughed out of the station.

Cameron Kasten was too smart by half, but even he wouldn't be able to take away the memories of a few good nights in Ben's arms. All she had to do was make sure those arms were hot, willing and ready for action.

Dropping the phone, she raced upstairs to look for those thigh-highs.

"FOR GOD'S SAKE, Mr. Wenner," Ben huffed. "Try to have a little dignity."

The man sobbed harder, arms curled around his bony knees. Ben was trying to be sympathetic, but he really just wanted to snap a picture of Mr. Wenner and make him look at it. His thin white hair stuck up in tufts around his head, and his bare legs were a melange of matted brown hair and pasty skin that contrasted sickeningly with the bright green of his parka. Of course, he'd looked worse before his wife had agreed to throw him the parka.

She hadn't appreciated coming home from her bridge game to find her husband on an extremely intimate— and interactive—phone call with another woman.

"Mr. Wenner, you need to calm down and think about where you can stay for a few days."

"I can't— I— There's nowhere to go! How can I survive without my sweet Olive?"

"Perhaps you should have thought about that before you took up with her best friend."

"Oh, God," old Mr. Wenner sobbed. "That meant nothing. It was just sex, I swear!"

Ben hid a wince behind his hand, trying very hard not to think of seventy-year-old Ellie Verstgard rolling around with Mr. Wenner. Despite his best resistance, the image scrolled across his brain and took some of his love for the world with it. He took a deep, cleansing breath and stood straighter, determined to get this spectacle over with.

"Does your brother still live over in Grand Valley?"

"Yes, but—"

The front door opened and Mr. Wenner whipped around with a pitiful cry of "Olive!" but it was only Frank, handing out the man's pants and an ancient pair of sneakers.

"And that's all you'll get out of me!" a woman's voice shrieked from inside.

Ben tried to make a soothing noise, but it was lost in the old man's renewed sobbing.

The door slammed shut behind them and Frank sauntered down the stairs. "She needs a little time, sir," he offered, and angled his head toward his truck. Ben nodded as he put a reassuring hand on Mr. Wenner's shoulders. He remembered the man as the kindly old barber who handed out butterscotch candies to kids who didn't cry during their haircuts. That memory would be crushed beneath the weight of this one, no doubt about it.

"How 'bout you put those pants on, Mr. Wenner, then we'll head over to the station and call your brother. See if he'll come pick you up."

"His wife won't like it. Olive already called her."

"Well, let's give it a try. Now…the pants? Please?"

By the time Mr. Wenner's brother drove to the rescue, forty-five minutes had passed and Ben was still an hour from the end of his shift, sitting in his office with nothing to do. He leaned back in his chair to catch a glimpse of the light flickering from The Bar.

Molly had thoroughly pissed him off with her flip attitude earlier in the day, and he'd known for a fact he wasn't going anywhere near her tonight. Except that the station was quiet and lonely, and he'd caught sight of Lori walking over to The Bar when he'd brought in Mr. Wenner earlier. Lori was there, which meant Molly was there, not to mention all the love-starved men in town, trying to drown their libidos in beer.

He thought of Molly stretched naked beneath him, her face lost in pure lust, then thought of her flirting with another man… His chair screamed its objection when he stood up and let it snap forward. He had an hour to kill; he might as well go check on the troublemakers across the street.

Ben opened the bar door to a rush of warm, beer-scented air and the tantalizing song of women's laughter. His eyes swept the bar, finding nothing but a couple of bundled-up ranchers, still hunched against the cold, trying to thaw out.

The giggling laughter swelled again, and his gaze shot to the back of the room and the stained pool table in the farthest corner.

He didn't blink for a long time. Molly leaned against a pool cue, the toe of one high-heeled shoe drawing little circles on the ground as she talked to Lori and Helen Stowe. The shoes were black patent leather with a strap across the instep…just like a little girl's dress shoes except for the thin, three-inch heel at the back.

Above that her legs were sheathed in sheer black stockings that led up to a red and gray plaid skirt that looked exactly like something a school girl would wear. A private-school girl. A very *naughty* private-school girl who was looking for trouble in a dingy bar.

She was about to find trouble, all right.

"Chief!" Juan called as Ben stalked past the bar.

Molly looked up, pink lips parted in surprise as she set her foot down and lifted the pool cue. "Hey, Ben," she breathed when he got closer.

"Aren't you cold in that skirt?" he barked, forgetting that he'd planned to ease into a cool and distant conversation.

She bit her lip and looked down in dismay over her hot little body. Sassy witch. "I'm wearing layers."

Boy, was she ever. A crisp white shirt that might have been demure two buttons ago. A black tank top peeked out underneath. He imagined her unbuttoning the white shirt and wearing nothing but the skirt and a slinky black tank. And the heels. And stockings.

"I promise I'm warm as can be," she added.

Fuck, he couldn't think of anything to say; he just stood there, staring at her like an idiot.

"Ben, I hate to interrupt," Lori interrupted from his side. "But it's Molly's turn. Think you can spare her for a moment?"

The naughty schoolgirl brushed by him and looked over the table. When she found a play she liked, she ran the cue through her fingers, shot him a smile over her shoulder, and then leaned over and poised herself above the felt.

Ben coughed, his spit drying up so fast he almost choked. The skirt had ridden all the way up to the darker strip of silk at the top of her stockings and Ben could just make out the pale flash of thigh above that.

"Breathe," Lori whispered, and he sucked in enough air to stop the spinning in his head, but not enough to keep the blood from rushing to his dick.

"I'm on duty," he said to no one in particular, and Lori just shook her head.

Molly made the shot and celebrated with a little squirm of pleasure that reminded Ben's dick just how good she was at squirming. Then she sashayed around to the other side of the table and cued up another shot, while Ben stared at her breasts overflowing the bra. She flipped her gold hair back. Ben caught a glimpse of a shimmery scarlet bra edged in black lace.

"Tell her I'll be back in an hour," he grumbled, and spun to flee the scene. He could've sworn he heard the cracking sound of his dignity crashing against the far wall.

One hour left in his shift and then he could retrieve Molly from The Bar, take her home, and they would work out the question of whether or not they were dating.

He made it to the door without looking back—just

barely. When he stepped outside, the cold air took his breath away. But no…that was just the anticipation of Molly.

AS SOON AS HE WALKED out, Molly rose up to a more dignified posture and adjusted her shirt. Ben probably thought she'd been flashing the whole bar all night.

"Oh, my God." Lori laughed. "That man is so hot for you it's funny."

"It's not funny to me," Molly said with a leer. "It's damn serious."

"Oh, I can see that, you little ho."

Helen Stowe gave her a thumbs-up from the other side of the table. "Work it, girl." Helen was forty, just divorced, and trying to find a new life. She'd been thrilled when Lori had invited her to meet them there for girls' night out. She'd also encouraged them to stop hiding behind highball glasses, so tonight they were drinking bright pink cosmos out of martini glasses with no shame at all.

"Speaking of working it," Molly drawled as she made her way around the table to Helen. "I think I've noticed you making a little eye contact."

"With who?" she asked, even as a blush worked its way up her cheeks. Funny that she seemed suddenly shy. She was showing cleavage out to there, not to mention her loads of eye makeup and some curvy hips that loved to shake to the music.

Molly winked and looked over her shoulder toward the bar. Juan immediately looked away.

"He's almost young enough to be my son," Helen hissed.

"Hey, I didn't say anything! But... Isn't your son nineteen?"

"Yes."

"Well, Juan just turned thirty. He's almost a full-grown man." She and Lori broke into laughter at that, but Helen just shook her head.

"His last girlfriend was probably a cheerleader. Nothing is going to happen. I'm just here to have a good time."

"Hmm. Looks like he's got the same idea." Helen's head shot up, her eyes locked with Juan's, and then they both looked quickly away.

Molly tapped her arm. "Just keep it in mind."

"Oh, I couldn't..." But her voice trailed off to nothing, which Molly took as an encouraging sign.

When their pool game ended, they cleared out for the group of men waiting and ordered another round brought to their small side table.

Molly caught sight of a cute stranger as soon as she took a seat. "You've been holding out on me, ladies. Who's that?"

Lori glanced toward a table near the front door. "Cute guy with black hair? That's Aaron."

"He's adorable!" The guy met her eyes just as she spoke, and she was convinced he read her lips. "Oops. *Awk-ward,*" she sang to her table.

"That boy *is* adorable and he knows it. Gets around like nobody's business. Aaron comes into heat as soon as tourist season starts."

"Is he one of the river guides?" Molly guessed.

"You got it. He gets depressed when the weather turns cold and he has to put on a shirt."

"Have you ever dated him?"

Lori snorted. "I do have some standards. Plus I'm over twenty-one and I don't giggle when he wraps his hands around his beer and flexes."

Looking through her lashes, she saw that Aaron was watching their table. "You sure you don't like him? I think he's looking at you."

"Thanks, but I listened to my gynecologist's lecture on HPV. I'm not walking on that wild side."

"Time for play interception then. He's coming this way."

He pulled up a chair and dropped into it with a poof of woodsy cologne. "Hello, ladies. How's everybody doing tonight?"

They engaged in a chorus of "hellos" and "greats" while Aaron nodded as if he were personally responsible for their good time. Up close he was even more gorgeous. His blue-green eyes twinkled over high cheekbones and a slim nose. His lips were almost feminine—wide and soft.

Molly thought of him in a sweet, ruffled, A-line dress and grinned.

Aaron grinned right back. "I don't think we've been introduced."

"I'm Molly."

"Hi, Molly." Holding her gaze, he crossed his arms and leaned back in his chair, showing off the bulge of muscles beneath the tight sleeves of his polo shirt. Okay, maybe not totally feminine. "I'm Aaron."

"Hi, Aaron," she answered in a breathy, little-girl voice that made Lori kick her under her chair. Molly bit the inside of her cheek to keep from laughing.

Aaron didn't notice. He was too busy seducing her with his eyes.

Pah. This guy had nothing on the domineering policeman eyes that Ben was always hitting her with. Aaron was a lightweight and he didn't even know it.

"Are you visiting?" he asked and his eyes flickered toward Lori and widened. "Oh, a friend of Lori's?"

"I sure am," Molly giggled, and Lori kicked her again.

"Oh." He slumped a little, but then his gaze darted back and forth between them a few times and his biceps flexed. The smile returned, even brighter than before. "Any friend of Lori's is a friend of mine. Let's keep this party going, huh? Can I buy another round of drinks?"

Lori snorted. "These drinks are kind of pricey for you, Aaron."

He nodded, totally unselfconscious. "How about a pitcher of beer then? Oof!" Aaron looked up at Juan who'd bumped him from behind. "Watch it there."

Juan glared at him, looking pretty threatening for a man who was carrying a tray of three pink drinks with cherries in them.

Aaron watched in dismay as Juan set the glasses down one by one.

"Oh, for God's sake," Lori huffed. "Don't worry, Aaron, we already paid for them."

"Thank you, Juan," Helen said softly.

"My pleasure," he whispered, not budging from his spot next to Aaron. Molly noticed that he had quite the view of Helen's substantial bosom from up there, judging by the slight glaze over his eyes.

Aaron elbowed him. Juan elbowed back, catching him in the side of the head. Before it could deteriorate from there, someone shouted "Beer!" from the bar. Juan gave Aaron one last glare, nodded his head to Helen, then went off to refill a pitcher.

"Hey, bring a pitcher over here too!" Aaron shouted. "These girls are thirsty!" He swiveled back around on his chair and aimed a brilliant smile in Molly's direction. "So, Molly…" When he leaned closer the brilliant white of his teeth made her squint. "Have you ever been with a man?"

CHAPTER EIGHT

CHATROOM SEX HOSTESS.

She wasn't an adult performer and she didn't do phone sex. Ben knew this because he'd seen her through her windows when he'd hiked up the trail to check on the mine. She'd been curled up on her bed, a laptop computer propped on the pillows, and a sexy little pair of black glasses perched on her nose. And when he'd hiked back down, she'd been in the exact same place, typing intently away. Doing…*what,* exactly?

He was determined to find out.

As he crossed the street, eyes locked on the door of The Bar, his brain was trying explain to his body—in patient detail—that he wasn't going to find his answers under that little plaid skirt of hers. No matter how long he looked or how hard, the tops of the stockings weren't going to offer any clues. Nor that naughty red bra.

But I'm wearing her down, his body replied. *I'm working on her until she…until she breaks.*

"Exactly," Ben agreed, taking a definite side and putting a stop to his brain's annoying chattering. He whipped the door open and swept the room for Molly's blond hair. And found her. Cozied up with that gigolo Aaron.

"Can't you arrest that guy or something?" Juan growled from behind the bar.

Ben looked over to be sure they were focused on the same guy. Judging from the direction of the bartender's narrow glare and the angry red color of his face, they were. "You got any good information?"

"No. Unfortunately."

"Well, I'll see what I can do." He grabbed the beer Juan held out and made a beeline for the stiff gelled spikes rising from the back of Aaron's head.

A small curl of satisfaction erased some of his jealousy when Molly looked up and saw him approaching. Her eyes crinkled in...was that delight? Still, no harm in getting rid of the vermin.

"Aaron!" Ben barked from right behind his head. The man jumped and spilled beer onto his lap.

"Shit!" He was too busy mopping up to look behind him.

"Hey, there's an eighteen-year-old girl outside looking for someone to buy her beer."

"Is it Jasmine?"

He leaned over until he caught Aaron's eye. *"Excuse me?"*

"Chief! Shit! I, uh... That was just a, uh, a joke."

Ben let anger show in his eyes and eased around the chair until he could meet Aaron's gaze head-on. "If I catch you in even a hint of a situation involving alcohol or sex and underage girls, I will drown you in that goddamn river you love so much, do you understand?"

"Yes, sir."

"Now get out of my fucking chair."

"Yes, sir," he repeated, scrambling away so fast that he stumbled and sloshed beer down the rest of his pants.

Ben dropped into the chair and glared at the table of women. "Ladies. One of you got a thing for pretty boys?"

"Me!" Molly piped up. "I like my men as smooth and perfumed as a harem girl!"

Lori rolled her eyes. "You're in luck then. Aaron sure smells pretty and I bet he waxes the hell out of his—"

"Stop. Right. There." Ben held up a hand. "I've already had my share of scary images today. That one would push me over the edge."

Molly leaned forward and his eyes fell to the spot where her cleavage had been, but she seemed to have buttoned up. He felt immense satisfaction that Aaron hadn't gotten the pleasure.

Her bottom lip sulked. "I sure hope you're not talking about me, Chief."

"Hmm?"

"Scary images?"

"Oh. Oh!" He met the bright laughter in her eyes and smiled in helpless response. "Well, there was that one moment when my life flashed before my eyes, but I wouldn't—"

"Stop. Right. There," Lori interrupted, waving her hands, and Ben blinked from a daze. He'd been talking to Lori not five seconds before. How the hell had he forgotten she was there?

He cleared his throat and tried to pretend he wasn't blushing again.

"But don't worry," Molly said. "Aaron thinks I'm Lori's girlfriend."

Lori rolled her eyes. "Thanks for that, by the way."

"Hey, he came to that conclusion all by himself."

Her annoyed frown melted slowly into a smile. "I may have encouraged him to think that last winter when he kept dropping by the garage to watch me do oil changes."

"Then why'd you kick me?"

"Did you really think picturing us in bed together was going to *dis*courage him?"

"I didn't know he was perverted."

Ben arched an eyebrow. "Nothing perverted about that." He raised his beer in a toast and drained half of it before Molly's shoe poked into his shin. "Did you just kick me?"

"Stop being pervy. You're a man of the law."

He had no idea what that made her think of, but she began to shake with laughter. "What?"

"Nothing. Just thinking of pervy lawmen."

"Like who?"

"No one. Just a sheriff I once knew."

Sheriff, my ass. She was thinking of Cameron Kasten. Being pervy. *Fucking A.* Ben wrapped his hands around his beer and squeezed. He glared at the tabletop in an effort to keep from demanding that Molly tell him everything *right now*.

A plate of sliced fruit suddenly clapped down in front of him, distracting him from his last thought. Irritated, he glanced up with the rest of the table and found Juan hovering.

"You ladies seem to like the little garnishes in your drinks. I thought maybe, you know... You always eat the oranges and cherries and..." His bronze face quickly warmed to bright red when they all just stared at him.

"You need any refills?" he stammered.

They shook their heads, and he spun to leave. Helen Stowe half stood, then dropped back down to her chair. "Thank you!" she called to Juan's retreating back. A few seconds passed before she looked back down to the fruit and whispered, "That was so sweet."

Ben just shook his head, his anger fading, but his determination growing by the second. "You ladies ready to go yet?"

"I don't need a ride," Lori protested, but Ben shrugged.

"Humor me. It's icy. And I have a new reputation to maintain, Sappho."

The cherry she'd popped into her mouth got lodged somewhere too far back, so Ben leaned over and slapped her a few times until she coughed and swallowed.

Molly snorted. "I feel like I should make a joke about you choking on your cherry, but I can't seem to put it together."

"Too bad," Lori rasped, "I was just thinking how much I miss high school humor."

"You're way off," Ben said. "That's junior high. And if you keep on chasing men away, you won't have to worry about your swallowing techniques anyway." Molly threw an orange rind at him while they both booed. "Hey, you said you were looking for high school humor."

Lori sat way back in her chair and gave him the once-over. "What in the world's gotten into Ben Lawson? Jokes? Flirting? Maybe I *should* sleep with Molly. I think she's got a magic hooha."

"Lori!" Molly yelped, laughing so hard that the table shook Ben's beer close to the edge. "That's top secret!"

Resigned to this round of mortification, Ben just finished his beer and stood to motion them up. "Come on, hussies, I'll take you home. You, too, Helen, if you need a ride."

Distracted, Helen continued her efforts to tie one cherry stem into ten knots. "No, thanks."

"You sure you're all right?"

"I'm fine. I think I'll just…um…"

"She's gonna hang out here for a while," Molly said as she shrugged into her coat. "Bye, Helen. Bye, Juan!" she added as they walked toward the bar.

Ben opened the door for the women and let them through. He was almost through himself when a man shouted, "Chief!" and hurried after them. Wilhelm Smythe, a fairly harmless drunk.

"Chief! Chief, you giving rides?"

Oh, Jesus. "No."

"I had seven beers, Chief, I don't think I can dr—"

"Walk."

"I'm living down by the south ridge now. It's a pretty good haul."

He glanced outside. Lori was nowhere in sight, but Molly was leaning over to fix her shoe. Way over. Good Lord. With a glare meant to burn the man alive, he motioned Wilhelm forward.

"This is the only time this will happen, is that clear?"

The man nodded as he staggered across the street toward Ben's truck.

"Where's Lori?" Ben asked.

"She walked home."

"Shit. I'm sorry about this."

"No, it'll be fun! Like we're on a date in high school taking your obnoxious friend home before we make out."

"A date? That's a great word for it, actually."

"I said 'like' a date, Chief. You didn't even buy me a drink."

Reaching out, he started to grab her to swing her back to the bar, but she danced away, skirt flipping up to tantalize and tempt him. "Nuh-uh. Too late."

"We're dating, Molly."

"It's called 'hooking up,' Ben. All the young kids are doing it."

"I'm not young and, despite your look tonight, you're not a kid."

"And aren't you glad about that?" she purred.

Boy, was he.

"I'm sure glad," Wilhelm slurred from his post by the truck.

Jesus Christ, he'd forgotten they weren't alone *again*. He was totally falling apart.

Stalking to the driver's side, he popped the locks and growled, "Get in the damn truck and don't say another word." Wilhelm obeyed, but Molly didn't. Big surprise.

"Thanks for giving us a ride, Chief Lawson. You're very generous," she said, climbing in.

She had to know her damn skirt had ridden up high enough to show her thighs. When she twisted to buckle the seat belt, it rode even higher.

"I can see your panties," Ben hissed in a voice he thought was soft.

"Oh, sorry, Chief!" Wilhelm called from the back. The truck shook when he bounced up and down to hitch up his jeans.

Molly collapsed against her door, hands pressed to her mouth to hold back laughter and, if anything, showing more of her bright-red panties.

Black stockings, red panties. Ben's heart began to thump faster. He thought of those shiny black heels, the black lace on her bra. He remembered how easily she'd made white and pink cotton look sexy the night before.

"Where the hell am I going, Wilhelm?" he barked.

"Mile and a half south. Take a left at Teddy's old trailer."

Ben forced himself not to peel out as he pulled from the curb. He kept his eyes on the road, and his thoughts on driving. There was no naked-thighed woman in the passenger seat, no promise of mind-blowing sex in her eyes. He wouldn't speed, wouldn't drive recklessly.

He even remembered to slow as he passed Lori's place to see that all her lights were blazing. He waited until he saw her shadow pass in front of one of the windows before he drove on. He was cool, impervious. Not the least bit sex-crazed.

And then Molly took his hand and placed it directly on her left thigh.

His pulse sped as his foot pressed harder on the pedal.

Warm and impossibly soft… His thumb and two fingers touched the satiny texture of one black stocking, but his last two fingers touched the skin of her thigh and all the promise that it held.

He could have jerked away, should have, but her hand was on his, her fingers spreading to cover him, hold him in place. He *needed* to pull away, but he *wanted* to edge his pinky finger over to rub the edge of her panties, so he chose the path of least resistance and just stayed still, absorbing her heat into his nerve endings.

Okay, he could do this. Despite her teasing, they weren't teenagers and he could control his libido. He could touch a woman's thigh and drive at the same time.

She shifted and her muscles tensed enough to remind him of her thighs shaking as she came. He'd been slightly hard since he'd caught a glimpse of her red panties, but now he was rock-hard and throbbing, and glaring at the blacktop as if it were his enemy.

"Slow down," Wilhelm called. "Turn's coming up."
Slow down, slow down.

Her fingers spread wider, shifting his pinky, and suddenly his finger was pressed snug against the edge of her panties and she was burning hot there, and her throat held back a little sigh that fought to get out.

Forcing his foot to ease down on the brake pedal, he tried to drive like a sane person and not a boy offered his first chance to get into a hot girl's pants. But he rubbed his finger over the fabric and found it damp, and he knew what was waiting for him. Heat and slippery desire. Tightness and moaning.

The old abandoned trailer appeared in his headlights and Ben slammed on the brakes. Gravel flew, pinging against the underside of the truck as he took the turn too fast.

Wilhelm grunted in shock, but Molly just tipped up her hips and let his finger slip beneath the satin. Sucking in a gulp of air, he tried to keep his mind on the road, but she was humming next to him, a sound of need so sweet he had to grind his teeth together to keep control.

Except he didn't keep control. He slowed the truck to a half-way safe speed and slid his hand down, easing all of his fingers under so he could cup her wetness in his hand.

"Yes," she whispered.

"Yep, this is it," Wilhelm agreed. "You can let me out right here, Chief."

The truck slid ten feet on the gravel before it finally rocked to a stop. Wilhelm grumbled about hotshot young drivers as he climbed out and slammed the door, but Ben barely noticed. He bent his middle finger and plunged it deep.

"Oh, yes," Molly said, pushing his hand harder against herself and grinding up.

"Are you trying to kill me or just get me fired?"

"I'm just trying to get you inside me."

"Damn it." He pulled his hand away with the effort of a man turning down eternal paradise. "Just hold on. Just…" He threw the truck in Reverse, hooked his arm around the back of his seat and backed halfway down the narrow quarter-mile road. When he drew just close enough to glimpse passing lights in the distance, but not near enough to be seen from the road or Wilhelm's place, he cut the lights, turned off the truck, and slid his seat as far back from the steering wheel as it would go.

"You seem determined to drive me crazy," he complained—or pretended to complain—as he lifted her from her seat to his.

"Only to distract you."

"From what?" Her knees settled on either side of him, skirt hiking up to show the tops of her thighs. God, he was beginning to love her.

No! his brain screamed. You're beginning to love her *skirts!* Not *her.*

His body almost physically shrugged off the problem. It didn't really give a damn about semantics.

"Distract me from what?" he repeated as his hands found her stockings and smoothed up to enjoy the contrast of silk against her skin.

Molly started to unbutton that white shirt, smart girl that she was. "I'm trying to distract you from the fact that you hate this."

"What?"

A brief glow of distant headlights illuminated her sad smile. "You hate this, just a little."

Giving up his exploration of her thighs, Ben reached to stop her hands from opening the last button of her shirt. "What the hell are you talking about, Moll?"

Laughing, she shook off his hands and slipped the button free to spread the shirt wide. "You wish you were doing this with someone else, someone with no secrets."

"No—"

"Someone you didn't have to worry so much about." She picked up his hands and cupped them to her breasts.

Despite his rising confusion, he rubbed his thumbs over her nipples, noting the way they tightened with each stroke. Her back arched and she leaned back into the steering wheel. Miraculously, the horn didn't sound.

"I don't want anyone but you here, Molly."

"You sure about that?"

"I wanted you even when I shouldn't have."

"Not true." She shrugged off the shirt and then took his hands to ease them beneath her black top. Ben found the front clasp of her bra and clicked it open. When he touched her bare breasts, squeezed her nipples between his fingers, Molly's breath caught.

Another faint pass of headlights showed her eyes closed, lips parted, cheeks flushed pink with pleasure. He wanted her like this always, wanting him, more of him, pink with happy lust.

"When you were in high school," he whispered, "I used to try to picture you, what you must look like naked, but that was… You were too young."

"Mmm. I'm not too young now."

"You look like you are, wicked girl."

Her husky laugh delighted him. "And you like it."

"That would be perverted, darlin'."

"Oh, I'll help you maintain your facade in public, but we both know you're really a bad boy."

The truth was that he wasn't, or never had been, but he wanted to be bad with Molly, that was for damn sure.

He flicked his thumbs over her again, pinched harder, loving the way her breath hitched.

"You had girlfriends," she said when she'd caught her breath, "when you were in high school."

"Yes."

Her knuckles brushed against his jeans, sending tiny jolts of electricity through his dick. "And what did you do with them in your dad's old truck?"

"I…" Her knuckles brushed more firmly, and then she was cupping him through his jeans, trying to wrap her fingers around his erection. Bright lights flashed behind his eyes, and this time it had nothing to do with sirens.

"Did any of those girls ever give you a hand job?"

"I…" He pictured her fingers wrapped around his flesh, could almost feel her stroking. "I really couldn't say."

"Mmm. Sounds like a chivalrous yes to me." She petted him slowly, up and down. "I missed out on you in high school, though not for lack of wanting."

She was doing a damn fine job of sending him back fifteen years, to those days when heavy petting was too much to handle and not nearly enough. That old desperate need fluttered back to his body, that crazed desire to find out what it would really feel like to have a girl's hand on his naked dick, even the idea of it too exciting to bear.

He'd forgotten how muffling and torturous simple denim could be. Her fingers sent tingles and shivers over his cock, tempting him to push her for more, please, more. Just a little. Just enough.

He rasped out, "You still have an hour before curfew," and was rewarded with that sexy laugh again.

"That's true," she whispered. "But what if someone finds out?"

"I won't tell a soul, I swear."

"Maybe… Maybe just for a second." Her hands stopped their torture and fumbled with the button of his jeans. And then, thank God, she was pulling his zipper down and the terrible pressure eased for a moment before twisting into an even sharper excitement.

Molly reached under the waistband of his underwear and her cool hand was a sudden, perfect vise around his cock.

"Oh, good Lord," he groaned.

"Mmm." She pulled him free and purred in excitement. "Did any of those girls ever tell you how big you are, Ben? How thick and hard and gorgeous?"

Jesus. No. No, he definitely would've remembered that because the evening would have ended right then with a big bang.

"You are," she whispered, just holding him. "You're perfect. Almost too big for my hand. Like steel under that silk skin. Just what I always imagined."

Loosening her hold, she trailed her hand lightly up, teasing again. Then down all the way, exploring. She turned her hand, easing lower to cup his balls. Ben hissed, grinding his teeth hard together.

"You like that?"

"Yes."

"Hmm." She tested the weight of him for a long moment, then explored his shaft again, stroking soft, then with increasing pressure.

God, how long had it been since he'd experienced something so simple and wicked and good? Her hand pumped a little faster and he groaned his approval.

"Does that feel good, Ben?"

Just the way she sighed his name... "Yes. *Yes*. Don't stop. Please, Molly."

A faint light flashed by again, showing her slight smile, bottom lip caught between her teeth, eyes narrowed in concentration. She looked like a young woman doing something she shouldn't.

Ben pushed her shirt up and cupped her small breasts. "God, you're beautiful."

Her hand stuttered for a moment before she found her rhythm again, faster now, more intent. "I want you inside me."

He shook his head, too far gone to speak.

"You're so big. I want you to fill me up. Make me scream."

A drop of sweat snaked down his temple. "I can't," he managed to say.

"Please."

"Molly... I would..." He forced his mind away from the goal of exploding in her pumping hand. "I don't have any condoms. I meant to buy some, but... You got any?"

"At home. I didn't bring my purse."

Fuck. Fuck. Her fingers found the perfect pressure, the sweetest path...

Molly shook her head and gave a rusty laugh. "I guess you'll just have to go again when we get home."

"I promise," he gasped, flying closer to heaven. Almost there.

"Chief!" a screeching, metal voice called from the dark.

Molly squealed and let him go, while Ben squeezed his eyes shut to will whatever it was away.

"Chief?" the radio screamed again.

"For God's sake." Ben took a deep breath and told himself not to reach out and put Molly's hand back where it belonged. "Someone had better be *dead*."

Molly was still looking around in confusion, but that didn't stop her from choking on laughter. "What the heck is that?"

"This," Ben barked and yanked the radio off its charger. "Chief Lawson here. What is it?"

"Chief," Brenda repeated. "Is everything okay?"

Hell no, he wanted to say, but he took one more deep breath before he pushed the button. "Yes. Is there a problem?"

"Sylvia Jones called in that she'd seen you turn onto South Ridge Road off Highway Ten, but she hadn't seen you come back. I worried you'd run into trouble."

Un-fucking-believable. "I'm off duty right now, Brenda."

"So… Everything's all right?"

"Yes!"

"But what are you doing out at the south ridge?"

He would not yell at her. And he would not strangle Molly for having to clap her hand over her mouth to keep from screaming with laughter.

When he'd gotten his raging temper under control,

he put the radio back to his mouth. "I was dropping off a friend, Brenda. Anything else?"

"No, I'm just glad you're okay. Have a good night, Chief."

"Thank you," he forced out and slammed the radio back into place.

Molly's laughter rained down over him as he laid his head against the seat back and tried not to die. "Tell me I am not sitting here in my official police vehicle with my dick out and my girlfriend laughing at me."

"I'm sorry," she choked out, wiping tears from her eyes.

"Oh, no. It's fine." Ah yes, he remembered this feeling from high school, too. Sexual frustration. Funny how you forgot things.

"We don't have very good luck in this truck. Or you don't, anyway."

"Right." Ben rearranged his clothing and zipped his jeans. "You're right. This truck is cursed. Invite me to your house. I've had damn good luck there. Plus I'm expecting one of my good citizens to stop and offer help at any moment." He shook his head, adding, "I figured if we couldn't be seen from the road we'd be fine." At least nobody really had stopped. He'd been into the high school fantasy, but not to the extent of being interrupted by an outraged elder.

Though his lust had cooled considerably, it sure as hell wasn't gone. It sizzled through his fingertips when he reached beneath Molly's shirt to refasten her bra.

"I can do that, you know."

"I know," he answered, smoothing her shirt back into place, feeling the curve of her body beneath his touch.

"You hate this," she said again, out of the blue, and Ben felt the words like a blow to his chest.

"Why would you say that?"

"Because it's true."

Smoothing a strand of hair back from her face, he tucked it behind her ear and shook his head. "Molly—"

"You can't help it. Just like I can't help my life, Ben, or my secrets. And it's okay."

"No, it's not okay. And I don't hate this. Just…" He was suddenly exhausted, weary and achy, and he didn't want to do this right now. He just wanted her, simple and sweet. "Just invite me home?"

The sadness vanished from her face, replaced with a grin. "Of course. Come home with me, Ben."

"Hmm." Leaning forward, he stole a quick kiss before her grin could vanish. "I don't know, Moll. What about your parents? What if they catch me sneaking in?"

His hands were curved around her ribs, and when she laughed the vibrations spread joy from her bones to his. "Don't worry. My parents are staying in the city tonight. But they made me promise to obey all the rules."

"Well…" Ben pulled her closer, ran his tongue over her bottom lip, sucked it until she sighed. When she tried to kiss him back, he pulled away. "We'll have to come up with some really good rules, then."

She scrambled up and over to the passenger seat. Her finger pointed at the steering wheel. "What the hell are you waiting for? Let's go."

Ben resisted the urge to turn on the siren and fly

through town, but just barely. Still, he managed to make it all the way to her driveway without braking once.

MOLLY RACED UP the stairs ahead of him, fully enjoying the fact that he could see straight up her skirt. He hadn't noticed the thong yet and—

"For the love of…" he murmured behind her, and Molly grinned. He'd finally noticed. "You are a very naughty girl."

"I try to be."

His fingers were just brushing her thigh when she lunged up the top step and sprinted to her room. She had her shirt half-unbuttoned before he rushed through the door. Then she started shivering.

Ben tossed off his coat and went to work on his own buttons before he looked her up and down and shook his head. "I guess I'll start the fire."

"It's already laid out."

"Good. I hadn't really pictured you hiding under the covers tonight." He set a match to the kindling and waved her over. "Why don't you come over here and get warm, sweetheart?"

One glance into those hot chocolate eyes and Molly's shivering stopped. She dropped the white blouse and gave her hips an extra shake as she walked toward him. His gaze devoured her, from her head all the way down to her toes. A surge of pure power crashed through her as she drew the spaghetti-strap tank up over her head and shook out her hair.

Ben's eyes narrowed, focusing on the red satin and

black lace that cupped her breasts. She stopped five feet away.

"Now the skirt," he said, his voice a deep rumble, but she wasn't interested in being obedient. Instead of unbuttoning her skirt, she gathered the pleats in her hands and inched the material up.

"First your shirt," she countered just as she showed him the tops of her stockings.

He tipped his head in a nod and tugged his shirt free of his jeans, eyes never leaving her thighs as he quickly unfastened his buttons. He wore a T-shirt underneath, but he whipped that off before she even had to ask.

My word, she'd never get used to that. He was sculpted flesh and crisp hair. Flat stomach and narrow hips.

"Now turn around," he said, and Molly turned, planting her heels a foot apart and inching the skirt up.

"Higher."

That one word zinged through her, bouncing around her belly until it sparked between her legs. She eased her skirt up, dragging it over the curve of her ass inch by slow inch, knowing he'd enjoy the torture.

She heard nothing behind her, aside from the quickening crackle of the fire. He held his breath or breathed so softly she couldn't hear.

Molly was just about to turn around when he touched her. Her muscles twitched at the soft feel of his palm on her ass, just before it slid up over her hip and straight down into her panties. His fingers slid right inside her, no hesitation, and she couldn't help but cry out at the invasion.

"It wouldn't matter if I did hate this," he murmured into her ear. "I couldn't stop it."

No, he couldn't. There'd been chemistry between them even when they were too young to know it.

Pulling her hips against his, Ben pressed himself against her naked ass, his jeans were rough and warm, his erection thick beneath the fabric. His hand began to stroke in and out of her, rubbing her clit with every pass, and Molly arched hard, grinding herself against his dick.

He bit her neck, licked the skin and bit again, and Molly's body was shimmering, shimmering.

"I don't want to…" she panted, then paused to try to remember what she'd meant to say. Ah, yes. "I don't want to come yet."

Ben made a sympathetic noise, but didn't pause in his attentions. His chest was so hot against her back, his arm so muscled where it curled around her waist. And his fingers…so slick and wide and merciless.

But she wanted more. *"Wait."*

When she grabbed his wrist, he let her pull his hand up, let his fingers slide free. "Wait," she said again.

She fumbled for the button of her skirt, trying to call back the sexual confidence she'd had just moments before, but it was a difficult task considering her shaking knees and melting brain. Still, she knew just what she wanted, had been planning it her whole adult life.

The knowledge that she was about to make her dreams come true gave her the composure she needed to drop the skirt and turn to him with a confident smile.

"Your turn," she said.

His mouth quirked up in a lopsided smile. "Sorry, sweetheart. I'm not wearing a thong."

Laughter burst from her throat, clearing away the last of the lust haze. "I can't tell you how glad I am."

"I don't know you well enough to bust out the thong. Yet."

Planting her fists on her hips, she put on her best glare. "Now is not the time to get funny."

Half smile still in place, he swept her naughty ensemble with a bone-melting gaze. The smile looked especially wicked when he met her eyes again. "You want serious?"

Almost afraid to say yes to that challenge, she went on the offensive instead. "Unbutton your jeans."

"Yes, ma'am."

He popped the button, exposing a new inch of skin, then he…stopped.

"Now the zipper." He lowered the zipper, and he was standing before her, jeans gaping a little, bare-chested, staring her down, just like the countless fantasies she'd cast him in for the past ten years.

Something dangerous turned in her heart, seeped into her veins. Something dark and heady and addictive. This was how people got hooked on seedy habits—drugs or danger or kinky sex. But she knew the refrain—everyone did… *I can handle it.*

She could do this once or twice or a few times. Keep it light. She could enjoy this and walk away from it when it became too much. No problem.

Forcing a small, distant smile, she strolled to him, touched her fingers to his collar bone, trailed them lower. A shudder spread through his muscles before he tamped it down. Molly pressed her lips to his jaw, then kissed her way down his neck. He seemed to know that she wanted control, because he kept his hands to himself, though she noticed them clenching at his sides. Good.

Molly skimmed her palms over his chest, around to his ribs. She licked his shoulder, scraped her teeth over his skin until he sighed. Then she braced her hands against his hips and lowered herself to her knees.

His belly jumped when she kissed it, or maybe that was the deep breath he took, but she couldn't hear because her heart was pounding in her ears, driving blood to all her nerve endings.

She took her time, knowing there'd never be another first like this, rubbing her cheek against his tight stomach, dipping her tongue into his navel. She breathed in his scent and tasted his skin as his muscles tensed beneath her.

Finally, she took him in her hand, freed him from his jeans, and he was heavy and hot in her grasp.

"Do you know how long I've wanted to do this?" she whispered.

He swallowed so hard she heard him even over her pulse.

"When I walked in and saw that girl..." She dragged an openmouthed kiss down his shaft in a quick, light caress. She let her breath touch him with every word. "I saw her kissing you, sucking you..."

His deep sigh cracked in half.

"And I watched, and I wanted to be her. I wanted

you to send her away and tell me to make it up to you, teach me how to please you."

She licked the tiny drop of fluid away from the head, tasting salt and sex, circled her tongue around the flared edge once, twice, before pressing a few tiny kisses to the moisture she'd created.

"I would've given anything to be the one on her knees for you, Ben. I wanted to take you into my mouth, wanted to make you come."

"Molly."

"Mmm," she hummed against his skin, then she parted her lips and took him inside her, slow at first, then as deep as she could.

He was a heavy, pulsing weight against her tongue. Perfect, just what she'd always wanted. She took him deeper than she'd taken any man and heard him groan her name. Licking, sucking, she felt him grow even bigger, just for her. His fingers tangled in her hair.

Tension wound through her belly and squeezed her sex tight. She'd masturbated to this fantasy so many times, she knew she'd hardly even need to touch herself to come. Her body had memorized him long ago in her dreams.

When his hand tightened in her hair, she moaned her approval, but he didn't play along. Ben was far too much a gentleman to be more aggressive than that. How could he know she didn't want tenderness? She hoped he could take a hint.

Molly eased off him, offering playful licks and kisses instead of the deep-throated ones he wanted. She teased and tortured until his fingers tightened and pulled her the slightest bit closer. She obliged, just until the pressure stopped, then she teased some more. They played through the whole cycle two more times until he finally gave in.

His hand spread across the nape of her neck, his fingers closed around her hair, and he guided her over his dick, pressing her deep, setting the rhythm he wanted.

Oh, God. Her clit felt tight as a bullet, sending out shards of pleasure each time her thighs rubbed together. Molly squeezed the muscles of her sex, keeping rhythm with Ben's dick sliding into her mouth.

When that wasn't enough, she slipped her hand into her panties and touched herself, groaning her ecstasy into his cock. Even over the flood of her own pleasure, she sensed his posture changing, tasted sweet saltiness on her tongue.

"Molly…" he groaned. "Molly, I'm going to come. Do you… Do you want to…?"

Oh, yes, she wanted to. In answer, she rubbed her tongue against the underside of his dick, sucked harder, and plunged her fingers deep inside herself. His hand fisted tight in her hair, holding her for his climax.

Rubbing, rubbing, she came just before he did, swallowed her own cries along with his come, and felt her dark need shatter into sparkling bits of light.

HIS HAND WAS STROKING the back of her head, and Molly felt like purring.

"Okay," he murmured. "Okay. I think I need to lie down."

Molly licked her lips and laughed.

"Not to mention it's time to take care of you."

"Oh, I'm taken care of," she answered, giving a little wave of her hand. He grabbed it and lifted her up to her feet.

"Why you sneaky little hussy. That's cheating. Not to mention incredibly hot."

"And to think I was doing it all for myself."

He tugged her toward the bed, where he collapsed on his back and proceeded to toe off his boots. "I think you've cured any lingering issues I might've had about blow jobs."

Still greedy for the sight of him, Molly tugged off his jeans and underwear and socks, then unfastened her heels and climbed on top of his big body. His eyes were already closed.

"Just give me a half hour," he said. "A half hour to pull my soul back from the brink of death and then we'll get down to business."

Molly blinked, leaning forward until he opened his eyes and met her gaze. "Did you really just say 'get down to business'?"

His eyes were clouded with confusion for a brief moment before they closed again. "Fuck, I think I just did."

"Wow. I mean… Jeez."

"I'm half dead!"

"Get down to business, huh?"

His chest began to shake with suppressed laughter.

"We could do that, I suppose, but I was really hoping we might 'do the nasty.' Or maybe 'hit a home run.' Or even…do you think we could play 'hide the sausage?' It's my favorite."

He was laughing so hard now that Molly was in danger of bouncing right off him, but she held on and grinned down at him until he wiped tears from his eyes.

"I'm supposed to feel manly and self-satisfied right now, Moll. You're kind of ruining it."

"Poor baby." Her fake sympathy evaporated when Ben flipped her onto her back and leaned over her.

"I really, really like this underwear."

"Thanks."

"But I'd rather see you naked. May I?"

The question was a little late considering he'd already unsnapped her bra and exposed her breasts, but she wasn't complaining.

He slid the panties down, all the way off, then rolled down each stocking and dropped them to the floor.

"That's better." His hand rubbed the marks the stockings had left on her thighs. "Poor baby," he murmured, echoing her, then he dipped his head to press kisses to the faint marks while Molly melted into the mattress.

When he paused, she waited, holding her breath.

"Is that apple pie still in the fridge?"

"What?" Molly popped her head up and looked down at his mouth poised so close to her sex. "What are you going to do with the pie?"

"Eat it. I'm starving. I never had dinner."

"Oh. Shoot, I thought we were going to have sex."

"Just a half hour! That's all I ask for."

"Need time to put on a suit and tie?" Her giggles turned to a yelp when he pushed her over and slapped her ass.

"Get me some pie, woman!"

"It's gone!" she squealed.

His hand rubbed her ass. "Gone where?"

"I ate it."

"You just made it yesterday! You ate a whole pie in one day?"

"Hey, you had a piece, too," she tossed over her shoulder. "And I live by myself. If I don't eat it fast, it goes to waste."

"What kind of girl eats a whole pie in twenty-four hours?"

"This booty you like doesn't make itself, you know."

He kissed the body part in question. "You got anything else to eat down there?"

"Mmm. Down *where?*"

"In the *kitchen,* Molly."

"Oh. Are you sure?"

He chuckled against her hip, his breath sending goose bumps chasing over her skin. "I'll get to that, too, I promise. Wouldn't miss it for the world." His growling stomach took the sexy edge off his words and made her snort.

"There's food in the fridge. Eat whatever you like."

He stood and pulled on his jeans. "Can I get you anything?"

Turning over, she stretched just to make him look at her again. He obliged and the long look set her skin tingling. "Maybe a cup of wine would be good."

"A *cup?*"

"I haven't found my wineglasses yet. Plus I'm just fancy like that."

"Speaking of fancy..." he muttered as he left. She

wondered what he'd think when he saw that her wine came in a box. Sophisticated city girl indeed.

Molly waited until she heard him reach the bottom of the stairs before she turned onto her stomach, buried her face in a pillow and screamed, "Oh. My. *God!*"

She'd died and gone to heaven. Even when she'd known she was moving back to town, even when she hoped she might have a fling with Ben, she'd never really believed he'd be anything like her fantasies. She'd assumed he'd be out of shape or inconsiderate or terrible at oral sex. Hell, he could have had bad breath or a hairy ass.

But no. He smelled and tasted and moved just like she'd hoped he would. Those childhood years of being up close and personal had informed her well. He was sweet, strong and dedicated in bed, just like he was in every part of his life. The lover she'd always wanted.

Her poor heart was going to take a beating.

She was busy imagining him walking around in her kitchen in just his jeans when the floor creaked not too far from her bed. Ben was back, but he wasn't holding a cup of wine.

"What the hell is this?" he asked, tossing a sheet of paper onto the bed.

Molly watched it float down, baffled as to what it could be. When it landed, she read the bold words and felt her heart drop. *Will you wear this for me?* it said. The curse of Cameron. Again.

"Where did you find that?"

"Tell me," he ground out. "Tell me this has nothing to do with tonight."

She shook her head, confused. "What do you mean?"

"Sexy underwear, stockings. Did you wear that for me or because someone else asked you to?"

"Who?"

"How the hell should I know? Who asks you to wear sexy clothes, Molly? Sergeant Kasten? One of your customers?"

Sergeant Kasten. "You looked him up, didn't you! After I asked you not to?"

"Just answer the question."

"No! I'm not a suspect in one of your cases! I haven't done anything wrong. I'm not even your girlfriend, so stop acting like you have a right to *anything*."

The frustration on his face blinked to pain for a moment, before he steeled his expression to ice. "I see. Thanks for reminding me that I'm nothing to you. I needed that."

Ben stalked past the bed and snatched his shirt off the floor.

Her stomach twisted with panicked regret as she yanked the sheets up over her breasts. "You can't honestly expect me to deal with these constant accusations. I've told you what I can, why can't you just leave it alone?"

"Because I can't."

"Just trust me."

"You have got to be kidding. What if I had some mystery job I refused to even hint at? What if I brushed off every personal question with a stupid joke? You think that wouldn't eat at you?"

"If you can't handle it, then just leave me the hell alone, Mr. Perfect."

"Fine." He shoved his feet into his boots and grabbed his coat. "And I'm hardly perfect, Molly, I'm just not living in the goddamn Witness Protection Program. I'm *normal,* which is apparently a state you lost touch with a long time ago."

"Screw you!" she shouted at his retreating back, as the panic continued scratching inside her. *Shit, shit, shit.* Why had she said those things? And how the hell had she missed that note in the front hall when she'd thrown everything else away?

She wanted to reach across the miles and punch Cameron in his perfectly moisturized face. And she wanted to hop on Ben's back and beg him to stay. She'd never forget that flash of pain when she'd thrown his affection back in his face.

"Shit." He'd stepped over the line, but he hadn't deserved that.

Molly jumped from the bed and raced naked for the stairs. "Ben! Wait!"

A rush of cold air wound around her from the front door, but when he looked up and saw her careening down the stairs in the nude, he shut the door with a snap.

"Go back to bed, Moll."

"Wait. I'm sorry. I shouldn't have said that."

"No need to apologize. The truth hurts sometimes."

"No, listen, just…"

When he finally looked her straight in the eyes, Molly wished she had some clothes on. There wasn't a drop of melted chocolate in that gaze. She was looking at a solid wall of espresso marble. He was the Chief of Police and she was a naked woman wreaking havoc on his world.

"Ben, I'm sorry. I know this is all hard to accept."

"It's impossible to accept. If we were *dating,* I'd say goodbye, explain why this is over. But since we're not… I guess I just leave."

"That note was nothing."

"Good to know." He reached for the doorknob.

"Wait! Ben, I'm sorry. You don't understand—"

"No shit. You wanna step away so I can open the door, or do you plan to flash the whole street?"

Molly looked from him to the door and back. Then she crossed her arms under her chest, pushing her breasts into more prominence. "I'm not going anywhere until you listen to me."

He seemed alarmingly unmoved by the mammary display. Her sex powers were useless in the face of his righteous anger. Her legs grew weak as the seconds passed and his gaze remained impassive.

"Do you actually have anything to say?" he finally asked, "Or are you just hoping to distract me again?"

Crap. "That…that note meant nothing and I've never worn those underwear for anyone. Except you."

"Great. Is that all?"

He was done with this game, that was clear. She could either let him go or concede something. But it was only Wednesday; she'd planned to have him until Saturday, at least. Time for a strategic surrender.

"Okay, you were right about Cameron. He's my ex-boyfriend. We broke up six months ago. It's completely over."

"Except that he sent you something special to wear. For him."

"He's deluded. And I threw his gift in the trash. It had nothing to do with tonight."

"So why all the secrecy? Why the lies?"

"I didn't—"

"You specifically told me he wasn't an ex-boyfriend."

"Right. Okay, that was a lie. But you and I hadn't even kissed then. I'm not obliged to give out my personal history to every person who asks."

Ben crossed his arms, too, though he didn't have any naked to distract from the anger of the pose. "And now?"

"Now? Now I told you."

"You haven't told me shit." He turned and reached for the door. "You'd better move."

The knob turned.

The door cracked and wind whooshed inside. He didn't even look to see if she'd hidden herself.

"All right! Stop! I dated Cameron for less than a year. He's a police officer, but you already know that. A hostage negotiator for the Denver PD. I broke it off with him six months ago because…because he was very manipulative. And I haven't dated much since."

Ben pushed the door shut very slowly, but he didn't turn around. His voice sounded as cold as before. "What does he have to do with your work?"

"Nothing. I never told him anything about it."

At last he looked at her, shooting her an incredulous glare. "Come on."

"It's true. Frankly, he never asked much about it, if that gives you any insight into the relationship."

"And you stayed with him for a *year?*"

"Not quite, but I was…confused."

"So if you broke up so long ago, why is he still sending you gifts?"

"A misunderstanding. He thought I was coming to visit. I'm not!" she added when his face flushed.

Ben ran a rough hand through his hair and leaned against the door. "Is that it? Are you gonna tell me anything more?"

The critical question. She had nothing more to tell him, so there was really no beating around the bush. He could either live with that or he couldn't. Or she could really be a bitch and just make something up.

Molly shrugged and rubbed her cold arms. "I've made it quite clear from the beginning, Ben. My work is private. I've been honest about that, don't pretend I haven't. You're the one who's been dishonest."

"Me?"

"You've been sneaky and underhanded. You've done background checks, you've called my brother, chased down leads like I've done something wrong. For all I know, you called Cameron."

"I did not."

"No? Okay, how many ways have you used Google to search my name in the past week?"

"That's…that's perfectly acceptable. Everyone does that."

"I haven't looked you up, asshole. If I want to know how many people you've shot or how many tourists you've pulled out of the river, I'll ask you."

"And I'd tell you!"

"That would be your choice. *Your* choice. Leave me mine, Ben, please. When I said…" She shivered again and Ben, cursing, took off his coat and threw it around her shoulders. She hugged his warmth to her and swallowed back the tears it thawed. "When I said you didn't have a right to anything, I just meant I wanted you to respect *my* rights.

"You knew me when I was child, but I have a whole life now and reasons for how I live. Can't you show some respect for that?"

He stared at her, still cool, still silent, but he was closer now and she could see the tension around his eyes, the slight tic in his jaw. Hands on hips, he dropped his head and stared at the floor.

Molly wrapped his uniform coat tighter around her, breathing in the smell of worn leather and Ben's soap. He'd had enough. She'd known it was coming, had even told him so. But, God, she just wanted a little more pleasure before they became polite neighbors. Just a little more undiluted Ben.

He sighed, a great heaving of his shoulders, and raised weary eyes to meet hers.

"I'm sorry," he said, but she didn't know what he meant. Sorry for what he'd done or sorry he had to end it? Molly felt as though she might pass out and bounce down the last two stairs.

Ben rolled his shoulders as if an ache had settled

there. "The secrecy has been eating at me and I stepped over the line. I apologize."

"Really?" she sniffed. She was trying to hold back her tears because she didn't even know why she was crying, but the more she tried to hold them back, the more teardrops rolled into her nose. She didn't want to cry, but she also didn't want to drip liquid out of her nostrils. She sniffed again, harder.

"Molly, no," Ben said, stepping closer. His hands framed her face and when she tried to wipe her nose, his arm was in the way.

"My nose is running!" she wailed.

"Shh, it's okay."

"No, it's not okay. I'm naked and snotty!" She finally managed to knock his hand away to swipe at her nose, but she'd forgotten she was wearing his coat. Oops.

"If I get you a tissue, will you stop crying?" Instead of waiting for an answer, he darted toward the kitchen, reappearing within two seconds with a giant wad of paper towels, which he immediately thrust into her hands.

Molly crushed the whole thing to her nose, then dabbed delicately at the arm of his coat. "Sorry."

"Don't cry."

"I'm just…I don't know. It's late."

"You want me to go?"

His words brought another rush of tears and Molly swiped futilely at her nose. "Do you want to go?"

Ben shook his head, eyebrows arched at an incredulous angle. "No, despite all my big words. Apparently I'm an idiot with no pride and very little self-control, because all I really want to do is hustle you back upstairs and throw some more wood on the fire."

She managed to look indifferent instead of victorious. "You haven't had your snack yet."

"I seem to have lost my appetite. But I will join you in a cup of wine if you're willing to share."

Molly finally let herself smile, but just a little. He had conceded only temporarily. This would be over soon. She was damn sure going to enjoy it now.

"I'll share with you," she said as she turned to go back upstairs. "The cups are above the dishwasher. Meet you in the bedroom?"

By the time she'd snuggled back under the covers, she heard Ben's footsteps on the stairs. He entered with two juice glasses filled to the rim with white wine.

"Your, uh, *box* is almost empty, fancy pants."

"There's another box in the pantry. And I'm not wearing any pants."

"Yes, I seem to recall that," he drawled as he sat on the bed next to her and handed her one cup.

"So… Is this a truce?"

Ben tapped his cup against hers and raised it in a quick salute. "Truce. I'll leave it, Moll, but only for a little while. At some point you'll have to decide—me or your secrets. I can't offer more than that."

"I never expected otherwise."

They both sipped quietly until the tension in the room began to soften and melt.

"Let me get you something to eat," Molly offered, but he shook his head.

"I'm tired. I just want to get some sleep."

"Really?"

Her alarm must have been crystal clear, because Ben chuckled. "No, not really. I was just looking for an excuse to take off these clothes and join you."

"An excuse, huh? Hey, I've got an idea! How about we have sex?"

"Darlin', you're a genius."

He was half-undressed before ten seconds had passed, though he had to sit back down to tug off the boots. "Condoms. I want to be prepared this time."

"Just like a Boy Scout!" She pointed at the table next to his leg, and he tugged it open.

Though he started to reach in, his hand jerked back at the last moment. "What the hell is that?"

Molly rose up on her knees to look over his naked shoulder. "Oh, that's Little Blue."

"It's not so damn little."

"Well…no. That would be kind of silly, wouldn't it."

He poked a finger gingerly at the sex toy, setting it rocking side to side. "So… You, um, use that thing?"

"I'm afraid so." Her face was growing warmer by the second, so Molly pointed at the box of condoms. "Just get the protection. The board meeting's starting in two minutes."

"Mmm." But he just looked down at the open drawer, then looked at her and back down again. "Can I watch?"

"*Watch?* Watch what?"

He reached in and picked up the vibrator, saying, "Never mind," but when he turned to her his grin was wide and wicked. "I'm not big on just watching."

His thumb nudged one of the buttons and the toy

buzzed to life. Ben's eyebrows twitched in surprise, but the grin didn't budge.

"Lie down, Molly. All work and no play makes Ben a dull boy."

"Wait a second, you pervert!" Her squeals of laughter faded quickly into a gasp and even more quickly into helpless moans as Ben tried out different angles and settings, thoroughly concentrating on the task at hand.

Molly's last coherent thought was that it was always the quiet men who surprised you. And Ben had clearly been living years in absolute silence.

THEY'D DISAPPEARED into the house hours before, completely unaware they were being watched. Molly hadn't looked the least bit nervous. In fact, she'd been giggling. She'd latched on to Ben Lawson like the little whore she was, thinking she had nothing to worry about now that a strong man was there to protect her.

Her sense of vulnerability needed to be ratcheted up, her security and confidence destroyed. But not right now. Not with the chief there. He was only in her house for sex. Surely he'd leave soon enough.

An opportunity had seemed to present itself soon after they'd gone in. Apparently the sex had been quick and dirty, because the front door had opened before half an hour had passed, the edge of it just visible from the blackness of the big mugo pine at the edge of Molly's property.

A shadow had moved in the light that spilled from the entryway. Voices drifted across the dying lawn, not quite audible, but edged with anger or distress. The sex was done and they were sick of each other, it seemed.

If Ben Lawson had left then, there'd have been the whole night to explore that bitch's house, decide on the best way to spook her, chase her away. But the door had closed, muffling the voices inside. Eventually the whole house had gone dark.

But that was fine. He would leave tonight or in the morning, and then Molly would be alone again. Vulnerable.

The coyote howling on the other side of the ridge seemed to take joy in the idea. Then a whole pack sent their voices up to the cold night, a warning of danger that Molly Jennings wouldn't even recognize.

CHAPTER NINE

SURROGATE MOTHER FOR HIRE.

Ben stopped the razor midstroke, leaned close to the steam-fogged mirror, and stared himself down. "You are losing your fucking mind."

He was.

Molly had been right. He'd been sneaky and under-handed, obsessed with her secrets. The information she was willing to give him might not be what he wanted, but she'd been honest about it from the start. Sure, she'd lied about the ex-boyfriend, but she hadn't been in-volved with Ben at the time, hadn't been anything but an old acquaintance.

If he wanted this relationship to go somewhere, Ben needed to back off. So did he want it to go somewhere?

Concentrating on his shaving, he tried not to meet his own gaze, but the tactic didn't work. There was no denying his feelings. He was halfway in love with a woman he knew nothing about.

Except that he did know her. Knew her past, who she'd been born and raised to be, knew her parents and friends. He knew the honesty in her eyes and the truth in her passion. But it just wasn't enough.

He needed more from her, and she'd never trust him

and share her secrets if he didn't give her space. Maybe he'd leave her alone for a couple of days. Send some flowers like a normal man.

But when the phone rang while he was wiping the last of the shaving cream from his face, her name popped up on the ID screen, and Ben knew he wouldn't leave her alone for more than twelve hours. Just the fact that she was calling sent his heart into overdrive.

"Good morning," he answered, trying to keep the thrill out of his tone. "Are you finally up?"

"Hey," she said, and that one cautious word made the hair on his neck stand up.

"What's wrong?" he asked.

"When you left this morning, did you go out the back door?"

"No, why?"

"My back door is open."

"Are you sure it was locked?"

"No, I mean it's *open,* did you—?"

"I was in the kitchen this morning, Moll, and it was closed. Where are you?"

"In the front hallway."

"Okay, put on a coat and wait for me on the front porch, all right? If you're scared, go to a neighbor's house. I'll be right there."

Ben tried hard not to panic as he threw on clothes and his gun belt and sprinted out of the house. Déjà vu, but last time had turned out just fine. Nothing dangerous or sinister. And this time... She'd probably left the door unlatched and the wind had simply blown it open.

He'd left only an hour before, and it was a bright, sunny morning. Molly was fine.

Still, he hit the lights before starting the truck, and had it in gear before he'd even slammed the door. Thirty seconds. Sixty. Ben turned off his street, drove one block down Main and took a hard right onto Molly's street. Two minutes flat and he was screeching to a halt and jumping out.

Molly stood up from her front steps, arms wrapped around her middle, face pale.

"Are you okay?" he demanded from halfway across the lawn.

"I'm fine, just freaked out."

"Did you see or hear anything inside?"

"Nothing."

Ben radioed the station and got through to James to explain the situation. He wouldn't need backup unless he found something suspicious, but it wasn't smart to enter a situation without touching base first.

After making Molly promise to stay on the porch, Ben drew his gun and started his walk-through. Second floor, then the first and finally the basement. No one inside, nothing suspicious and the lock on the back door looked clean as a whistle. He opened the front door and waved her in.

"Is there anything missing?" he asked.

She shrugged. "I have no idea."

"I want you to take a careful look around and let me know."

He stayed with her as she studied each room. When they reached the dining room, Ben took his own time

looking around. This was her office, uncluttered, yet
still slightly messy with pens and sticky notes and a few
books. A big armoire stood off to one side, but when he
quietly tried the door it was locked. Two massive bookshelves held tons of paperbacks and a few thick hardcovers. The laptop sat open and dark on top of a small desk.

Seated at the desk, Molly looked up at him with troubled eyes. "Did you look through my desk this morning?"

"Of course not."

"Sorry, I just… This bottom drawer was a little
open."

"Anything missing?"

"Nope. It's just a few files and some printer paper."

Ben moved closer and tried the top drawer. "This
one's still locked."

"It's always locked, otherwise it slides open."

"So maybe the other slid open, too."

"Maybe. But my laptop…when I turn it off, I close
it. You didn't open it?"

"Why the hell would I do that?"

She shot him a doubtful look.

"I didn't look through your things! What is going on
here? I'm trying not to pry, Molly, but you're going to
have to be honest and tell me why someone would want
to break in and search through your desk."

"I don't know!"

"What do you do and who exactly knows about it?"

"This has nothing to do with my work. No one knows
what I do. No one but the person I report to."

Ben ran both hands through his hair in frustration.

"If you're involved in something dangerous, you have to tell me. I am not screwing around this time. This isn't a game."

"Listen to me. I am not a spy or a cop or…whatever you've got in that head of yours. I'm self-employed in a completely danger-free profession. Even my family doesn't know what I do. This is *not* about my work."

He had no choice but to believe her, so he dropped it and moved on. "Did you change your locks when you moved in?"

Her eyes widened in shocked realization. "I didn't."

"Okay, that's the first thing to do. I'll call Carl and have him come out with some good quality locks. And dead bolts. They're only usable when you're in the home, but I'm more concerned about your safety than your property. Next, you need to make arrangements for an alarm system, but that could take a little while. Call the—"

"Whoa, there. I'm not ready to burrow underground just yet. Of course I should have had my locks changed. For all I know my aunt has given out keys to every repairman and delivery boy in the county. I'll have the locks changed, have dead bolts installed and we'll take it from there."

"And see if you're raped or killed before we move forward?"

She yelled, "Freak out much?" and Ben realized he was scaring her, probably because he was scared himself.

Molly took a deep breath and stood, holding up her

hands. "If I were a normal, everyday citizen you weren't sleeping with, what would you advise?"

He thought about guns and attack dogs, bars on the windows, motion detectors, video cameras at every door, but if he mentioned those ideas there was a chance she'd see through to the overreaction beneath. Being a disciple of logic, in the end Ben surrendered to it. "Change your locks."

"Anything else?"

"If you have a reason to be particularly concerned, you might consider getting a security system."

"But?" She raised one eyebrow and tapped her foot.

Shit. This honesty of his really was a problem. "But it's probably some kid looking for a credit card or a bank account number."

Her shoulders fell, slumping with relief. "Okay. Thank you. And I'm sorry I keep panicking and calling you and—"

"First of all, it's my job. Second, give me a fucking break, Moll. Now, listen. This is a small town, but it's not the same small town you grew up in. Things have changed in the world. Methamphetamines, Internet porn, prescription drugs. These are huge problems in rural America right now. We haven't had big trouble here, but I've had to be vigilant."

"Don't worry. I'll be careful. Really. Haven't I panicked at every given opportunity?"

"Yeah, so keep it up. It makes me feel big and useful."

She finally cracked a smile. "Good. But…" The smile turned a little sickly.

"What is it?"

"I was just thinking…if it was just a thief, they probably would've taken my laptop."

Ben had been thinking the same thing, but despite his earlier panic, he didn't want her living in complete fear. And as a cop, he knew bad things could happen, but he also knew that the simplest explanation for a crime was almost always the right one.

"If I put on my 'boyfriend who's not really dating you' hat, I'd say that it's weird. But I put on my cop hat at your insistence, and my cop hat says that laptops aren't exactly easy to unload up here and you probably came downstairs and surprised him before he could think straight. That's why the door was open. He left in a hurry." He glanced at the little clock on her desk. "You usually don't get up until, what? Ten? Twelve?"

"Nine! Sometimes. And I'm getting better."

"Regardless, anyone who's been paying attention would know you're not an early riser, and anyone watching would know when I'd left."

"Okay, so… Call Carl."

"Call Carl. I'm going to file a report. Why don't you come to the station with me? Just for a little while."

He wasn't happy when she shook her head. He couldn't exactly drag her around in his truck through his whole shift, but it seemed impossible that he'd just leave her here alone for eight hours.

He glanced at his watch. "I'll be back in about forty-five minutes to dust for prints around the back door and your laptop."

"Oh, that's good. I didn't think the police usually did that for something so minor."

"Not usually, but I don't like this pattern. I'll take prints just in case."

"Thanks, Ben."

Done with being a cop, he reached for her and pulled her into his arms. "Are you okay?" He breathed in the sweet citrus scent of her hair. "Really okay?"

"I think so." Her body slowly relaxed into his, her arms snuck under his coat to tighten around his waist.

"I'm sorry about last night."

She sighed, "Me, too," and nuzzled her mouth against his neck.

"Why don't I trade shifts with Frank today? We can go to Grand Valley. Have lunch. Act like normal people."

She shook her head. "I don't think anyone would buy it."

"I would."

When she leaned back, Ben thought she was pulling away, but instead she framed his face with her hands and tugged him down for a kiss. He gladly gave her one, kissing her until she pulled away with a loud sigh.

"I'd love to spend the day with you, but I'm going to lose a lot of time this morning what with the pacing around, waiting for the locksmith, wondering if I was safer in the big city... So this afternoon... I'll have to...you know."

"Work." He made very sure to sound neutral.

"Yes. But maybe tomorrow? Are you working?"

Yesterday he would've given her a hard time, but

today he was being reasonable, mature. "I'm off tomorrow. How about we go out for dinner and a movie?"

She narrowed her eyes and frowned.

"I won't call it a date."

"Promise?"

"I promise."

"That old movie theater's still open?"

"Still showing only the best of the month-old movies."

She looked him over, measuring him before she smiled and nodded. "Yes, I'll go to dinner and a non-date movie with you."

Pulling her back into his body, Ben leaned in to kiss her neck just below her ear. "I'll bring condoms," he whispered, just to make her shiver against him. "You bring your blue friend."

"Ohmigod," she laughed, pressing her palms hard to his chest to shove him away. "Shut up."

"What? I might need backup. You're kind of an insatiable beast once you get going."

"Shut *up*." The blush bloomed over her cheeks, spreading in a slow stain of rose pink until Ben had to kiss her again.

He moved his lips to her jaw and worked his way back to her ear. "I think there's really a good girl underneath all that naughtiness."

"Dream on."

After pressing a quick kiss to her nose, Ben turned and headed for the front door before she made him forget he had a job. Plus he didn't want half the police force breaking down the door to rescue him when he failed to report for duty. And after the past week, he had no doubt that was exactly what would happen.

CHAPTER TEN

THE PITCH BLACK night had swallowed everything except the occasional porch lights of the ranches they passed. Even the stars were hiding tonight, and the moon seemed to have forgotten to rise. Molly stared through the truck window into the darkness, too lost in thought to care that she could see nothing.

"You've been quiet tonight. Didn't like the movie?" Ben asked.

Yes, she'd been quiet. Confused and freaked out and quiet. "No, I thought the movie was great. Better than the reviews said."

"Are you upset about the paper today?"

"I should ask you that."

"My thoughts on that are a given. You're supposed to make a joke so it all seems inconsequential."

She flashed him a smile. "It is inconsequential. Everyone knows you're not really the personal bodyguard to a spy queen."

"But?"

She didn't know what to tell him and what not to share anymore. Heck, she didn't even know where to start. Her writing was going well at least, mostly because she couldn't sleep and she felt tense and anxious enough to pass that tension on to her story in a good way.

She'd sent her editor the first three chapters and she was over the moon, pushing for Molly to get it in as quickly as possible. She had a spot to fill in only three weeks—some other writer had a child in the hospital and couldn't make her deadline. Molly had promised to finish it in five days' time, and her editor had sworn she'd have it read and edited in a record forty-eight hours. They were already working on a cover. All in all, it was going to be a roller-coaster ride in hurricane-force winds, but she was thankful for the distraction.

"What's wrong, Molly?"

"I'm sorry," she sighed. "I didn't mean to ruin our first non-date."

"Has something else gone on at your house?"

"No," she said truthfully. Nothing had gone on at the house, per se. But everywhere else... "My mom's been reading the *Tribune* online and she's totally freaked out thanks to Miles listening in on the police radio frequency and reporting every detail. Even Quinn is worried."

"Yeah, he's been in touch."

"I knew when I saw the paper this morning that you'd be pissed, but you don't seem upset. Half the paper was about me, *us*. Why aren't you upset?"

"I have issues, Molly, but I'm working through them. Being associated with you isn't the problem."

"What is?"

"I'd rather jump off a cliff than be dragged into an-other scandal in my life. So far, our relationship is nothing more than amusement for the neighbors. As far as your secrets go… I'm not happy about that, but if I can't ferret them out, then Miles probably can't, either. You say you're not doing anything illegal or immoral, and I have to believe it's nothing that would ruin my career or my reputation."

She hoped he meant *professional* reputation. "I'm no danger to your career, I promise."

The faint light from the dashboard let her see the serious look he gave her. "Plus," he went on after a moment, "Miles let everyone know there'd been a possible break-in at your house and maybe a Peeping Tom. With the whole town on alert, you'll be safer."

That made sense. Except she hadn't told him everything and didn't know how much to reveal. If it did have something to do with Cameron, she'd tell him Saturday. Or after Saturday. Next week for sure.

"I'm sorry your family's so worried," he sighed. "I let your brother know it was almost certainly a crime of opportunity, and an unsuccessful one at that."

"Yeah."

He glanced at her again, and Molly turned back to the window.

"Why do I feel like you're keeping something important from me?"

Despite evidence to the contrary, she'd never been any good at lying, so Molly gave in to the inevitable and faced him. "I walked over to The Bar yesterday to get my car and it wouldn't start."

"Yeah, I saw it at the garage. I figured the engine threw a rubber band or something."

"Funny." Molly swallowed hard and took a deep breath. "Lori called this morning. It wasn't the battery or the ignition. Someone cut the electrical line. And the brake line."

"What?"

"She wasn't sure if someone meant to cut both or just didn't know their way around the car."

"You mean someone might have meant to cut *just* the brake line? So you could start the car and drive it far enough for the brakes to fail?"

"I don't know."

His voice lowered to a dangerously quiet rasp. "Why didn't you call me?"

"At first…it just seemed like it must have been a prank. It doesn't make any sense."

"Someone wants to scare you or hurt you, Moll. Why?"

"I don't know."

"You must have an idea."

Yes, she did have an idea, but she'd checked it out. She wasn't an idiot. She'd spent the morning calling all of Cameron's Merry Men, browbeating them. No one had sounded the least bit guilty.

She'd even broken down and phoned Cameron's lieutenant. The man had barely tolerated her call, but after receiving Cameron's amused consent, the lieutenant had given her the details of Cameron's schedule for the past week. There simply hadn't been time for him to drive the four hours to Tumble Creek, cut her brake line, spy on her, break into her house and get back to Denver.

Heck, he'd been at work an hour after she'd found her back door open.

"Shit," Ben growled, and grabbed his cell phone from the console. He dialed and waited, cursing again when no one answered. Molly heard the faint sound of Lori's answering machine message. "Lori," he barked. "I'll be there in the morning to look at Molly's car. Leave it the hell alone in the meantime." His hand moved to push the call button, then hesitated and put the phone back to his ear. "And I can't believe you didn't call me."

He tossed the phone back onto the crowded console. "And *you*."

Molly cringed at his fury.

"You are going to tell me why someone would want to hurt you, *right now*."

"I don't know! I swear! Nothing like this ever happened when I lived in Denver. It's someone here or something to do with this town."

"Like who?"

She threw her hands up in frustrated bafflement.

"I don't remember you having any enemies or rivals in high school."

"I was fairly unnoticeable."

Ben shook his head, his knuckles blue-white against the steering wheel in the dashboard lights. "I can't think of any obvious suspects for violent crimes. We've got one reformed car thief in town, but he's seventy-five now. And one registered sex offender, but he preferred teenage boys."

"Oh, good. Well, not good, but…"

"It occurred to me this morning that Miles could

have been the one sneaking around your place, look-ing for a big story, but I definitely can't see him doing something like this. Have you noticed him more often than you'd expect?"

"No," she answered on a whisper. Her anxiety had been building up and up all day, doubt and fear and anger reacting together inside her chest until she thought she would explode. She'd turned down Ben's offer to come over last night, wanting to be independent, prove something to herself. She'd been independent to a fault her whole life.

But now she could see the occasional tiny light wink-ing in the distance as they drew closer to Tumble Creek. They were almost home. Almost to her big, creaky, lonely house. And she had no idea who could be try-ing to hurt her.

The tension wound tighter until she couldn't take it anymore. *"Can I stay at your place tonight?"* she screeched.

Ben jumped, the car skittered a foot over the yel-low line before he composed himself. Then he reached over and took her fisted hand in his. She appreciated his failed attempt at a smile, but was much more comforted by the largeness of his warm fingers surrounding hers.

"Of course you can come to my place." He picked up her hand and kissed it. "It's either that or I get my sleeping bag and camp out on your porch."

"Either way. Whatever you want."

He kissed her hand again, brushing his mouth over her knuckles in an absentminded gesture that made the hair stand up on her arm. "We found a couple sets of prints at your place that weren't yours or mine. Probably your aunt's or one of the movers, but I'm going to send them into state forensics. Were either of the movers paying too much attention to you?"

"Not that I noticed. Nothing creepy."

"All right. I'll go check out your car in the morning." He took a deep, long breath and let it out slowly. "Jeez, Molly."

"Yeah, I know."

He held her hand the whole way to her house, stood sentry while she gathered up a few of her things and locked her brand-new hardened-steel locks, and before she knew it, they were pulling into his garage.

Excited that she was going to be protected by a big, sexy policeman all night, Molly forgot her tension and hopped out of the truck. She'd been to this house when it had been his mother's, but now it was *his*.

She expected typical male decor, meaning not much at all, and that was true for the most part. When his mother had lived here, the walls had been faded colors. Mauve, pink and gray with an occasional splash of mossy green. The carpets had been dusky pink and textured. Classic early eighties stuff. Molly had been damned impressed as an eleven-year-old girl.

The pink was gone now. She wondered how many minutes had passed between his mom selling him the house and Ben tearing up the carpet. It was all wood floors now, not even a throw rug in sight, and the walls were white.

A giant couch of distressed brown leather took up most of a living room wall, facing a big ol' television.

She'd bet her life savings that the couch had at least one reclining seat, if not two. Typical single-male furniture except for two noticeable things.

There were humongous bookshelves on either side of the couch, and two more flanking the TV. She'd forgotten that about Ben, his love of reading. The shelves were packed with books, overflowing with them. Hardcovers filled the first bookshelf, and the remaining three held stacks and stacks of paperbacks. A quick glance showed her a few of her favorites and some she'd never heard of.

A memory blanketed her, of Ben reclining on her brother's bed, waiting for Quinn to finish his chores. He'd been absorbed in some science fiction book, hadn't even noticed Molly standing in the doorway, and she'd had the luxury of just watching him. A little frown had slowly formed between his brows, and she'd tried to imagine what he was reading, what could make him look so concerned. Then he'd scratched idly at his stomach, and she'd started watching his long fingers instead, as they curled slightly into his body. When she'd sighed, he'd looked up, and the spell had been broken.

The sight of all these books in his house made her glad…and hopeful. Maybe, just maybe, he would actually be impressed with her job. Maybe he wouldn't be horrified or disgusted. Maybe he'd be *happy*.

She'd have to think it over.

The second thing she noticed about his living room, the more startling sight by far, were the pictures. Framed black-and-white photos covered the walls. Dozens of them. Most of them were nature photos. A dark crocus caught in snow. Round rocks curtained by rushing water. The reflection of a sunlit cloud in a pool of clear ice.

And more: A deer raced across a field of pure white. A lone aspen leaf clung to a slumbering tree.

"Ben, these are gorgeous!"

He grunted a response as he brought her bag in from the truck and walked past her to tote it down the hallway. Molly didn't bother following. She was too busy moving from picture to picture, taking them in.

When she heard him re-enter the room, she gawked at him. "Did you take these?"

"Yeah."

"Oh, my God, Ben! When did you start doing photography? These are amazing."

"I started snapping pictures a few years ago. It's not hard to get into it these days with digital cameras and photo printers." He shrugged. "It's nothing special. Makes my hikes more interesting."

"Nothing special? You're kidding me. Do you sell these?"

"No, though I put some up on stock photography sites. It helps offset the cost of cameras and paper and ink."

She noticed the faint pink flush to his face and just wanted to squeeze him. "You should show at the Aspen Art Fair."

"Ha!" He shook his head again, the blush deepening. "Did you want a drink? I've only got bottled wine, I hope you don't mind."

"Wow. Fancy art and bottled wine. You're like a metrosexual or something."

"Yeah, my cuticles have gotten a little rough since the pass closed, but I try to make do."

Unable to resist his adorableness for another moment, Molly bounced over to him and threw herself into his arms. He caught her with an unnecessarily loud "Oof!" but she forgave him that.

"Do you know how sexy you are?" she murmured.

"Huh, I haven't had my eyebrows waxed in ages."

She kissed him to shut him up, and it worked. His tongue got busy fast. His hands curved under her ass and pulled her against him, and they kissed until Molly leaned back and grinned at him. "I missed you last night."

"Me, too."

"Will you take naked pictures of me?"

He let her go so fast she almost fell down. "Absolutely not."

"Aw, come on."

"You're out of your mind."

"It'll be fun."

"The last thing I need is evidence of my sex life floating all over the Internet."

Okay. Maybe he wouldn't appreciate her books after all. "You don't have to e-mail them to me or anything. And you're the one man in the world I'd trust with my nude photos."

"Dream on."

"Don't you want to have a memento of our affair when it's over?"

He spun on his heel and stalked to the kitchen, and

Molly bit back her request for a picture of him as a keepsake. He didn't seem in a modeling mood.

The thought of Ben modeling for nude photos was so hilarious though that she chuckled as she followed him into the kitchen. Her laughter died when she saw him, hands braced on either side of the sink, head bowed. His shoulders were tense and still; he definitely wasn't doubled over with laughter.

She felt a moment's panic when he turned around to watch her with eyes dark as a stormy night. She didn't want to have a serious conversation, didn't want to be forced to clarify exactly how she felt or what their future might be.

"Let me see this fancy bottled wine you've got," she said, willing him to give in and let it go. She thought he wouldn't. The lines on either side of his mouth deepened. He crossed his arms, hot gaze boring into her.

Shoving her hands into her pockets, she tried not to look guilty, but in the end, he just pushed off the counter and went to take a bottle of white wine from the fridge, offering her a chance to flee the kitchen and begin a self-guided tour through the rest of the house. The short hallway held more photos between the doors leading to the one bathroom and three bedrooms. She stopped at the largest bedroom.

It was clean, but not perfect. His bed wasn't made. A pair of sweatpants lay on the floor. The headboard of the bed was made of thick, polished pine logs in a simple ladderback pattern accented by a chocolate-colored bedspread.

The room fit him. It was simple, a little rough around the edges, and softened in surprising ways.

A photo graced the wall next to his bed, larger than the others she'd seen, and this one in color. The setting sun, glowing behind black-shadowed mountains under a lapis sky.

Ben's hand snuck past her to offer the wineglass.

"Ben, you're really gifted. You should—"

"I do it for myself. It's one thing I never feel on guard about."

"Well, I had no idea you were an artist. You just get sexier every day, Professor. Wanna go to bed?"

He raised an irritated eyebrow, not the reaction she'd been expecting. "I thought maybe we'd talk. Have a conversation."

"Oh." It wasn't that she didn't want to talk to him. But bed was definitely safer territory. Conversation with Ben was sincere and complicated and emotionally involved. Dangerous. She considered just whipping her shirt off, but he wandered back toward the living room and she had no choice but to follow.

He sat at one end of the couch, ankle on one knee, wineglass balanced on the other. She paused just to take him in, because there might not be another night like this and he was so handsome. Impossible as it seemed, she'd noticed earlier that his charcoal-gray slacks made his ass look even hotter than his jeans did, and the dusky-green button-down shirt set off his brown eyes perfectly.

He'd dressed up for her, and turned her on in the process. Like that was hard.

Seeming to pull himself from his troubling thoughts, Ben finally looked up at her and patted the couch beside him. "Come on. I promise I'm not going to fish for background information."

She considered taking her shirt off for two more seconds, then decided she could employ that option at any time during the conversation if she had to. If he asked about Cameron, for instance, or her life in the sex trade.

"How's your mom?" she asked as she plopped onto the cushions next to him.

"Good. She's going to retire this year. She called to ask about you."

"Is she keeping notes on the mystery?"

"Apparently I'm the last to know that the *Tribune*'s online. She saw the stories, and called to tell me how much she's always liked you."

The way her heart leapt was completely uncalled for in Molly's opinion. "Your mom is such a sweetheart."

"She's been dating someone for a year," he blurted, as if it was still a surprise to him.

"That's great!" She laughed at his doubtful look. "Don't tell me this is her first boyfriend since your father? Come on."

"I think it is. She very unfortunately mentioned to me that she felt like a virgin again. So I think, you know…" He cleared his throat.

"Wow! Well, she's overdue for fun then."

"I guess. Hey, what did you mean about Ricky Nowell?"

After she choked on her wine, she managed to gasp, "Huh?"

"You said something about him being really horrible to you."

"Oh, I… Nothing. Teenage stuff."

He leaned back against the cushions and gave her the cop look. Shit. "You said you lost your virginity that night, Molly. Did you?"

"Oh, were you paying attention to that? Ha."

"You lost your virginity that night and you came to talk to your brother about it?"

"No…"

"I was worried about you when you left. I couldn't even come after you. My date…and I wasn't dressed."

"Oh, I remember."

"Please tell me what happened."

"I, uh… Right now?" He nodded. "Okay. I was fine. I just, I came by that night because I'd gotten in a fight with Ricky. We were on a date, and he said if I didn't put out it was over. I was outraged and I came to your place because… I don't know. I thought I'd tell you and you'd be outraged, too."

"Damn straight."

"So I stormed in and, yowza! There you were. Naked. And very busy."

"Right."

"And I'd been thinking about you naked. I couldn't really… I couldn't look away. My heart was breaking and all I wanted to do was stay there and watch."

"Oh, Molly."

"I know! It was terrible!" She slapped his arm to break the tension. "But it also kind of freed me. I'd never consciously told myself I was waiting for you, but in that moment I realized I was. And seeing you with that other girl released me from that. It also totally turned me on, so I decided to do it."

"With Ricky."

Molly cringed. "Ugh. Yeah. Big mistake. Or little one, really. End of story."

Ben arched a doubtful eyebrow. "Aren't I supposed to be the one with communication issues? You're a girl, Molly."

"As far as you know. They can do amazing things with surgery these days."

"Yeah? Well, it feels real, and that's all that matters. Plus you swam naked in your kiddie pool until your were five. I'd have remembered any dangly parts."

Unfortunately, that made her snort wine up her nose, and it burned like crazy as she coughed and blinked. Boy, she was sexy. Ben was probably rock hard now and finding it difficult to resist ripping off her jeans.

"So you said Ricky was horrible to you."

"That was ten years ago, and I was so, so stupid. Why do you care now?"

"Because I do."

"Fine," she groaned. "I found Ricky hanging out outside The Bar. I told him I wanted to do it, and he was happy to oblige. Thankfully, he's a member of the little boys' club, so it was disappointing, but only slightly uncomfortable. I had a lot more fun once I got to college."

"And he was an asshole?"

"Yeah, after one and a half minutes in heaven, he rolled off me and told me I had a whole lot to learn about pleasing a man."

"No fucking way."

"But it exempted me from any guilt I might have had about mocking him."

Ben ran his hand down her hair and twirled a strand around his finger. "He comes home every year for Thanksgiving. I'll set up a drunk-driving checkpoint just for him."

"Aw, you're so sweet."

"I wish I'd caught up when you ran."

She shook her head even as his sweetness relaxed her bones. "No." She leaned into him and his arm curled around her. "I used to fantasize that maybe you'd have pushed that woman off you and come after me, but you're not that guy, Ben. Regardless of what she was to you, a one-night stand or a girlfriend, you'd never have treated her like that. And if you had, I wouldn't have wanted you to catch me."

His fingers traced patterns over her shoulder. "You're a sweet girl, Molly. You always have been."

"You wish," she murmured. "Are we done talking? Can we go to bed now?"

He sighed in exasperation. "I thought we'd—"

Molly shoved away from him. "I see I have no choice here," she grumbled and finally gave in to the urge to whip off her shirt. Ben looked at her like she was crazy, so she took off the bra, too, and that did the job real good. Ben gave up his mission to talk, and Molly got just what she wanted.

CHAPTER ELEVEN

MOLLY WOKE TO the low rumble of distant explosions.
The sound vibrated through her ears before fading to
an eerie stillness. A few minutes passed before a new
pack of dynamite blew, shaking the ground enough to
sense but not quite feel. It had been ten years since she'd
awoken to that, and the sound made her smile before
she'd even opened her eyes.

They must have had a major snowfall in Aspen to
get the avalanche crews out this early in the year. The
otherworldly silence in between the avalanche blasting
told her it had snowed here as well, but there weren't
enough back country skiers on this side of the mountain
to warrant dynamiting the fragile snow pack.

She thought about sleeping in, then remembered that
she was in Ben's house, in Ben's bed. That made her
smile even wider. Last night had been slow and sensual,
as if their chemistry were different here in his home.
He'd been in charge, he'd set the pace. She hadn't been
able to do anything but hang on for the long, fantasti-
cally good ride.

And though she'd asked him twice more if he'd take
dirty pictures of her—when would she have another

lover who was both a photographer *and* an honorable man?—Ben had refused.

Meaning to hug her pillow to her chest, she started to roll to her side, but something crinkled under her arm. She blinked her eyes open to slits. The blinds were still closed, but the sun was high enough to brighten the room anyway. Apparently she'd already slept late.

Ben's pillow was empty beside her, so she sat up to look around, which was when she found the source of the crinkle. A photo lay beside her elbow, a color photo that seemed abstract at first. She picked it up and turned it slowly until she recognized it as a close-up photo of a woman's foot disappearing beneath a twist of white sheet. She flipped the paper over to find it blank on the back.

Frowning, she scooted farther up on the bed, and her hip touched another piece of stiff paper. She looked down, reaching for the photo even as her gaze caught on another one farther down the bed. Her eyes widened as she curled her legs beneath her and looked around, really looked around. Four, five, six…more than half a dozen pictures were scattered about. All of them close-ups of…*her*.

Holding her breath, she snatched up the picture closest to her knees. Just her ear, the curve of her neck, and her blond hair spread across the pillow. She turned it over. *This is as naked as it's going to get, so I hope you like it. —B.*

Her pulse beat so hard that she felt the separate thumps of her heart muscle bringing blood in and sending it out. She grabbed another photo. This was her hand, curled in sleep against a crumpled fold of sheet. Another showed her shoulder curving down to her arm and just the faint swell of the top of her breast. The last one she gathered up showed the top of one hip and the curve of her belly, her navel dipping in just above the startling white of the sheet. Tears blurred her eyes as she turned over the picture.

You, in morning light, it read in his black, spiky writing.

Molly dropped the whole stack of photos and pressed her hands to her mouth. This was too serious. Too lovely. She'd wanted dirty pictures, not beautiful ones.

Frightened by the continued, panicked patter of her heart, Molly jumped from the bed to pull on her clothes. She needed coffee and a clear head, anything but this soft mushiness that wrapped her thoughts up in…in *feelings*.

She couldn't fall in love with Ben. Even if she wanted to she couldn't.

Unable to find her shirt or bra, Molly covered her breasts with her hands and went to the living room to find them on the couch. Once she was decently covered, she went to raid the kitchen for caffeine.

She didn't have far to look. There on the round kitchen table sat a thermal carafe. Next to it were a mug, a bowl, a spoon, a banana and a box of cereal. Ben had made her breakfast.

"Shit." Molly collapsed into one of the sturdy chairs and stared in dismay at the box of Apple Jacks. Why did he have to do every single thing right? Not even in a creepy way. If Cameron had decided to lay breakfast out, he'd have gone with fresh-squeezed orange juice and croissants. Maybe some fresh berries and a quiche.

But Ben wasn't trying to impress her; he was just taking care of her, because that was what he did. He was gruff and quiet. Serious. Private. And he took care of people.

And the horrible truth was that she *was* in love with him. Thinking they could just have fun sex had been idiotic. Of course she was in love with him. She'd been half in love with the man her whole life.

Damn it, if she'd never written that first story, if she hadn't authored something so obviously about him, she could have just told him the truth up front, and let him decide if her career was too much to take. But now… she'd not only violated his annoying sense of privacy, she'd also hidden a problem that involved him.

Now what the hell was she supposed to do?

"Crap." Maybe she wouldn't have to do anything. Maybe Cameron would come up here and romance Ben, and it would be over anyway. They'd probably bond over cop talk, then shake their heads over Molly's quirks and agree that she needed to work through her obvious intimacy issues before she got seriously involved with anyone. Ben would nod when Cameron said that she shouldn't enter into one relationship until she'd put the last one behind her. And the angrier she got, the more obvious it would be that she wasn't over Cameron.

Mad at just the thought of it, Molly peeled the banana and began to chomp it down as she poured herself a cup of coffee.

Men. If she'd never written her first book, she'd be

good enough for Ben, but she wouldn't have this career she loved. She'd be slaving away in the back room of a marketing firm or working in sales at a big company. She certainly wouldn't have been able to move back to Tumble Creek, so she wouldn't have had this chance with Ben anyway.

God, she hated guilt. And she hated obligation and compromise and arguments. She'd figured out early on that she wasn't really cut out for serious relationships, and that had worked fine for her until Cameron Kasten came along. Then she'd found herself suddenly swept up into a relationship with no idea how she'd gotten there. The man was good at trickery, but she'd clawed her way out of that black hole through sheer force of will.

Maybe she could do the same thing with this unfortunate well of sticky emotion she'd fallen into. Figure out a way to scramble out of it as quickly as possible. A great idea, except that she was hoping like crazy that Ben wouldn't run into Cameron and she'd be able to keep this going for a while.

Shit, she was totally screwed.

Molly downed the rest of her coffee like a shot and hurried over to her bag. She dug out the boots she'd packed, tugged on her hat and grabbed her coat off the chair she'd tossed it over.

She had to get out of his house. It felt too personal hanging around here, like she was sinking into quicksand and not bothering to struggle. But regardless of her panic, she darted back to his bedroom to snatch up the photos. They were works of art, poetry he'd created for her, and she wanted them no matter what.

When she opened the door, she was glad she'd brought the boots. At least five inches of snow covered everything. Well, not Ben's driveway, of course. He'd shoveled that. Old Mrs. Lantern's drive was shoveled, too, and Molly didn't have to think to know who'd done it.

She slung her bag over her shoulder and began to trudge home. She'd lose herself in her book, see if she couldn't get all the way through the first draft today. She had work to do, and there were other important people in her life; she didn't have to think about Ben Lawson 24/7.

"That's right," she muttered, watching her breath fall toward the white ground. "You're independent. Educated. Well-rounded. A fascinating conversationalist. Financially comfortable."

Thoughts of money prompted her to dig her phone out from the bag and turn it on. Her editor had promised to call with the numbers from her last release, and Molly was thrilled when she saw the message icon blink at her.

"Ooo. Money, money, money."

Except that it wasn't from her editor. The message was from her mother. All three messages were from her mother. Molly listened halfway through the second one, then deleted them all and called her mom.

"Molly!" her mother cried. "I was so worried about you last night!"

"Sorry, Mom. I was out with Ben and—"

"I know. He called me this morning to let me know you were fine."

"He what?"

"Oh, I left a message at the police station."

"Mom. You are kidding me, right?"

"I wouldn't joke about something like that."

Molly took a deep breath and told herself not to yell at her mom. "Are we quite clear on all the trouble you caused by talking with Cameron about me?"

"Ben Lawson is a good man. I wiped his nose when he was little."

Grateful there hadn't been any talk of wiping his ass, Molly made a face of sheer relief. "Yeah, well you loved Cameron like a son, or that's what you said when I broke up with him."

"I didn't appreciate it when he invited your father on that fishing trip. I'd planned a nice anniversary dinner."

Oh, Cameron had misstepped with that one. Hard to believe he hadn't memorized an important date like her parents' anniversary. He'd been the golden boy for weeks after their breakup, but he'd turned into persona non grata once he'd stolen her dad away for an impromptu fly-fishing trip. Mom had been deeply peeved, finally owning up to the truth. "He's not even your boyfriend anymore!" she'd screeched.

Molly smiled at the memory.

"I've been thinking…" her mom offered in an ominously quiet voice. "It could be Cameron spying on you. You said—"

"Tell me you did not say anything to Ben."

"Molly, he's the police. If—"

"Tell me!"

Her mom huffed, clearly outraged. "I didn't even

think of it until half an hour ago. So, no, I didn't tell him."

Thank the sweet Lord. She did not need Ben participating in a long, drawn out, intense discussion with Cameron, especially when there wasn't any chance he was the stalker.

Her mom was still silent, broadcasting invisible rays of hurt across the phone. When Molly rolled her eyes, she caught sight of Wilhelm Smythe walking in the opposite direction on the other side of the street.

"Morning, Ms. Jennings," he called out.

Molly waved to him, then finally gave in to her mom's silent treatment. "I'm sorry, Mom. It's just… This Cameron thing has been a living nightmare. And it's not him. It's not. So…"

"Well…" Her mom's sigh echoed through the phone. "I'm sorry I kept taking Cameron's calls—"

"And a visit," Molly interrupted.

Another sigh. "Okay, and a visit. I'm sorry I was friendly with him after you two broke up. It wasn't right."

Molly didn't realize how angry she'd been until her mom said those words, but half of that anger was self-directed. She shook her head and kicked at a chunk of snow on the road. "It's all right. The man is a force of nature. I understand."

"Good. So why don't you think about moving in with Quinn for a little while? There's no reason—"

"No."

"With Ben, then."

"Mom, we've been seeing each other for a week.

Surely you're not suggesting I move on to living in sin so quickly."

"Oh, you've been sinning enough from what I hear."

"Yeah, we've been going at it like rabbits from the moment I hit town." Actually, they had been, which made it kind of funny when her mom gasped.

"When was the last time you went to church, Molly Jennings?"

Her smile faded. "I love you, Mom. Don't keep trying to call. I leave my cell off most of the time and you'll just worry."

Molly hung up just as she reached Main and paused at the edge of the newer blacktop.

What the hell was Wilhelm Smythe doing strolling down Ben's street anyway? She spun around, thinking she might catch him watching her, but no… Wilhelm was shuffling along, paying no attention to Molly at all. Just to be safe, she watched him for a full thirty seconds, but aside from scratching his butt, he didn't make any sneaky moves. Still, she had been slightly creeped out by him when she'd dated his son for two weeks in high school, but the cause of that had been Wilhelm's constant whiskey smell.

Or maybe she'd been picking up on some sleazy vibes. Maybe he liked to look through women's windows at night.

Molly watched suspiciously until he disappeared around the curve of the street. He didn't really look healthy enough to hike the ridge behind her house in the middle of the night. Actually, he looked like he'd come close to liver failure sometime in the next few years, and that made Molly wonder if his son had followed in his footsteps.

The hushed rumble of the river crept into her sad thoughts, and Molly glanced to the narrow, rutted lane to her left. The access ramp led to the deepest part of the river, and she considered following the road down instead of heading straight home. She wanted to stand on the bank and watch the swift, tumbling crystal of the water and think, think, think. But she was scared to go down there by herself. Someone might push her into the icy water and nobody would even know.

That pissed her off so much that she stomped across Main Street and up her hill in record time, and barely even paused when she saw the note taped to her front door.

Get out of Tumble Creek or die, it demanded in dark, ugly writing.

Molly was furious when sick fear iced through the pit of her stomach. So enraged that she ignored the note as she twisted the key in the new lock and stormed inside. She left the ragged paper where it was and slammed the door; Ben would want to see it and check for fingerprints, and she couldn't deal with that right now.

Instead, she headed straight for the kitchen to grab her sharpest butcher knife. Some coward was ruining her life and she couldn't take it anymore, so instead of calling and crying to Ben, she checked the back door—locked—and the cellar door—also locked—then searched her home from top to bottom.

By the time she got back to her desk and sat down, the anger had melted away to reveal the fear beneath, and her knees gave out, dropping her like a rock into her ergonomic desk chair.

Coming back to Tumble Creek was supposed to have brought peace to her life. Her hometown was secure and stable, a refuge from the city. So what the hell had she unleashed when she'd moved back? She hadn't stolen anyone's boyfriend in high school, hadn't voted anybody off the cheerleading squad. She hadn't even *been* on the cheerleading squad. No one in Tumble Creek should have a grudge against her. She hadn't come to town and taken someone's job. The only thing she'd done was get it on with the hot police chief.

"Hey…" Molly planted her boots on the floor and sat up straight. Maybe this had nothing to do with her. Maybe it was all about responsible, upstanding Ben and whatever women were in *his* past. Sure, he'd claimed that he didn't date in town, but he'd been "not dating" her for a week now, after all, and they'd gotten pretty personal. Oh, the man might have some 'splaining to do.

Smirking at the thought of knocking him off his high horse, Molly rubbed her hands together. Yeah, he'd come over sometime in the next few hours, all outraged and protective, then she'd confront him about just how many women in town he *hadn't* dated.

Energized by the thought of being the one in the right, Molly unlocked the bottom drawer of her desk and took her laptop out. She fired it up, signed on and zeroed in on an e-mail from her publisher.

First, her editor assured her that, no, they hadn't received any unusually creepy letters about Molly or her stories. Just the usual diatribes from Mrs. Gibson.

Then... Ah-ha! Molly's new sales numbers. The lovely, luscious new sales numbers that she really needed right now. This was her *career*. She was good at it and she enjoyed it. A secret career, yes, but nothing to be ashamed of, and nothing to regret.

She'd tell Ben about it some day soon, and he'd try to make her feel bad, and they'd be done.

"I can handle this," she said to her computer, happy with the surety in her voice. "I will be fine."

THIS WASN'T WORKING. Instead of running out of town, Molly Jennings had run straight into the bed of Ben Lawson. But what else could be expected of a whore like her?

Now Chief Lawson was on the case like a pit bull with a fresh bone, and that wouldn't do at all. They had to be separated. There *had* to be a way to separate them.

After days of frustration, trying to find a solution, some *weapon,* the *Tumble Creek Tribune* offered a gift.

Lo and behold, Molly Jennings had a secret. A secret even the Chief didn't know, if the *Tribune* was correct. Whatever it was...nobody kept a secret like that unless it was harmful. Sordid even.

Whatever she was hiding, that was the key. The wedge to pry them apart. The club she could be beaten with. But how to ferret it out?

She had an office in her home, had a computer and locked cabinets. As far as access... Well, the woman had got herself a fancy new set of locks, but the place wasn't exactly Fort Knox. The department just happened to have received a brand-new bump key, the latest in lock-picking convenience. The bump key looked like any other household key, but once inserted, all it needed was a good whack to disrupt the tumblers of any lock.

So if Molly continued to spend her nights away—and there was no reason to think she wouldn't—there'd be time to page leisurely through her files and find out exactly what embarrassing truth she was hiding from her new boyfriend.

And when Chief Lawson dropped her like a hot potato, she'd hit the ground running until she was out of Tumble Creek and back where she belonged.

CHAPTER TWELVE

MORE LIKE HERSELF than she'd felt in days, Molly got tired of waiting for Ben and breezed into the police station, ready to solve this mystery once and for all. She'd been sulking around, guilty, thinking this was all her fault just because she had a dirty secret and a crazy ex-boyfriend. But she was now convinced the crux of the problem lay with her new, non-crazy lover.

Ben was sexy enough to drive any woman to a life of crime, wasn't he?

Ready to blow him away with her surprise theory, Molly sauntered over to the station, Tupperware container in hand, then stopped short to find his office empty. Well, crap.

She spun in a slow circle, taking in Brenda's empty desk and the deserted hallway. All this genius floating around in her head and no one nearby to hear it. But they couldn't have gone far.

After one last glance toward the front door, Molly stepped past the threshold of Ben's office, a swirl of anticipation twisting around her stomach. She felt sneaky as a spy, looking over this space where Ben spent so much time.

The room smelled of him, clean skin and leather. A

faint touch of some oil that made her think of guns. His desk was organized, but not clear, and two paperbacks perched on one corner weighted by a stained coffee cup.

She eased the first book out from under the cup, turned it over in her hand. A Western. Definitely not a sexy romance, but almost as romantic at heart, really. A time when men were men and women liked to be tied up. Oh, wait. That was *her* version of a Western.

Grinning, she eased the book back into place and put the mug carefully back on top.

"What do you think you're doing?" an angry voice barked.

Guilty fear hit her in the gut as she swung toward the sound. Something hard struck her knuckles, and a crash boomed through the room just as Molly registered Brenda's broad shoulders filling up the doorway.

"Oh!" Molly yelped, looking from Brenda to the shards of ceramic mug spread across the floor. "Brenda, you scared me!"

"What are you doing, sneaking around in here?"

"Not, uh, *sneaking.* I'm just looking for Ben and... Oh! Here!" She thrust the Tupperware bowl toward Brenda, a light-blue peace offering.

The woman snatched the bowl away, but she didn't seem to understand its symbolism. Her mouth twisted in a sneer. "You shouldn't be in here by yourself."

"Sorry. There was no one around."

"And you've broken Ben's favorite mug. His mother gave that to him when he made chief."

"His..." Hand over her mouth in horror, Molly looked back to the floor. Of course the damn thing had hit at the exact wrong angle. Instead of splitting into two or three big chunks, it had shattered like glass. "Oh, shit. Do you…do you think I could find another one?"

"And then what?" Brenda snapped. "Lie to him about it?"

"No! I just meant I could give it as a peace offering! Are you having a bad day or something?"

Instead of answering, Brenda just huffed and spun away. "I'll get a broom. You need to wait in the reception area."

"Jeez Louise," Molly muttered. Brenda was turning out to be just as grumpy as her mom had been. Brenda's mother had always had a cigarette in her hand and a chip on her shoulder.

Molly wanted to tell Brenda that she didn't have to stay in Tumble Creek and become her mother. She could move anywhere and be anyone, just like Molly had done, but the woman didn't look in the mood to have a heart-to-heart. A tactical retreat to the reception area seemed in order.

As soon as her butt hit one of uncomfortable chairs, the main door opened and Ben walked in, carrying the bright scent of snow with him.

His eyebrows rose. "Is everything all right?"

"Sure. I just wanted to talk with you."

His eyebrows lowered to the frown he'd been wearing before he'd seen her. "The electrical and brake lines were cut, just like Lori said. I dusted for prints, but…" He jerked his head toward his office, indicating Molly should follow him toward the sound of tinkling ceramic.

"Uh, Ben." She hurried after him. "I broke your mug,

and I'm really, really sorry. If there's a way I can replace it…"

"Hi, Brenda," he said before he glanced back at Molly. "What mug?"

Brenda finished sweeping and hustled past them both, nodding to Ben and totally ignoring Molly, who stood there helpless, wringing her hands.

"The mug your mom gave you when you became chief. I'm so sorry!" She stopped wringing her hands when he gave her an exasperated look that strongly impugned her sanity.

"I'm sure I'll survive the loss. I'm not even sure which mug you're talking about. My mom sends me one for every holiday. I think that's the default for grown men who don't wear ties to work."

"Oh. Okay. Good." Though she tossed a glare over her shoulder for Brenda, the woman seemed uncowed. She glared right back.

"Anyhoo…" Molly dropped into one of his chairs. "I have an idea of who the stalker could be."

Ben stuttered on his descent into his own chair. "Who?"

"Well." Reaching blindly back, she grabbed the edge of the door and swung it closed. "You know how we're not dating?"

"No."

"Yes, you do. And you said you never date women in Tumble Creek."

"I don't."

She rolled her eyes at his grumpy reticence. "So do you 'not date' them in the same way you're 'not dating' me? You know, with a lot of sex and making out and flirting?"

He hardly moved at all, but he went so tense that his chair squeaked beneath him.

"Because a mere mortal woman could take that the wrong way."

"Molly." Oh, he'd learned that tone from hanging around her parents in his youth. Teeth ground together, he added a simple, conversation-ending, "No."

"Whatever. I think there's a woman in this town you used to get it on with. And I think she's after me. So who is it?"

"There's no one," he growled.

"There's got to be someone! You're telling me you haven't had sex once during the winter in the past ten years? Give me a break."

He blinked twice, some of the certainty leaving his gaze.

"A-ha!" Molly pounced, leaning forward to point a finger at his give-away eyes. "Liar!"

"Oh, for God's sake. It's not her."

Just that little word. Three letters. H-E-R. And an ulcer drilled straight through Molly's stomach. "Ow," she muttered, rubbing her waist. She thought she'd been certain of her theory, but clearly she hadn't been, or that word wouldn't have speared her with such pointy jealousy.

"There's only been one woman," Ben insisted. "And it couldn't be her."

"Who? And why not?" *And who?*

"Because she's been married for six years and has four children."

"So maybe she's hanging on to her youthful fantasies. Who was it?" Molly repeated. "And just having children doesn't take away any stalking skills, as far as I've heard."

"Aside from the fact that she had her fourth child last Monday, I guess that'd be true."

"Oh." Damn. "Okay. Who is she?"

"Jealous?"

"She just gave birth! No, I'm not jealous." Much.

Ben's half smile rubbed her pride like sandpaper. He was all arrogance and triumph. "Shall we get back to some real theories about why someone's stalking you? Or do you have something else?" he drawled.

"Wilhelm Smythe!" she blurted. "I saw him walking down your street this morning, and I can't imagine why—"

"His ex-daughter-in-law lives on my street. He comes to visit his grandson."

"Oh." Another theory shot down. Molly didn't like to think of herself as petty, but she was feeling pretty petty right now. Both her pitiful theories had been shot down and Ben had some wholesome ex-flame he wouldn't tell her about. So she aimed her own smirk right at his. "Well, I've got nothing else except the threatening note taped to my front door."

His chair screamed as his knee thumped against the underside of the desk. "What?"

She waved her hand. "Just go over and take your pic-

tures and your prints. I don't know anything more than
you do. Maybe I'll call you later, Chief."

His stunned frustration went a long way toward making her feel better as she walked out, which proved just
how petty she was.

Big words and delusions of independence aside, Molly
would spend the night at Ben's house again. She didn't
even suffer guilt over her helpless dependence on him,
because he made it quite clear he'd handcuff her and
drag her bodily out of her house before he'd let her sleep
there. Plus, the next day was Saturday and she so did
not want to be home. So Molly got into Ben's truck, pre-
tending to begrudge him, and thinking of those handcuffs the whole time.

"Your car will be out of commission for a while. I'll
take you wherever you need to go."

She glanced at him, but he wasn't looking at her. His
jaw was rough steel. He hadn't shaved this morning, and
now he looked menacing. Dark. Furious.

Sexy.

Molly gave her head a shake. "I think Lori has a car
I can borrow, actually."

His eyes slanted toward her, narrowed against her
words. "I'll take you wherever you need to go," he repeated.

Had his mouth even moved when he said that? Man,
he was in a bad mood. "'Kay," she chirped.

She didn't need him to start bitching about the note
and how she hadn't called him, and why had she gone
half the day without telling him, and when the hell was

she gonna start taking this seriously? Molly sighed just at the thought of it, and wondered how she was going to get her own car the next day.

But when she woke up on Saturday morning, ass pressed to Ben's hip, a brilliant idea hit her smack between the eyes. Cameron would be in town sometime in the next few hours, and she didn't want him crossing Ben's path. So she would take Ben's path straight out of town.

"Ben!"

"Mmm?"

"I need to go to Grand Valley this morning."

"Mmm." He rolled to his side and snuck an arm around her hip to pull her against his morning glory.

"Hellooo," she crooned, then yelped, "Oh, hello!" when his hand delved between her legs with no preliminaries. Not that she needed any. He had her purring in seconds.

Oh, God. Gaaaawd, that felt so good, and his thick length was pressing against her ass, promising even better stuff to come. But… "Wait, I need to…take a shower. I've gotta go to…oh…I…I need to go to Grand Valley."

"Don't worry, this'll only take a minute."

She snorted in delight, happy with any excuse to stay.

"Just hold still, darlin'."

"Stop!" She was shaking now, laughing hard even as her body sang.

His lips teased her neck as he guided her knee up and pulled her leg over his thigh. "Count to ten and this will all be over."

"Hey, I'm not supposed to be laughing when you—Oh! Mmm…"

But he was a sneaky liar, after all, and they spent a good twenty minutes laughing and groaning and sighing before he was done with her. Then he stole the shower while she sprawled bonelessly across his bed, breathing in the scent of his sweat on the pillow. Damn that man had some awesome pheromones. And fingering skills. Those years in the junior-high trombone section had paid off for him. Finger, slide. Finger, slide.

Molly laughed so hard at her own joke that she had to sprint to the bathroom to pee. A little too intimate with Ben showering right there, but he didn't seem to mind. He just stepped out of the tub when she flushed the toilet, wrapped a towel around his waist—sadly—and gestured her toward the steamy spray.

"Still hot," he said, always the gentleman. "I'm only working a few hours tonight, so I'm at your disposal for the rest of the day. What's got you so fired up to go to Grand Valley?"

Molly was glad she had the excuse of stepping into the tub and adjusting the shower head to buy some time. "Uh… I need some office supplies." Well, she'd stepped right into a sticky subject, but at least it sounded true. And she always needed ink and paper, so it wasn't even really a lie. Jackpot. "And, you know, I've got some work to do this afternoon, so I wanted to get out there this morning. Maybe we could have breakfast!" And lunch.

"Sure."

She could hear the purposeful neutrality in his answer. He really was trying, which only made her feel worse. She'd lulled herself to sleep last night by thinking of all the ways she could ease him into the truth, imagining the unlikely scenarios in which he might react positively to her writing. Maybe she could feed him bits and pieces of the real story. She could tell him she was a writer, then later explain exactly what she did write.

Maybe he wouldn't accuse her of producing smut or trash or women's porn. Maybe he'd be interested. He loved books *and* he loved sex, after all. If the conversation went well, she could give him one of her novellas. But not the one she'd written about him. She could pull him deeper with another book and then another. And when he was waxing poetic about her gorgeous imagination, her impressive use of craft, her impeccable sense of language, when he'd been brought fully over to the dark side...then she'd spring the Story of Ben on him. Hell, at that point he might even be flattered!

When she snorted water into her nose at the thought and choked, Ben tapped on the shower curtain. "Want me to get your water wings?"

"I think every time we have sex, more of my sense of humor rubs off on you."

"I think I'm really damn relaxed. And naturally witty."

"Ha! Actually, you always did make me laugh. When you used to come camping with my family, you'd have me laughing so hard my stomach hurt." She smiled at the memory. "I remember thinking it was strange that people at school thought you were shy. But when you and Quinn both made varsity basketball and we started coming to the games, I saw you interacting with other people and I realized you *were* shy."

"I prefer to think of it as reserved," he countered. "And dignified, if you know what that means."

She splashed water over the curtain rod, kind of hoping he'd retaliate by lunging back into the shower with her, but she washed on unmolested. Soon enough she was dried and dressed and they were on their way.

The day was gorgeous; bright and crisp, the sun glinting off rapidly melting snow. A perfect fall day, and she was making a brilliant escape, and her heart was flying, flying.

They had breakfast, then went to the little office supply store wedged between the insurance office and the VFW Hall. After a quick stop at the drugstore so that Molly could stock up on exotic items like face moisturizer, they drove. Just drove.

Ben took her through the whole valley, a place she hadn't explored since she was a teen. They followed the river, passing herds of elk that seemed unconcerned with the nearness of the truck. Molly watched a family of foxes playing on the opposite bank, darting in and out of dried reeds, and she felt so, so glad to be home.

Next summer she would come and walk in the water here, revel in the contrast of snow-melt water and impossibly hot sun. She'd get sunburned and tipsy on mountain air, and she'd go home and…and Ben wouldn't be there.

But he was here now, holding her hand, giving her

back the life she thought she'd left too far behind. He was here, and it was perfect.

Until Cameron called. That day-ruining bastard.

To be fair, it wasn't actually Cameron who called, because Molly had turned off her phone and was unreachable. She'd thought that would be enough, being out of town and unreachable. But Cameron Kasten was no mere mortal man bound by the rules of wireless technology and societal norms. He was a magic manipulator, able to bend time and space, or at least able to bend small-town cops to his will.

"Hey, Andrew," Ben answered his phone. "What's up?"

She knew as soon as Ben looked at her, knew he was hearing something about Cameron. He made a lot of "uh-huh" noises, eyes getting narrower as each second ticked by. When he slowed the truck and swung it in a tight circle to head back the way they'd come, her heart dropped.

"What are you doing?" she demanded.

But Ben was busy snarling something to Andrew that ended with, "He'll just have to fucking wait and see, won't he?" before he closed the phone with a snap and hit the accelerator.

"What's going on?" No answer, just glowering silence. "Ben?"

"Your *boyfriend.* Is sitting. In my place of employment. Telling *my* employees—"

"Ben—"

"No. He's telling *my* employees that he's *worried*

about you, Molly. Because you were supposed to have a big date with him, and you've gone missing."

"I'm so sorry, I didn't—"

"You knew he was coming, didn't you?"

"Uh…"

He bit out, *"Office supplies,"* as if he were cursing some cruel god, and Molly flinched.

"I'm not there," she said in a rush. "I knew he might come and I'm not there because I don't want to see him."

"Jesus Christ, Molly, this isn't grade school. If you don't like someone, you tell him. You don't run away and hide, just to avoid having an actual adult conversation!"

Molly sucked in a deep breath full of outrage. "Excuse me?"

"I know you've got communication issues, but—"

"You've got to be kidding me," she gasped.

"You're clearly reluctant to tell anybody the truth about anything—"

She made a high-pitched noise of frustration that cut him off. "Why," she bit out, "do you always think the worst of me?"

"Oh, for God's sake. Your supposedly *ex*-boyfriend comes up to take you out on a date, and you run away like a kid who's trying to avoid punishment! You don't even think about what might happen while you're hiding in blissful ignorance, and now all my officers think I'm a fool who can't keep an eye on his girlfriend, much less a whole town. What the hell isn't 'worst' about that?"

"Screw you, Ben Lawson." She twisted toward her window and stared pointedly out.

Perfect day, my ass. Hard to have a perfect day when you were out with an arrogant, judgmental control freak. Not that she was surprised. No one in her life ever expected much from her, and then they all had the nerve to wonder why she wouldn't share the important parts of her world.

Just because she tried not to take life too seriously, her friends and family assumed she *couldn't* be serious. Or mature. Or responsible. Fuck, she couldn't even handle one lowly ex-boyfriend, how the hell could they trust her with her whole *life?*

That was one reason she reveled in her secrets. There was nothing for her father to point at, exasperated, demanding an explanation. Nothing for her mother to cluck over and shake her head with that look in her eye. That "Oh, what else could we expect from Molly?" look.

So she'd changed majors eleven times in college; she hadn't found her passion yet. So she'd stranded herself in Mexico once; a driver's license was an easy thing to misplace. And so she wasn't her genius brother who'd always known what he wanted, who'd scored nearly perfect on his SATs, who was well on his way to being rich as hell, who'd never dated a cute biker dude with tattoos on his neck, who was carving a name for himself out of granite and hardwood and years of hard work.

Yes, she was irresponsible sometimes, and irreverent, and she'd failed trigonometry and couldn't build a fucking house out of Lincoln Logs, much less iron and rare timber. And she hovered on the razor's edge of constant scandal and didn't really give a shit if or when she tumbled over. Yes, she was imperfect. But that didn't mean she wasn't also spectacular.

It took thirty minutes of thick silence to reach Tumble Creek. Molly slammed out of the truck without waiting for Ben and stomped up the steps and into the police station.

Cameron, resplendent in a black suit and lavender tie, stood from the chair he'd pulled close to Brenda's desk, and had the nerve to smile at Molly as if she'd just shit a pot of gold, complete with rainbow. His sculpted dark blond hair didn't budge despite his movements.

"Molly, you're all right!"

"Not even close."

"Well, you look terrific."

The door opened and closed behind her, sucking the air from the room and leaving tension in its place. Molly caught sight of at least two officers shifting in the hallway to her left. No one was going to miss this little show.

"Chief," Brenda said, standing also. She made a jerky gesture toward Cameron, her mouth wavering between a tight smile and a sneer. "This is *Sergeant* Kasten from the Denver P.D. Ms. Jennings's *boyfriend,* it seems."

"Not even close," Molly repeated, but Cameron was already moving past her, hand outstretched, green eyes sparkling, his trust-me smile in place.

"Chief Lawson," he beamed, and he was on.

Create normalcy, Molly thought, keeping track of the negotiation steps in her head. She'd memorized them once she'd realized that she was stuck in a relationship she'd never even been interested in. Cameron was an expert, but she'd be damned if she'd let him create any normalcy here.

She turned toward the men as they shook hands. "Ben, meet Cameron, my ex-boyfriend. *Ex.* Cameron meet Ben, the man I'm now having sex with. Lots of sex. Lots of hot, hard sex as often as I can."

Brenda gasped, but her desperate grab for air was the only sound in the room. Everyone else had frozen, though Cameron thawed within seconds.

"Chief," he said easily, then rolled his eyes toward Molly, an exasperated smile in place. "She's a real handful, huh?"

Allow the subject to save face.

Ben ended the handshake quickly, but Cameron just shoved his hands into his pockets and rocked forward. "Listen, Chief Lawson, could I speak with you in private for a few minutes?"

Isolate the subject.

"No," Molly said.

Ben's face was stone, but his eyes were burning ice when he looked at her. "I think private would be just fine."

"No," she repeated. "Let's discuss this right here. Cameron, I told you not to come here."

"Molly," he chuckled. *Display calmness.* "Molly, you agreed to be my date." He turned toward Ben. "Policemen's Ball. I'm honored to be receiving a small award and even more honored that Molly's agreed to attend with me."

"I agreed before I broke up with you. I told you last

week that I wasn't ever going to see you again. It's been over for six months, Cameron."

"Not quite six months." His face was all pleasantness, but his eyes offered a warning. *Threat of force.* Easy enough to neutralize that.

"Yes, Cameron," she sneered, "there was that little incident five months ago. You want me to tell these people what happened? Fine. I had sex with my ex-boyfriend a month after we broke up. Oh, the humanity!"

"Come on, Molly," he sighed. "We don't want to go into those details here." Another warning.

"Oh, let's just get it all out, Cameron. That's why you're here isn't it? Listen everyone! I had sex with him in an alley, behind a club, against a brick wall. I was drunk and angry and lonely, because Mr. Magic here kept stealing all my friends away, and so I did something trashy. What else have you got, Cameron?"

"I'm not here to fight with you—"

"No, you're here to screw up my life again! Haven't I made it clear that I want nothing to do with you?"

He raised one perfectly shaped eyebrow. "Molly, you called me in the middle of the night last Tuesday. You also called me two days before that. If we're over, why do you constantly reach out to me?"

"I called to tell you to leave me alone!"

Cameron shook his head again, allowing a hint of sadness to leak through. *Show empathy and understanding.* "I know you've got commitment issues. I know you're no good at relationships. I'd imagine Chief Lawson sees that about you, too. But I love you. And you can have sex with all these different guys—"

"Hey!"

"But it won't change how I feel about you." He turned back to Ben. "Chief, I'm really sorry you've become involved in all this. Molly and I have been going back and forth for a while, and I hate that you've been pulled into our argument. I'm sure you've seen she has commitment issues. You've known her for years, right?" *Encourage the subject to do the talking.* "You've seen how nervous she gets about genuine emotions?"

But Ben was the strong and silent type. "Enough," he growled. "Sergeant Kasten, my office. Now."

She grabbed Ben's arm as he moved past her. "Please don't. You don't understand. He's got…he manipulates people, changes how they see me. I know you don't like me very much right now, but don't listen to him. Just…"

Ben shook off her grasping hands. "Go home, Molly. I'll be there in a few minutes."

"I'm not leaving! I won't—"

He swung back toward her, and Molly actually took a step away from his vicious frown.

"You just spilled the details of your sex life to the whole police force, not to mention a few details of mine. So get the hell out of my workplace, *please,* and I will speak with you when I'm done here."

Shit. Well, she'd managed to thwart Cameron's plan, but only because she'd done the deed for him. Alienated Ben. Proved everything he thought about her true. "You don't have the right to send me away so you can discuss me. This isn't medieval England."

Not even a flicker of sympathy sparked through his

eyes. "This is my police station. You don't have to go home, but you can't stay here. Leave. Now."

She could argue for hours and he wouldn't back down, not after she'd humiliated him like this. His eyes made that clear.

"Fine," she whispered, then speared Cameron with a look she wished could kill. "And Cameron? Don't ever contact me again. Is that clear? Will one of you good police officers take that down as evidence? I do not want this man calling me or knocking on my door or sending me gifts. I'll be in to file a restraining order when I'm allowed back on police property."

Her vision blurred with tears, and the room swung blindly around her when she turned, but she clearly saw Cameron slap a friendly hand against Ben's back. And there was no missing the decidedly unfriendly smirk on Brenda's face as she watched Molly leave.

So it was done. But as Molly trudged home under the annoyingly cheerful sun, there was a tiny spark of triumph under her misery. Her fling with Ben was over, but she'd pushed it under the train herself before Cameron could manage to tie it to the tracks.

Sadly, that was a big improvement.

CHAPTER THIRTEEN

PROFESSIONAL SEX fiend determined to ruin his reputation, murder his sanity and trample his heart. Yes, that sounded about right. Ben had finally solved the Molly Jennings Question.

The engine starting just outside his office window grated against Ben's nerves like ground glass. The sound was all the more irritating for being the smooth purr of an expensive sports car. Sergeant Cameron Kasten had impeccable taste in cars, if not women.

Ben shoved up from his chair and stalked into the hallway, barking, "Is there anything else you need from me this afternoon?" to no one in particular. A chorus of negative responses greeted him. Apparently his off-duty officers had felt a sudden need to come in and organize their paperwork today.

When he reached the front door, Ben stopped, turned and glared at the far wall. "If any of this ends up in the *Tribune,* I'll know it came from one of you. I would not appreciate that in the least."

"Yes, sir," Brenda and the men responded.

Nodding, Ben started to leave, but Brenda rushed over with one hand out to stop him.

"Are you okay, Chief?"

"I'm fine."

"I'm sorry. I'm sorry for what that woman did to you. Why don't I drop off a plate of my lasagna tonight? You'll feel better with some good food in your gut."

"It's all right, Brenda. Honestly."

"I knew that girl was trouble as soon as she flounced back into town. She—"

"Whoa." Ben shook his head. "I appreciate your friendship. I always have. But I need you to give Molly a break here, okay? For me?"

She took one of his hands and held it between both of hers; her lips disappeared in a thin line. "Of course. You're right. You sure about the lasagna?"

Ben assured her he was, and managed to hold his anger down to a simmer until he was outside and in his truck. Then he ground his teeth together, wrapped his fists around the steering wheel and spewed out every single curse word he knew. Just to be thorough, he combined a few of them, repeated a few more and finally felt calm enough to start the truck and back out into the street. By the time he got to Molly's house, he could almost feel the ends of his fingers again, though his blood pressure was still affecting his hearing. The world sounded wrapped in cotton, though the sun was too fucking bright. He wished his vision was still darkened by rage.

She opened the door before he'd finished pounding and seemed startled when he brushed by her and closed it behind him. He paced to the kitchen, pulled out a chair and then walked away without sitting in it. His eye fell on the back door, so he checked to make sure it was locked, then finally turned to face her.

"I can't believe you dated that guy."

Molly's hands dropped from her hips. Her face lost its anger. "Huh?"

"He's a complete ass, Molly. What the hell were you thinking?"

Her eyelids fluttered. "Uh, what?"

Ben held up his hands in exasperation, glanced around the kitchen. "Did you have a drink when you came home?"

"I... I... Didn't you talk to him?"

"Yes, I talked to him. I talked to him for a half hour. That's thirty minutes of my life that I will never get back."

"And?"

Why was she looking at him like he was speaking in tongues? Was she pissed about being thrown out? Because he was sure as hell still pissed at her, and if she wanted to—

"Ben!" she screeched. "Are you saying you didn't *like* him?"

He felt his face twist in disgust. "Jesus Christ, did you want us to be friends or something?"

She slapped both her hands over her mouth, muffling a little cry.

"Molly, I—" He wasn't quite sure what he meant to say, but whatever it was, he lost the words when she launched herself at him. He had to step one foot back to save his balance, and when she wrapped her legs around him, he had no choice but to hold on to her ass.

And then she was pressing kisses to his mouth and jaw and neck, which was pretty damned distracting.

"Oh, Ben," she whispered against his ear. "I know you must hate me, but I don't care. You're my hero." Her tongue licked at his pulse, urging it to quicken. It did.

"Hey… What…?" But her hands were under his shirt, caressing his naked back, nails biting him just like they did when— "Wait."

"You're amazing. A miracle. I should've known…"

"Molly." He had to clear his throat, because he meant to sound authoritative, but he sounded simply aroused. "Molly. Why was he really here?"

She bit his shoulder, tightened her legs around him. "To ruin my life."

"What?" He let her go abruptly, but her legs were strong enough to hold her, and her hips just dropped more snugly against his groin. "Ah! Just a second. You are not going to distract me this time."

"Don't worry. This'll only take a minute."

He grabbed her waist and pulled her off like a stubborn burr. "Could you stop cracking jokes for a few seconds and be serious?"

That cut through her mood like a knife. She set her feet down, crossed her arms and glared, hero worship forgotten.

"Tell me what you meant about Cameron ruining your life."

She shrugged, looking like a rebellious teenager. He expected her to start cracking gum when she cocked her chin up. "He's been stalking me."

Those words hit him right between the eyes. "What?

Stalking? No. No, that can't be right, because *you would have told me about that when someone started breaking into your house.*"

"It wasn't him."

He couldn't strangle her. First of all, that would be wrong. Second, everyone would know it was him. What to do? Ben took a deep breath and tried to let it out slowly. "Please. *Please.* Say something that makes sense. Anything."

"It wasn't him! He never did anything like that in Denver, plus the reason I've been calling him is to check on his whereabouts. It couldn't have been him. That morning my house was broken into, he was at his desk in Denver."

"Shit. You're sure? So what do you mean by stalking? I knew I should have arrested that bastard just for being cheesy."

"You think Cameron's cheesy?" She started to laugh. "God, Ben, I think I love you."

The air left his lungs at the same speed as all the blood left her face.

"I mean…you know…" she stammered, while his stomach sunk to the floor in a sickening rush. "I didn't mean *love* love. I just…"

Ben nodded, wanting to skim over that just as much as she apparently did. "I get it."

"It's just that everyone adores Cameron. *Worships* him. He's got this power… I'm not sure I ever even liked him, he just…sucked me in. And then one day I woke up and realized I was so relieved he hadn't stayed the night. I didn't want to have to see him. But every time I tried to break it off..." She shook her head. "He talked me out of it."

"But you did break it off."

"Finally! After I started looking into his work and realized I was being constantly manipulated. Talked down."

"Handled," he added, thinking of the way the man had tried to put off an aura of instant friendship.

"Handled, exactly! Like I was practice for his job, keeping his skills honed. When he realized I was done with it... I don't know. He needs to feel that he's in control, that's why he loves his work so much. And he couldn't stand not pulling my strings anymore."

Ben's stomach was back in place, but it was starting to burn with anxiety. "What did he do?"

She collapsed into a kitchen chair and propped her chin on her hand. "It started small. He was suddenly hanging out at *my* places. The bar in my building. My favorite restaurant. The coffee place on my block. And my friends kept in contact with him, invited him to their parties, urged me to give him another shot. It was like they were all hypnotized, you know?"

"Yeah."

"It's what he does! He's trained to bring people around to his point of view. Even my family...well, Quinn was too distracted to get sucked in, though he was constantly giving out information he shouldn't have. But my dad, my mom..." She pressed a hand to her eyes. "They couldn't get enough of him. 'Come on, Molly. He's like a son to us. He loves you. Why don't you grow up and make a good choice for once?'"

"Ouch."

"Yeah. Ouch. I had to skip Memorial Day with my parents in St. George because they'd invited him."

"I'm sorry, Moll."

"And then I started seeing him in places he really shouldn't have been, like the bookstore on the other side of town. Or in a women's clothing boutique. Why would he be there? I complained to his superior, complained to everyone I could, but it didn't matter. Everyone loves him. And he made it clear that I was the problem. Sending mixed signals. Blowing hot and cold. He even... After that night at the club... I just wanted to go home and pass out, but he said he needed to settle his tab, so I went back in with him, and he made a big production out of it, tucking his shirt in, grinning like a damned ape.

"In the end, I just tried to ignore it. I started dating again, hoping he'd fade away but, boy, was I mistaken."

Ben's anger at her was subsiding, and he noticed now how tired she looked. Drawn and miserable. Ben grabbed a Frappucino from the fridge and popped it open for her. She smiled at him, and he couldn't resist trailing his fingers down her cheek.

"I'm sorry I accused you of being childish, Molly."

She shook her head, but Ben saw the tears she swiped from her eyes and felt like a complete jerk. He should have just asked her about it instead of jumping down her throat. But he always felt on edge with her, waiting for the other stiletto-heeled shoe to drop.

Molly took a long drink and slumped back in the chair. "I didn't tell you because...well, I knew he couldn't be the stalker, but if I told you, you'd look into it anyway. You'd have to. And I thought if you called him…"

"Yeah?"

She let her breath out in a long, sad sigh. "Every single man I've dated in the past six months has fallen for Cameron like a ton of bricks."

"*Fallen* for him?"

"It sounds crazy, but he steals them away from me faster than you can say 'homoerotic bonding.'"

"And you thought *I*… You…"

"No, no. I didn't think you'd want to spoon with him or anything. I just thought he'd come up here spewing about my 'issues,' and how screwed up I was, and how I clearly wasn't over him yet. And then you guys would exchange cop stories and have a few beers, and you'd have the excuse you've been looking for to bow out. The end."

"I *guess*," Ben drawled in disgust. "Sure, I could see that if I were some kind of wussy pushover with mommy issues."

"I've had a rough six months, okay?" she cried. "Little Blue was my last friend, and frankly the last time his batteries ran out I had a fleeting moment of panic that he'd been compromised!"

"Nice," he snorted and had to dodge the fist she threw at his hip.

"So I didn't want to tell you about Cameron, and I made it clear to that crazy bastard that I wasn't going to Denver with him, but I knew he'd show up anyway. I didn't want to be around, and I didn't want you around, either. I'm sorry. I had no idea he'd go to the station and… God, I'm sorry."

He shook his head, pushing down his mortification at the whole incident. She wasn't exactly wise and dignified, but Molly had her reasons…and her own special brand of charm. "I don't need some over-groomed city cop to tell me about your issues, Moll. I lived half my summers at your house. I like your parents a lot, but I cringed every time they sang Quinn's praises, even when I was a kid. I was there that day his SAT scores came in—"

"Gack," she choked out.

"And I remember that look on your face when your dad laughed and told you to plan on taking the ACT so you wouldn't feel bad. And when your debate team made the district finals and your mom and dad came to our basketball game instead. Christ, if I'd known about the debate I would've skipped the game and come myself."

Molly shook her head frantically. "Please say you didn't tell Cameron any of that!"

"I'm not one of those so-called men you dated in Denver. I wouldn't yell 'fire' at that slimeball if his ass was in flames."

"Thank God."

"My point is that I can see you have trust issues, and I know why. I even understand your need to keep your secrets close, but just for future reference, some of the things *I* like to keep secret are how often and how hard I have sex with you."

"Uh…right. I'll, um, keep that in mind."

"Because that was more than a little out of line."

"Yes. I agree. I have a bit of a temper."

He arched an eyebrow. "Hard to tell."

She gave a mumbled, "Sorry," then grabbed her drink as if it were a lifeline and gulped it down.

Sighing, Ben dropped into the other chair and ran a hand through his hair. "All right. Let's go through all of it."

Molly's eyes went wide. "All of *what?* I don't think it's a good idea to discuss past relationships with—"

"All the incidents since your return to Tumble Creek, and exactly why you think Cameron couldn't be responsible."

"Oh, that makes more sense. So… Are we…?" She looked up from her study of her hands, and Ben had to suck in a quick breath to feed the rush of his heart. Her hazel eyes were soft with anxiety, uncertain instead of bold, and she looked like the girl she used to be, the one who'd never been quite enough in her parents' eyes. The one who could walk into her house without anyone noticing. How many times had Ben wandered back to her room just so she'd know someone had looked up when she came through the door?

"So we're okay?" she asked.

He wanted to say no. No, of course they weren't okay. She didn't trust him any more than she trusted anyone. She was still keeping secrets, revealing things only when forced to, hiding behind a wall of humor and distance.

But he couldn't say that when she looked at him with those lonely eyes. "We're okay," he said instead and resisted the need to gather her in his arms and hold her. "So tell me everything."

Of course she didn't. But she told him a little.

Ben called Kasten's superior officer to confirm what he could, and then they were right back where they started: uncertain, possibly in danger, and soon enough, back in bed.

CHAPTER FOURTEEN

WELL, SHE WAS STUCK now. Trapped. Totally screwed.

Ben had proven himself immune to the Kasten charm. He'd seen right through it. Added to everything else, that made Ben the perfect man. Which made Molly a perfect idiot.

She should have told him everything from the start, then they could have eased into a relationship with all the cards on the table. But they hadn't, and now she was in love, and she didn't know where to go from there.

She'd never been in love before. Never. And now there was a very good chance she'd have her heart broken before she even got a chance to enjoy the little pink stars floating above her head.

In the four days since Cameron had invaded Tumble Creek, Molly had buried herself in her work in an attempt to avoid making a decision. And she did have to make a decision, she knew that. She just couldn't bear it. She'd either have to break it off with Ben or tell him the truth. And if she told the truth and he turned his back on her...oh, that was going to hurt like hell.

Her stomach hurt just the way it used to when she'd been a kid and her brother had—once again—gotten the highest GPA in his class. Molly knew now that she

had been smart enough to make any parent proud...
any parents but her own anyway. But she'd been a girl,
and both her parents had been raised on ranches where
girls were expected to be useful. So her modest intelli-
gence had never compensated for her innate silliness.
Her time on the debate team and her interest in the arts
had been nothing more than a waste of time. Her sense
of humor and love of reading and night-owl hours had
been a constant irritation to her mom and dad.

Quinn was the smart one—the really smart one. The
one whose studying was offset by a healthy dose of ath-
leticism and seriousness. Molly had just been...not what
they'd wanted in a daughter. Flighty, too loud, messy,
always asking for attention. Not a girl who'd make a
good, hard-working wife and mother. Not good enough.

Just like she wasn't good enough for Ben. She was
flighty, too loud and really good at creating a mess that
would draw attention. And it hurt just as much as it had
when she was younger. But the hope...the hope that
he'd be proud was still there, too. And that was worse.

She needed to tell him the truth, and it scared the
devil out of her, so she just kept writing and pretend-
ing that everything was fine.

At least on that front, everything *was* fine. She'd
finished *The Wicked West* and sent it off. It was done,
and it was good, and that was something to be proud of.
So she had talked Lori into driving to Grand Valley for
dinner and a late movie, but not before Molly stopped
by Ben's office for a farewell kiss.

After carefully locking her house, Molly clomped
down the hill in her favorite stacked-heel leather boots

and her hottest pair of jeans. She was an award-win-
ning writer, an expert at erotic titillation and a master
at turning on one stuffy police chief; she deserved a hot
night out on the town with her girlfriend. After tugging
open the heavy door of the police station, she sashayed
in with a grin on her face. And ran smack into the wall
of ice that was Brenda Hamilton.

Ouch.

"Hi, Brenda."

The woman's lowered eyebrows sent a message of
thick, dark hatred. "Ms. Jennings."

"Is the chief in?"

"He's busy. If you'd care to leave a message, I'd be
pleased to convey it." Pleased as a serial killer bent
on torture, if the tone of her voice was any indication.

"Brenda, I'm really sorry about that scene the other
day. I'm sure Ben's already told you, but the truth is
that Cameron and I were over a long time ago and he's
been causing me some problems. I'm sorry it boiled
over here in your office."

Instead of answering, she swept a cold look over
Molly's outfit, ending with a pointed sneer at her boots.

Molly sighed and shrugged. "Look, if I could just
see Ben for a minute—"

"Chief Lawson is busy. Perhaps you don't understand the meaning of a good, honest day's work, but he
does. So either leave your message or get out of my—"

"Brenda," Ben's voice rang out, startling both
women into a little jump.

"Chief," Brenda wheezed, but she quickly recovered
herself. "I was just explaining to Ms. Jennings that you

were on the phone with the State Police and couldn't be disturbed."

Using some of that discretion no one seemed to think her capable of, Molly kept her thoughts to herself, and Ben proved that he didn't need her help. He looked straight at Brenda with his cold cop eyes and didn't show a flicker of sympathy.

"Brenda, your shift is now officially over. I'll talk to you in the morning."

"But—"

"Tomorrow. Shut down and go home."

Brenda's face reddened to a mottled crimson. "Fine. But that girl is nothing but trash and everyone knows it. They're laughing at you, Chief."

Though his face was quickly approaching the same shade as Brenda's, Ben's voice held its cool tone. "Out. And don't come in tomorrow if you can't keep your professional behavior elevated above your personal bias. Is that clear?"

Brenda's muttered "yes" belied the pure fury on her face, but she stood and rushed into the hallway toward one of the back rooms.

Ben took Molly's arm and led her in the other direction, out the office door into the cool evening air.

"I'm sorry, Ben," she started, but he jerked back as if she'd smacked him.

"No, *I'm* sorry. Christ, that was terrible and completely uncalled for."

"Oh, not completely," she laughed, though her insides trembled just a little with adrenaline.

"Molly," he said, his mouth a flat line. "I'm pissed at

her on a personal level, but more than that, I'm furious as her employer. That was unprofessional and unkind."

"Well, I am a citizen of this town."

"Exactly."

Okay, she'd been kidding about that, but the man took his job seriously.

"I'm sorry, Moll. Not a nice start to your evening. Are you on your way to Lori's?"

"Yep. She says my car is ready, but she wants to do a longer test drive to be sure, so we're taking her truck."

"Good." His eyes stayed on the station door. "There might be a few flurries tonight. Be careful."

"Okay."

"She'll drop you off here?"

Molly lost her patience with discretion. "Ben, I think Brenda's in love with you," she blurted.

That got his attention. "What?" His wide-eyed gaze collided with hers.

"She's in love with you."

"She is not!"

Rolling her eyes, Molly considered, not for the first time in her life, that men were truly dense creatures. "Brenda has been very strange to me since the first minute I moved back to town, and now she's practically frothing at the mouth. She's jealous."

Ben was shaking his head through her whole speech. "No, Brenda and I are friends. She thinks she's looking out for me, that's all."

"Put on your police cap," she whispered when the station door opened. Brenda, bundled up in a long down coat and thick cap, hurried out. Her head jerked back a little when she saw them standing a few feet away, but she kept moving, veering away to rush down the sidewalk toward her small house. Ben stared after her.

Molly leaned in a little closer. "It could be Brenda," she ventured, expecting him to shoot the idea down.

He watched as Brenda disappeared around the corner, her long coat flapping ungracefully in her wake. "Her prints are in the system. I would've gotten a hit."

"She works at a police station, Ben. I'm sure she'd know to wear gloves."

He turned troubled eyes back to Molly. "It can't be Brenda. Actually, I've been thinking about Miles again. Maybe he's gone over the edge. Maybe he's trying to create his own stories now."

She waved his idea away. "You want it to be Miles because you hate him. It's clearly Brenda."

"No way. I've known her my whole life. And she's not in love with me!"

"Why else would she hate me?"

"Don't women have little tiffs like that all the time?"

"I barely even know her!" Molly insisted. "Just think about it, okay?"

"I'll look into it, but it seems highly unlikely. That first night, you said it was a man you saw on the hill, not a woman."

She crinkled her nose at his logic. "Well, not to be rude, but Brenda is a tiny bit, um, stocky. I wouldn't want to meet her in a dark alley, especially in her current mood."

"I'll try to keep an open mind," he promised, running a hand through already mussed hair. "I'll check her schedule for the past month and try to recall any suspicious actions. But she's not in love with me."

"Uh-huh. I make dinner for random men all the time. 'Cause that's normal."

"Isn't it time for you to get over to Lori's?"

"Aw, you're blushing. I can't imagine Brenda's the only woman in this town with a serious case of unrequited love for you. Man in uniform. Stoic loneliness. Steady strength. You're a thirtysomething's wet dream, Chief Lawson. Hey…" She got up on her tiptoes to whisper in his ear. "You haven't been picking any other women up with those big, strong arms, have you? Because, personally, *I'd* kill for that."

"No."

She dropped back down and gave him a suspect look. "You're sure you haven't slept with anyone else? That Jennifer who manages the grocery store is pretty cute."

"Well, that *is* all it takes."

"Exactly."

Done with her, Ben crossed his arms and narrowed his gaze. "Have fun with your girlfriend tonight. I'll see you around eleven."

She made sure to give her ass some extra sway as she twirled around and stepped past his truck and into the street.

"Molly," he said almost immediately.

Her grin gave away her self-satisfaction when she turned back around. Ben stepped off the curb and took a few slow steps toward her. His finger brushed her chin and sent little sparks skittering down her neck.

"Don't talk to any boys."

"Mmm. If I do, are you gonna spank me?"

That chased the worry from his brown eyes and made them glitter as his eyelids dipped low enough to make her melt. The edge of his index finger returned to stroke the skin just under her jaw. "As long as you're good I won't have to."

"But you know how much trouble I have being good."

He tilted her chin up, feathered a tiny kiss over her bottom lip. "I do."

Molly shivered when he let her go, wondering if she'd be able to make it across the street without stumbling. He sounded as dangerous as her dark sheriff, and all the hours she'd spent on that story had left her feeling edgy and on fire.

"Try to be good now, Molly girl," he murmured, and she vowed to talk to as many boys as she could find.

"I CAN'T BELIEVE you still won't tell me what you do for a living!" Lori cried.

"I can't."

"Well, how the hell am I supposed to help you with no details?"

"You've got the info you need. Secret career that Ben won't like. Nothing illegal or immoral. How should I tell him?"

Lori took her hand off the wheel long enough to wave it around. "That's not information. I need some good stuff here."

"Nope. Sorry. It doesn't matter anyway," she sighed. "I know I just need to tell him straight out and I don't want to."

"If there's nothing wrong with it then he's not going to break it off. Why are you worried?"

"It's sort of tailor-made to fit neatly into all his issues. Privacy. Fear of sexual scandal—"

"What do you *do,* you little hussy?"

"I mean, I guess if I worked for the *National Enquirer* that would be worse, but..."

"Ugh," Lori groaned. "Just tell him already, so you can tell me."

"Good Lord, you're the soul of selflessness, you know that?"

"Yeah. Hey!" Lori perked up. "Did I tell you that Juan ran out of gas about thirty minutes south of town yesterday?"

"No, but that *is* fascinating tow-truck-driver gossip."

Lori snorted as they bounced over a dip in the road. "Bite your tongue, girl. The interesting part is who he was with when he ran out of gas."

"Who?"

"Helen!" she shrieked, already laughing.

"Nuh-uh. Are you serious?"

"Oh, my God, you should have seen Helen's face when I pulled up. She actually tried to slouch into the hood of her coat so I wouldn't see her. And poor Juan looked like he was going to cry from embarrassment that he'd run out of gas on their date."

Molly gasped. "Did he call it a date?"

"No, but he was wearing nice pants and a button-down shirt and it was nine o'clock. I'm thinking Helen didn't want to go to Grand Valley, so they went to that lodge restaurant down in the canyon."

"Good for her! Helen's getting her groove back."

"Let's take her to The Bar this weekend and get all the details. I live vicariously through others."

Molly slanted a look at her friend. "I thought that waiter was giving you the eye."

"He was nineteen if he was a day."

"But he had big hands, did you notice?"

"Maybe," Lori muttered.

"Not as big as Ben's," Molly added just to be cruel, and Lori groaned as if she were being roasted over a pit fire. "Has it really been that long?"

"Sooo…" her friend crooned, tossing her curls a little as she shook off the question. "You really think the stalker could be Brenda?"

"Maybe. So either you're a virgin—" she elbowed Lori in the arm "—or you had sex recently with someone totally inappropriate. Which is it?"

"I'm pure as the driven snow."

"Oh, my God, who was it? Was it Aaron?"

"No! It's no one you know and it was months ago anyway. But you could be right about Brenda. That woman's wound tighter than a…well, you don't know what a valve spring is, but trust me. And her mother is a judgmental old biddy and Brenda lives with her. That'd be enough to drive anyone to desperation."

"Ben's doubtful."

"He's a man and she's female. Plus he wouldn't like to think he'd been deceived so thoroughly."

Molly winced at that. Yeah, that would really hit him where it hurt.

As they began to ease into the lights of Tumble

Creek, Lori sent her a worried glance. "I'm not taking you to your house, am I? You're still staying with Ben?"

"Until I tell him the truth and he kicks me out. Another good reason to put it off for a few more days. If you'll drop me at the station, he should still be there."

"Look, Molly, I was just kidding about needing to know everything. You don't have to tell me, but Ben... He's a good guy and he's serious about you. Tell him. Whatever it is, he'll get over it."

Molly drew a slow deep breath. "I didn't mean to fall for him. I really didn't."

"Yeah. Well. You're totally screwed. And you'd better make it work, or this town's going to get really small for the two of you."

"Thanks. You're like a little angel baby sent from heaven to cheer me up."

"That's me." She pulled to an abrupt stop about two inches from the bumper of Ben's SUV. "I should have your car ready tomorrow by noon. I'll give you a call. Until then, please be careful. If it is Brenda, she's probably freaking out right about now. Don't go checking out strange noises in the backyard by yourself."

"Duh. Ben checks the backyard. I take the basement." She stepped out of Lori's truck and Ben was already there, reaching for her hand. "Bye, Lori!"

Ben eased his warm—and big—fingers between hers and angled his head toward the station. "Andrew's already here. You ready to head over to my place?"

Turning into his body, she leaned up for a kiss that started out simple and sweet, but quickly devolved to her tongue in his mouth and his hands in her hair. Yes, she was ready to get to his place. And he didn't seem in the mood to talk, which suited her just fine.

"I was a very naughty girl," she whispered against his mouth.

Ben stood straighter so that she couldn't reach him. He jerked his head toward his truck. "Get in."

Thoroughly wet already, Molly jogged around to the passenger side and leapt in. He was already turning the key in the ignition.

"Take me by my place first? I forgot my bag."

"Naughty *and* irresponsible."

"I'm a total delinquent." She reached across the space to rub her palm over his thigh and then farther, and by the time he pulled into her driveway, he was hard as steel.

"You're not wearing a skirt," he rasped. "Another infraction."

Giggling, Molly hopped out of the truck while Ben stepped more stiffly to the driveway.

"I'll run in. It's right on the kitchen table."

"I'll come with," he countered, clearly inviting no argument.

But that was fine with Molly. Maybe they wouldn't even make it to his place. Maybe they'd do it on the kitchen counter, half-dressed and loud with lust. She'd never done it on the kitchen counter before.

Her little plan took on new hope when she reached to unlock the door and Ben stopped her by putting his hands to her waist and turning her to face him. Molly leaned willingly against the door and watched him from beneath her lashes. He wouldn't do anything nasty right here, surely. But he *could* do something subtle. Something discreet.

He did.

Leaning one arm against the wood above her head, Ben curled around her, not touching, but surrounding. His lips brushed the barest kiss against the crown of her head, and she was suddenly breathing hard.

"Molly…" he started.

"Yeah?" Oh, yeah.

"I thought maybe we could go up to my cabin this weekend. It's nothing fancy, but there's a small kitchen, a bathroom."

"And that hot spring?"

"Yes."

She raised a doubtful eyebrow. "I'd love to. But you said…about the cabin."

"Yeah." He dropped his head a little, and his forehead touched hers as he dragged one calloused finger down her temple, along her jaw, over the sensitive skin of her neck. That precious stroke curled through her until it squeezed her heart into mush. "I'd like to be alone with you, just for a little while. Even if you won't admit to being my girlfriend. And it would help to clear my head a little, think through this Brenda thing."

"So you are taking it seriously?"

"Of course I am. I'd never dismiss anything to do with your safety just because I think it's ridiculous."

"Ha! I'll bet you it's her. Hey! How about a real wager? If I'm right, you wear your cowboy hat for me. Just your hat and a whole lotta nekkid."

"My official uniform hat? I don't think that's an authorized use. But since you won't be right…fine. And if I'm right?"

"How about I put on a private show for you…costarring Little Blue?"

"That's a fucking deal." He winked down at her. "Better buy some new batteries."

Snorting in amusement, Molly spun around to unlock the door, but her hand froze with the key in the lock, her nerves protesting her casualness.

Ben was right about her. She joked about everything, tried very hard not to take anything seriously, but she could be serious if she wanted. She was sure she could, even if she'd never done it before.

So Molly left the keys dangling and turned slowly back to Ben to commit herself to doing the right thing.

"This weekend," she started, not quite able to meet his eyes. "This weekend when we're alone…we'll talk, okay? I mean, I'll talk. To you. About me."

She stared at his throat, at his steady pulse, while her own heart pattered in rising panic. She'd do it. Tell him this weekend. And it was kind of brilliant, actually. If she spilled the beans when they first arrived, he'd have time to adjust to it before he ever had the chance to read her work. She'd ease him into it just as she should have done from the start.

"Molly," he whispered, drawing her gaze to his. His eyes melted to sweet chocolate as she watched, so sweet it hurt her deep inside. His cheeks flushed a little, pink rising up his jaw. "Molly, I love you."

Oh, God. Ohgod, ohgod, ohgod. "Ben, I…I…"

"We'll talk this weekend, Moll. There's no rush. Honestly."

Her hopes overrode her fears for the first time in days, weeks, months. Something loosened inside her chest, making her want to sob with relief. But she smiled past her tears and nodded and turned to unlock the door. She couldn't say it yet, was scared to say it, but she'd show him how she felt as soon as they got to his house. Or to her kitchen. Or anywhere outside the reach of the porch light.

She was floating on his words and his touch as she pushed open the door. High on Ben.

They were both inside before she heard it. A strange, low mumbling. Ben's hand snaked around her and he pressed it flat against her breastbone to pull her back against him. As he eased her backward toward the open door, Molly saw that a faint light glowed from the wide doorway of the dining room, and a distorted shadow moved across the floor in jerky motion. It looked like a devil, she thought, dancing out its fury to silent music.

Molly's heel caught on Ben's shoe and she gasped. His mouth was right against her ear, breathing out the barest whisper to be quiet, but it was too late. The shadow passed just then, and stopped dead at the sight of them. Ben pulled her back more quickly, but a gun rose in that shadow hand and froze them both.

"What are you doing here?" a cracked voice sobbed.

Molly heard the barest intake of his breath in her ear and then Ben murmured, "Brenda?"

"What are you doing here?" she screamed in response, the sound of an animal in pain.

"Brenda, put the gun down so we can talk about this."

His hand was steady against her, which was a good thing. Despite her earlier words, Molly was still shocked enough that she might fall right down to the ground. And that was before she noticed the scrawled black writing on the walls behind Brenda, who was now waving the gun instead of putting it down.

"Oh, we're going to talk," she sneered. "Close that door."

"I don't think—" he started, but Brenda gave a high-pitched scream and pointed the gun straight at Molly's chest. Ben shut the door.

"Get your hands off of her," Brenda ordered. "You don't know anything about her. She's nothing but a whore."

Molly muttered, "Jeez," which prompted Ben to dig his fingers into her chest just before he let her go. She moved slowly away, mouthing *I told you so* over her shoulder, but the look he gave her could've singed rock.

Come on, she wanted to say. *Brenda is not going to shoot me or she'd have to shoot you.*

Ben held up a subtle hand to let her know she'd moved far enough away, then twitched his fingers to get her moving backward instead of sideways. "Okay, Brenda. What do you want to talk about?"

With the door closed, it was dark, but Molly could see Brenda more clearly now in the glow of the desk lamp in the office. In one hand she held the gun in an unwavering grip. In the other she held a…marker?

"This woman," Brenda rasped, her eyebrows beetling down to a crooked line. "This woman is not good enough for you. She's a liar and a pornographer."

Oh, shit.

"Brenda, come on." Ben's voice was smooth and low. Totally calm. "We're friends. I have no idea what you mean, but let's just go get a beer and talk about it."

"I don't drink," she spat. "I don't drink and I don't wear slutty clothes and *I don't lie to you.* Not like *her.*"

His big hands rose in a reconciling gesture while Molly tried to slide invisibly closer to him and nearer the door.

"It's okay," he soothed, but Brenda shook her head in furious denial.

"Do you know what she does? Do you know how she earns her filthy money?"

Ben's eyes shot toward Molly for a brief moment, but Brenda didn't give him time to answer.

"Come in here. Come in here and I'll show you."

Ben stepped forward immediately, nodding. "Show me."

But Brenda didn't fall for it. The gun jumped in anger. "You first," she spat at Molly as he shook his head.

"Let her go. If you let her go, I'll sit with you and you can show me anything. That's what you want, right? To show me the truth?"

"Yes." Brenda began to cry in a strange, wordless growl, and Molly realized it was the sound they'd heard from the doorway. But Brenda wasn't distracted by her grief. She kept the gun pointed straight at Molly and

swiped at her teary eyes. "But she can't go. Not until you see her for what she is."

"Okay. All right. Show me, and then she'll go."

Hell, yeah, Molly was smart enough not to say. Slutty pornographer she might be, but she'd be a *live* pornographer. She was getting more scared now, even though she knew that Ben wouldn't let anything happen to her and Brenda wouldn't hurt Ben.

So when the gun waved her forward, Molly walked. The closer she came to the dining room, the more words seemed to appear on the walls. Words like writhing snakes that danced and jerked, and Molly couldn't read a thing.

Until Brenda hit the light switch. The little desk lamp hadn't revealed much, but the dining room chandelier sure did. Words like *wet* and *tremble* and *tongue* leapt from the wall. *Fingers* and *thighs* and *cock* written so hard that she'd gouged out the drywall in crumbly dust.

"Oh, shit," Molly muttered. There was no doubt what the words meant. Her laptop was open and glowing on the desk, and she recognized most of the phrases.

"This is her," Brenda said. "This is what she is."

Ben was shaking his head when Molly looked at him. "I don't understand."

"She writes this, this…this *smut.*"

Ben still looked only confused.

"She writes this!" Brenda shouted, gesturing a wide circle with the marker. Then she stalked over to the armoire. The doors lay broken beside it, and stacks of books were displayed inside. Brenda grabbed one and tossed it at Ben.

Molly watched him turn it over in his hands for a moment before she looked back to the black scratches on the wall.

"Holly Summers." Brenda's voice made the name sound like a sin. "That's her. Holly Summers. She writes these books, these disgusting stories."

Molly walked closer to one of the walls, wrinkling her nose. "You know this really isn't my best work. And it's not fair to take it out of context. 'His tongue touched the pink peak,' is never gonna sound good if you just blurt it out like that. You've got to build tension and characterization and..."

Blinking from the hypnosis of self-critique, Molly turned to find them both frowning at her. She took a deep breath and squared her shoulders. "It's true, Ben. I write erotic romance. That's it. End of story."

Brenda rolled her eyes. "Oh, you wish. That's just the start of it."

Patting the flat of the book against his palm, Ben offered the woman a careful smile. "You've solved the mystery. Good job. I had no idea."

"Don't humor me! I'm not stupid. You think I don't know how you see me? I've worked for you for five years! I've made your coffee and brought you lunch and noticed when you're tired. I've been there for you and I know you, Ben Lawson. I may not be cute or sexy. I may not wear short skirts and high heels. I'm not the type of woman that men notice, but I *know* you. I take care of you."

"You do," Ben agreed in a soft voice.

Brenda nodded. "But I misunderstood. My mother

always says that even good men fall for the showy girls, the sluts who put out. Like *her*." She glared at Molly.

Despite the nasty words, Molly was starting to feel bad for the woman. It wasn't Brenda's fault that she looked exactly like her mother. And Molly would have spent a lot more time looking stern and dour if she'd been stuck in a little house with a harpy like Brenda's mom. If she would just wear some tailored clothing and pluck those brows, maybe she'd change her life a little. Molly was opening her mouth to suggest a makeover when Brenda stabbed the gun in her direction.

"She may be skinny and easy and enticing, but she doesn't care about you."

"Brenda, let's just—"

"She must know how much you value your privacy. She knows about your father. And still she—"

"Oh, no," Molly groaned as Ben waved her back and took a step toward Brenda.

"She doesn't just write smut, Ben! She wrote smut about *you!*"

His hands were up again, a sign of good will. "None of this matters, Brenda."

"Of course it matters! She's using you, feeding her sick muse to write more sex stories about you. The whole time you were in her bed she was recording it, writing it down. She's going to ruin you, but not before I ruin her."

Her arm tensed, and Molly let out a little squeak of terror as she scrambled away to hide behind Ben. She wasn't thinking about defending her work anymore, that was for sure. Trying to make herself smaller, she curled

her arms tight to her belly and crouched just a foot behind Ben. His hand drifted behind his back, pinky finger trembling a little as he flattened his palm, signing
her to stay still.

Like she was going anywhere.

"She wrote about me?" he asked in a near-whisper.

Brenda cried out, "Yes!" as if he'd just sprouted
wings of glory. "Yes. Do you see? She wrote about
you, some ridiculous story of having sex with you in
that apartment above the feed store. And the new one's
even worse..."

Molly cringed, telling herself not to care about that
right now. Ben took a step forward, and she wanted to
follow, but he showed her his palm again and she obeyed
like a loyal hound.

"Tell me," Ben urged, moving farther away from
Molly.

"You wouldn't believe it. Disgusting stuff with ropes
and whips. Horrible. As if she were trying to bring you
as low as possible. Ruin you. Everyone's going to be
laughing at you, Ben."

"But not you."

"No," she sobbed, the tears finally returning. "No,
I knew from the start that she was bad news. I knew."

Ben bowed his head, shaking it slowly from side to
side. "You did. You tried to tell me."

"I'd never—"

His arm moved faster than light, faster than anything Molly had ever seen. One minute he was gesturing at Brenda, fingers relaxed, friendly. And the next

the gun was tumbling through the air, Brenda squealing her pain and denial.

Molly should have left. Ben was yelling for her to
run, but she felt entranced by the slow somersault of the
dull black weapon as if arched toward the floor. *That
woman could have killed me.*

Knowing she'd feel more frightened later, Molly was
damned grateful for the strange shock that had settled
over her. The scene between Ben and Brenda was a
movie playing out for her as the gun finally banged
to the floor and he pushed Brenda down and onto her
stomach so he could click handcuffs into place.

"Don't do this," Brenda was sobbing. "Don't do this.
I love you."

Ben muttered a pained curse under his breath, then
patted her down. He didn't find any other weapons it
seemed, because he lunged to his feet to pull Molly
into his arms.

"I win," she said into his chest. "Don't lose that hat,
Chief."

"Good God, are you okay?"

"I'm fine, but I think your hands are shaking."

"No shit." One of his arms made strange movements near her side and then she heard the click of his
radio. He spoke in code, or else Molly was in more serious shock than she realized. The man on the other
end seemed to understand the garbled message if the
shocked reply was any indication.

Molly eased out from his distracted hold and looked
toward Brenda. She was watching them, ruddy cheek
pressed to the geometric rug Molly had bought three

months before. Her forest-green Henley shirt clashed horribly with the red and slate-blue rectangles, and Molly felt a terrible need to get out of that room. She began to back away, Brenda's eyes following every step.

"He won't love you now," she growled. "He might not love me, but he won't love you, either."

"I know," Molly whispered.

Ben's radio finally ceased to squawk and he eased his arm around her to pull her into the front room. Sirens twittered faintly somewhere, growing louder as each heartbeat passed.

"You're pale as hell," he complained. "In shock."

"No shit. But I'm fine. I'll be fine."

Guiding her over to a big chair, Ben grabbed a throw from the love seat and wrapped it around her. "I've got to keep an eye on Brenda. Will you be all right here? It should only be a—"

"I'm fine."

"Andrew will be here in just a moment."

"I hear that."

He didn't seem comforted by her flip attitude. His eyes lingered on her as he moved toward the dining room, but he had a criminal to watch, after all. He couldn't babysit a shockey girlfriend.

The desperate protests from Brenda continued, but Ben didn't utter a word. He was probably too busy thumbing through the print copies of Molly's books. She hugged the blanket tighter and hunkered down in the chair, trying to fend off the invading feeling that this was not going to end well. The increasing racket of the siren wasn't helping her tension. She pulled a corner of the blanket over her head.

When Andrew finally arrived, another officer in tow, slow chaos ensued around Molly's cocoon. There were questions and curses and barked orders. Ben checked on her for a moment, then someone began snapping pictures of the nasty black words that had destroyed her walls, and he was busy again.

She was just starting to be lulled by the buzz around her, when it blinked to a brief stop.

"Call Jake for her. She'll need a lawyer," Ben was saying as he and Andrew walked Brenda out of the dining room between them. She seemed more subdued, but when her eyes landed on Molly, she puffed up long enough to snap, "Whore!" as they whisked her past.

Ben jerked her along to the front door and opened it to guide her through, but they were all blinded by an explosion of flashbulbs. Molly jumped up and ran to the front window, but it was actually only one flashbulb. Miles stood there snapping picture after picture as Brenda tried to turn away. Then she seemed to reconsider and turned to look full at him.

"She's Holly Summers," she yelled. "She won't be able to hide the truth anymore. She's Holly Summers, you hear me, Miles?"

"Got it!" he called cheerfully back, and Molly's stomach dropped through the floor.

Right. This had been the ax hanging over her head as she'd sat numbly on the couch. Why she'd been so quick to agree with Brenda's assertion that Ben wouldn't love her. Even if Miles hadn't been out there waiting like a buzzard, an arrest and trial were public record.

Ben knowing about her books was one thing. She'd meant to tell him in a few days anyway. But Ben knowing that everyone else knew? Not so fucking great.

Maybe she could run Miles off the road over by Killer Curve and nip this problem in the bud. Hmm. How to lure him the five miles out of town?

Molly forced her weak legs to carry her back to the couch where she collapsed in her blanket like a fuzzy red burrito. Actually, setting Miles up would be easy. She could just offer to show him something that would incriminate Ben in a huge scandal. Hell, he'd probably drive off the curve himself for that.

"Molly?"

She squeezed her eyes tighter shut, imagining a bright, sunny morning in a place where no one knew her secrets.

"Molly?"

The urgent note in Ben's voice snapped her awake and she sat up so fast she cracked his jaw with the crown of her head. "Ow."

"You okay?"

"I think I fell asleep."

"We're finished up here."

"Then I definitely fell asleep."

Ben nodded, his eyes more distracted than they should have been, in her opinion. "I really hate to do this to you, but I need to interview Brenda tonight. As soon as possible. I'm sorry. Can I call Lori or…?"

She shouldn't have felt hurt by that. He was the chief

of police, of course he had to go. But it was more than just his leaving her alone tonight. She didn't want to give him any time to think, wanted to make an attempt to hold this sand castle together right now, and the tide was coming in, and everything was crumbling. If he left now…it would disappear.

And there was nothing she could do.

So Molly pasted a smile on her face and did what she'd always done. "Hey, I've been waiting for you to leave so I could call Lori over for our weekly pillow fight."

"Moll." That word spoke volumes of hurt and worry, but she blew it off with a laugh.

"I don't need Lori to come over. I'm fine. The threat has been eliminated. Go do what you need to do."

He shook his head, elbows on his knees, hands clasped loosely between them. He looked tired and lost and very lovable, damn him. "I'll be back as soon as I can. Let me call Lori."

"Ben, I'm a big girl. I'll see you in a few hours. Go."

So he went, and Molly called Lori anyway to cry and tell her what had happened, and then she went to sleep on the couch.

She woke to bright morning light and a granite stone rolling through her gut. Ben didn't come back until nearly eleven, and then everything was as bad as she'd imagined.

CHAPTER FIFTEEN

WRITER OF WOMEN'S PORN.

Okay, so she wasn't naked on the Internet or helping perverts masturbate over the phone. Nothing sinister or illegal. She was just writing sexy stories. About him.

Ben hadn't wanted to go back to her house, despite his promise to come by when he was done. At the moment he was utterly exhausted, nowhere near his bed, and his relief that Molly was safe had begun to wear off hours ago.

Brenda had spewed bitter words about Molly's stories, and given the first opportunity, he'd gone online to check them out. Yep, they were there. All sixteen of them (more than half now available in print!). The publisher touted her amazing reviews, her many awards and her bestselling numbers. The woman was a star. And Ben was the leading man in at least one of her novellas.

He hadn't wanted to believe that part of it. If she'd just been a writer of naughty stories… Okay. Strange, but okay. But *Stolen Kisses* was undoubtedly about him. Hell, he could see that in just the two-page excerpt on the Web site. A small mountain town. A girl and her brother's best friend. An apartment above a *feed store,* for God's sake. It seemed that the only thing she'd changed were their names and ages. Oh, and if the description was correct, she'd drastically changed the outcome of that evening. Not that anyone else would know that.

His stomach burned with acid as he tapped on Molly's door and hoped that she was still sleeping. No such luck. She opened the door looking fresh and innocent as a daffodil. Comfortable jeans and a yellow sweater and her hair in those braided pigtails that made his mouth water. Aside from the dark circles under her eyes, she looked like the teenager she'd once been.

"Sorry I'm so late," he muttered.

Her gaze sharpened. She stared at him, studied his face until Ben looked down. Then she opened the door wider. "Come on in," she offered with a wry politeness that set his teeth on edge. As if she knew what he'd come to say, but she didn't. He had no idea what he was going to say.

"Brenda's confessed to almost everything." He stood there in the entry with his hat in hand, like he'd never been in her house, her bed. Molly crossed her arms and nodded.

"She claims she didn't cut the lines on your car, but that could bring a charge of attempted murder, and no doubt she's aware of that."

"Smart girl."

"But it's clear she's been the one breaking into your house, and she was up-front about it. She used the department's equipment to break in."

"Bad publicity."

He raised an eyebrow, and Molly squeezed her arms

tighter. For once, he was sure she wasn't attempting to distract him.

"So what happens now?" she asked in a rush.

Maybe she was asking about their relationship, but Ben chose to take it another way. "The D.A. will review the case and decide what charges to file. Sometimes there's more investigation to be done first, but this is pretty cut-and-dried. I wouldn't be surprised if Brenda filed a plea soon thereafter. This could all be over quickly." He flinched at his own words, and Molly's eyes flashed cold.

"Oh, I'd imagine."

He turned his hat over, straightened the brim. "Well, I'd better go. I've gotta grab a shower and lunch. The D.A. wants to meet at three. You're doing okay?"

"I'm fine."

"It was a traumatic night. Maybe you should go stay with your parents for a few days."

"Let the furor die down?"

"Something like that."

"Or," she countered, smiling widely. "You could take me up to your cabin like we'd planned and we could recuperate together."

"I, uh…" Shit. "I don't think I can take the weekend off now. It's gonna be pretty crazy around here. I'm sorry."

"Sure. Of course. I'm sorry, too. I really am."

"Molly…"

Offering a tight smile, she shook her head. "We both know this is about my books."

His gut clenched to painful tightness. "I don't have time for this right now."

"Oh, I bet it won't take long."

"What the hell does that mean?"

"It means," she ground out, "that you want this to be over, and you don't know how to end it. It wouldn't really be appropriate to break up with your girlfriend the morning after someone tried to kill her, would it?"

"I can't... You..." The tightness in his stomach finally unwound and let free a torrent of fury that surged through his muscles. He didn't want to do this now, didn't want to speak to her. "You..."

"Just say it, Ben."

She looked so self-righteous he wanted to yell. So he did. "I never thought your dirty little secret had anything to do with *me!* You can keep the rest of your life locked up as tight as you want, but you had no right to keep that from me. No right to fucking drag me into it in the first place."

She nodded as if the words rolled right off her back, but her face was tight and wooden. He was past the point of caring.

"How the hell did you justify keeping that from me?"

Molly shrugged and shook her head.

"How the hell did you justify climbing into my fucking bed without mentioning that you'd been writing *smut* about me?"

"It's not smut," she muttered.

"Oh, I'm sorry. You prefer the word porn? Or trash? Or perverted fantasy?"

"Screw you."

"Well, I would," he shot back, "but you'd probably write another story about it!"

Throwing her shoulders back, she drew a deep breath as if to calm her anger. And what the hell did *she* have to be angry about?

"It's not smut," she said again. "I understand why you'd say that, but if you'd just read my work—"

"Me and every other damn person in this town?"

"I... I know it's bad, but—"

"Bad. Yeah, I'd say it's bad. Did I not make it clear to you just how determined I was not to involve my family in another sex scandal?"

"Yes—"

"You knew that from the moment you stepped back into this town."

"I—"

Ben slapped his hat against his thigh to cut her off. "You knew that when you wrote that damned story in the first place."

She clenched both of her fists into tight little balls. "I never thought the story would get published! I wasn't thinking at all. And even when I got the contract... e-publishing was a brand-new business. I thought maybe a few hundred people would read it, and I'd make a few dollars, and it would be done. By the time I realized..."

"So you could've told me anytime in the past two weeks. Hell, anytime in the past ten years!"

"I couldn't!"

He was so mad he could actually feel his muscles

trembling. "Why the fuck not? And tell me the truth for once, Molly."

She stepped back a little, letting her clenched hands loosen into a pleading gesture. Her eyes looked unnaturally bright, shiny with pain, as she pled silently for some little bit of mercy.

"Ben… I should've told you. I knew a long time ago that I should tell you, but I couldn't. I liked you, I always have, and I couldn't stand to let you read my personal fantasies."

"You didn't mind thousands of others doing it."

"No one knew it was me! And nobody knew it was you. It's not real, so it seemed—"

"How the hell am I supposed to convince my friends and family and *every person I've ever known* that it's not real?"

"I'll tell them!" she answered quickly.

"And they'll believe *you?*"

"I guess…I guess they'd have no reason to."

"No, they wouldn't. It's done, Molly." He looked down to his hands, the fingers that had clenched the hat brim into a crooked mess. "It's done. Over."

He heard her deep sigh. "You mean we're over. But this morning… This morning you said you loved me, and I thought we could try—"

"This morning I had no idea you'd betrayed me, that you had kept something from me you knew was damned important. This morning I had no idea that you were going to drag my name through the mud just because you were too much of a coward to tell me the truth. And none of this would have happened if you hadn't let me fall for you, Molly. So no, we can't *try*."

Jesus, he'd known Molly was going to ruin him, and now, watching her wipe tears from her cheeks, he felt it starting. He'd been numb and angry and exhausted, but now he felt sheer pain stutter through him. He had told her he'd loved her, and he'd meant it, and now his heart was shredding itself to pieces.

"Okay," she managed to say, nodding. "Okay. I'm sorry."

It's not okay, he wanted to scream, but he couldn't stand the tears on her face and the terrible need to lash out that boiled through him. So Ben just turned and reached for escape. He was out the door and back in his truck before he could say something he'd really regret. Something that would hurt her as much as he was hurting inside.

MOLLY VERY CALMLY went to the kitchen, drank a glass of lukewarm water, and washed the dishes. Then she checked her e-mail, downloaded the editing suggestions in her Inbox, and updated her Web site with the coming release date.

It was only noon. She couldn't just go to bed, could she? The world didn't stop because her little universe was crumbling. Still, at least she'd been bracing herself for weeks. Ben must be reeling, coldcocked by a woman he might have loved.

She was staring out the back window, watching a magpie hop around the empty bird feeder when the phone rang. Her heart jumped so hard she slapped a hand to her chest. Then she sprinted for the phone. Panting, she squinted down at her brand-spanking-new caller ID display. *Love's Garage,* read the letters that floated by, and Molly slumped in despair. Not Ben, and she didn't want to talk to anyone else.

When she found herself kneeling in front of the phone, sobbing her heart out into the caller ID display, she decided that perhaps bed was a good idea after all.

She didn't get up for two days. Didn't work. Hardly ate.

But the forty-eight hours of depression served her well. She thought about her life and her future. She thought about Ben and what he meant to her. There was something between them, something special and important, and they'd be fools to let that go. So how to convince Ben he was being a fool?

When she finally threw off those funky sheets, Molly Jennings was depressed, dirty and hungry. But she had a plan.

CHAPTER SIXTEEN

WORK DIDN'T EXACTLY bring him comfort, but Ben threw himself into it anyway. He found that if he stayed in his office, the hours blurred into whole days that passed by without him giving in to the temptation to call Molly.

But that afternoon when he stepped into the work-room, the illusion that his office was a refuge popped like a bubble. Frank, Ben's senior officer, looked up from the book he was reading, gulped in a strangled breath of air, and successfully completed a graceful fall from his desk chair onto the cheap office carpet. "Chief!" he squeaked as his rump hit the ground.

There was no need to ask what book he was reading. "*Et tu,* Frank?" Ben muttered as he backed out of the doorway and went back to his own office.

Un-fucking-believable.

After two weeks of gossip and giggling, things had just started to die down around Tumble Creek. Then Holly Summers's new release had hit computer screens across the county. Ben had thought the good citizens of his town had been titillated by *Stolen Kisses*. Oh, they'd loved pouring over those details, debating whether or not Ben and Molly had really been an item back then or whether it had just been a dirty, wicked fling acted out on a hot summer night.

No one had believed his early explanations that there hadn't been any fling, so Ben had shut up about it, theorizing that silence would help the furor die down. It had. Even Miles had lost interest about ten days in.

All in all, it hadn't been a complete nightmare. He'd started to relax back into the normalcy of his life. Whatever normalcy he could scrape up, anyway. He'd been betrayed in the space of one night by the two women in town he'd been closest to. Those feelings were still raw enough that he made very sure not to touch them, but he was muddling through.

Then *The Wicked West* had debuted.

Ben dropped into his desk chair, then almost immediately rose to pace the small confines of his office. He felt restless and desperate, as if he might explode at any moment. And it was snowing like mad outside, keeping him from one of the long walks he'd been indulging in every day. He ran a rough hand through his hair, huffed out an impatient sigh.

Andrew suddenly stopped in Ben's doorway, lost in his study of a thick report. His foot crossed the threshold before he glanced up and jerked to a stop.

"Chief!" he choked out. His chubby cheeks flashed to a sudden, bright pink. "I didn't know you were here!" His gaze began to dart from the report in his hand to Ben's desk, then to the floor and back again.

His own men couldn't even look at him. A good reason he shouldn't have come in four hours early, but he couldn't stand sitting in his house, thinking. Couldn't take it anymore.

"This storm wasn't expected," he muttered. "I thought you guys might get overloaded."

"Oh. Yeah. Good thinking." Andrew rushed forward to drop the file on Ben's desk. "Here's that info you requested from the sheriff. I mean, uh, from Creek County."

Ben stood and grabbed his coat. "I'll look it over later." He couldn't go for a walk, but there was no reason he couldn't go on patrol. Andrew scrambled quickly out of the way, flush still firmly in place. Ben wondered what scene he was picturing. Probably the one involving knotted ropes and candle wax.

Christ.

Gritty snow blew straight into his eyes when he stepped outside. The wind burned through his skin, a needed counter to the hot weight pressing from the inside of his chest. He dashed to his truck, and the relative silence of his lonely SUV swallowed him up.

During her official police interview, Molly had made it clear that Brenda was wrong, that the new story wasn't about Ben or Molly or anyone real. It was a story. Pure fiction. And it was. Ben had read it—closely—just two nights ago. He didn't recognize himself in the cold-hearted, hot-blooded sheriff. And Molly wasn't anything like the defiant widow who distracted herself from her heartbreak with pain and sex.

He had expected to find some familiar phrases or remnants of his and Molly's nights together. He'd expected that she'd been mining him like a damned gold strike, but there was nothing in that story that they'd ever done.

Not that anyone else knew that.

Fuming, Ben prowled the city until the snow stopped. After that he wasn't patrolling for stranded motorists so much as he was stalking Lori in her snowplow. He crossed paths with her purple truck every other block or so, until she finally rolled down her window, waved him over, and ordered him to either go have a damn beer or get the hell over to Molly's house to work it out.

"As if," he muttered, feeling increasingly like the angry teenager he'd been long ago. Maybe he should just go home and sulk in his room.

That turned out to have been a better idea than he could've imagined. He should have just gone straight home. Instead, he drove around—avoiding Lori—for another fifteen minutes, then pulled up to the station an hour before his seven o'clock shift and sat in his truck, brooding. The parking space gave him the perfect vantage point to watch the spotty traffic on Main Street, not to mention a good view of The Bar's lot. When an unfamiliar pickup pulled in, Ben watched with only a small amount of interest…until the passenger door opened.

Molly—*Molly!* Ben's traitorous heart cried—jumped from the cab, all bundled up in her white coat and fuzzy pink hat. His heart groaned out its misery. That fucking pink hat was gonna kill him.

No, scratch that. The pink glove *resting on some other guy's arm* was going to kill him.

Ben hadn't even noticed the driver getting out, he'd been too busy watching Molly's mouth curve into a smile. But there he was, some *man,* escorting her to the front door of The Bar. Ben angled over to the right, squinting, trying to get a better view. The guy glanced toward a passing car, and Ben felt his jaw drop.

Holy fucking shit, Molly was on a date with one of the deputies from Grand Valley! No. No, no, no. He was clearly mistaken. No way was she dating this soon. No way was she dating a fellow law enforcement officer.

Ben heard the steering wheel creak in warning and looked down to see his hands strangling the leather cover. He eased his hold and watched The Bar door close slowly on the scene within. What were they doing? Playing pool? Leaning into each other, flirting?

Maybe the guy was a relative. Did the Jennings family have any cousins in Grand Valley? Quinn would know. Maybe he was just a friend.

Molly's words began flashing through his head. He'd vowed not to read any of her books, but it hadn't taken more than three days for him to break. He'd read *Stolen Kisses* first, horrified, angry and completely turned-on by the fantasy scene she'd woven. In her version of that night, she'd secretly watched Ben finish his "date," and then teased and taunted him until he'd let her have a turn. And that had just been the first three chapters.

In each of her following books, he'd noticed her craft improving, her words growing more poetic, her stories getting edgier. He'd been grudgingly impressed, and increasingly doubtful that he could have kept a girl like Holly Summers satisfied. But maybe that deputy—what the fuck was his name?—maybe he was less uptight. Maybe he didn't worry what the neighbors would say.

Maybe he liked it hot and scandalous and dangerous and public.

Ben pictured hot wax and began to wheeze. His vision was just starting to darken, or maybe that was the sun setting, when The Bar door opened again and Juan slipped out with an unlit cigarette already in hand. Ben snapped to attention and rolled down his window.

"Juan!" he yelled as softly as he could.

The bartender's head popped up and he responded to Ben's wave by trotting across the street.

"Hey, Chief. What's up?"

"Not much," Ben lied. "What's going on?"

"Just, uh…" He gestured with the cigarette. "You mind?"

"Go right ahead. Slow day?"

"You'd think." He took a deep, happy drag. "But that storm blew in and kept the dinner stragglers on their stools."

"Mmm. Yeah." How the hell was he supposed to be subtle about this? "I thought I saw one of McTeague's deputies go in a few minutes ago."

Juan's eyes went wide. So much for subtlety. "Uh… Sure. Griffin? I think I saw him."

"He come in very often?"

"No," he answered quickly, then winced when Ben narrowed his eyes in frustration. "Okay, look. He's in there with Molly Jennings, but I've never seen her with him before."

"The girls still coming in a couple times a week?"

"Er… Sure. Yeah."

His tone was off. There was more information to be

had. Info Juan was sure Ben didn't want to hear. "Juan, you want me to beg for it or something?"

He realized that he'd quoted nearly word for word a line from Molly's ninth book and fought the urge to bang his head on the steering wheel. Luckily, Juan must have been the one person in town who hadn't downloaded her whole backlist. He didn't even blink.

"Sorry, Chief. It's just that… She had a date last Thursday, too. That sculptor who lives in the valley. James Something-or-other."

"The *sculptor?*" Oh, she'd probably really gone for that sensitive, I-work-with-my-hands shit. "What kind of man brings a woman to The Bar for a first date? Jesus! No offense, Juan."

"None taken." But the poor guy was squirming now, desperate to get away.

"Never mind, Juan. Hey, how's it going with Helen?"

He did blush then, shuffling his feet and mumbling an answer that Ben couldn't quite work out, so he let Juan off the hook and waved him on his way before slouching down in the driver's seat.

Molly was officially dating, damn her pink-capped head. What the hell was he supposed to do with *that?*

It had been hard enough seeing her around town these past weeks. At the grocery store, the post office, sauntering down the street. They never spoke, but she *looked* at him, made it obvious, challenged him with her hazel eyes. *Get over yourself,* that gaze said. *Take me on, big guy.*

Those eyes never once apologized or looked ashamed or begged for forgiveness. In fact, they'd been shouting to him that she was going to start dating again, and he had ignored the warning, so here he was hiding in his truck, spying on the pickup across the street. It mocked him with its tinted windows and double-deep cab. There was probably no computer equipment between those seats. A man could really stretch out and enjoy himself while—

"Somebody just kill me," Ben groaned aloud. He was doomed. He'd known from the start that this would end in disaster, but he hadn't anticipated that he'd know just what Molly was thinking when she touched a man or took him inside her. He hadn't anticipated that she was an author who'd continue writing books, stories about the man she'd invited to her bed that year or month or week. Stories *not* about him.

How the hell could that actually be *worse* than everyone reading the details of Ben's sex life? Impossible, but he suddenly saw that it would be worse. Much, much worse if they were whispering about Griffin the Perverted Deputy instead of Ben the Hot-Blooded Sheriff.

"Damn," he breathed out, hardly able to put any force behind the word because he couldn't get his lungs to expand. *"Damn."*

He'd thought the pressure in his chest unbearable before, but it was only getting worse. Pressing in on him, squeezing him into some shape he feared he wouldn't recognize. For the first time in his career, he didn't want to go into work, didn't want to face his officers. He could take a personal day. They'd understand. Hell, they couldn't stand looking at him anyway.

His head suddenly exploded with a high-pitched

blast. Ben actually grabbed his temples before he looked around, but when he spotted Lori in her truck, laughing her ass off, he dropped his hands and glared. After conquering the brief impulse to walk over and put a bullet through that damned air-horn of hers, Ben gave her the finger and slammed out of his truck.

She'd saved him from being a complete pussy and calling in sick to work, anyway. For that alone he wouldn't give her a ticket for disturbing the peace.

"You didn't have that beer, did you?" she yelled at his back. "You know, you could just go see her!"

Ben heard the snap of a camera just as he gave Lori the finger again. Miles Webster's chuckle carried easily across the street.

But Ben had noticed just this morning that Miles's tags had expired three weeks before, so he was smiling as he slammed the station door. *Screw you, old man.*

"THANK YOU. I had a lovely time," Molly said honestly, if not enthusiastically.

"I'm the one who should be thanking you," Griffin responded.

She shook her head. "I wish you didn't have to do this."

"Hey, I had a great evening, even if you did stare at Aaron for a good half an hour."

"I was hyp-mo-tized by his shiny, tight T-shirt. I thought you would be, too."

Griffin grinned. "He is so not my type. I like a more natural guy."

"Really? Because when I saw you at that bar in Denver, I got the impression you liked club boys."

"No! That was a very bad, very short phase in my life, I swear. I like strong, smart men in flannel."

"Like James?"

The grin remained, framed by reddening cheeks. "Like James."

"He's so sweet. I don't doubt you make a great couple. Are you sure you need to cover it up? This is the twenty-first century, even in Creek County. You shouldn't have to go on pretend dates with shameless hussies."

"I like shameless hussies. And my parents, my job… It's just hard. I'm working up to it."

Molly patted his muscled arm. "You'd better work quick. James showed me his new collection. I think those sculptures might give him away."

Impossibly, his cheeks deepened to an even darker red.

She leaned in and gave him a kiss on his scarlet jaw. "I thought I recognized those biceps. You make for a very impressive work of art, Griffin."

"Stop," he protested, but his eyes sparkled with pleasure. "Do you want me to come in?" he asked. "You've had a lot of weird stuff going on. If you'd feel safer, I'd be happy to take a look around."

"I'm fine now. Brenda's still in the slammer. But thank you."

When she got inside, Molly closed the door and leaned hard against it. This making-Ben-jealous plan was exhausting. And she didn't even know if he was aware of it, which made it doubly hard.

She'd made a strategic retreat in the face of his anger. But she hadn't given up. Far from it. Molly was in love for the first time and she wanted it with all the righteous tenacity of a seventh-grader crushing on a freshman. The freshman refusing to speak when he passed had no effect on that kind of devotion. None at all.

But her plan wasn't perfect. There were only so many closeted men around. If Miles didn't pick up on this story soon, she was going to have to put it off 'til summer. Or go out with Aaron.

"Gah," she choked and went to check her answering machine. Nothing. At least Cameron had given up the ghost. He hadn't called once since his trip to Tumble Creek. Some of the Merry Men had been in touch, but she hadn't detected any puppet strings. She'd finally freed herself, but unfortunately she'd cut Ben loose in the process.

It was only nine o'clock and she wasn't the least bit tired, so she called Lori Love to keep from moping about Ben. "Hey, Lori," she sighed.

"Hey, yourself! Were you by any chance on one of your dates tonight?"

Molly perked up. "Are the rumors starting?"

"I'm not sure, but I saw a certain police chief sitting in his truck, glowering at The Bar about two hours ago."

She gasped and nearly dropped the phone. "Are you kidding me? He saw it *himself*?"

"I think so. He looked pretty damned tortured."

"Oh, that's so perfect," Molly groaned.

"You are a cruel, cruel woman."

"Maybe, but he won't even talk to me. I can take it right back to junior high just as easily as he can."

Lori snorted out a laugh. "You two are pitiful. Why don't you just put on that schoolgirl outfit and break into his house while he's sleeping? Impasse over."

"He has a gun, Lori."

"A nice one, from what I heard. Oh, you mean a *gun* gun. Right. I guess we shouldn't set him up for a lifetime of sorrow and regret. Good thinking."

"Thanks. Just let me know what you hear. And I hope to God he comes to his senses soon."

"Of course. And send me more fan mail tonight, please? I'm bored out of my mind."

"Well…only because you spied on Ben for me." Hanging up, she went straight to her laptop and logged in to her Holly Summers e-mail account. Thirty-one new messages. She sorted quickly through, setting aside the majority to answer later. Most of the e-mails were kind and generous, the type of mail that kept her writing. And she really needed the encouragement right now.

One was laugh-out-loud hilarious and another totally bizarre—apparently some men were into clown costumes and grease paint. Molly deleted the name of the writer from that one and forwarded it to Lori. The last three would have been perfectly normal except that they were addressed to "Molly" instead of "Holly." Damn Miles Webster and his online paper. Her real name was now just a click away for fans and stalkers alike. Not to mention friends and family.

Quinn had been horrified as only a brother could be, meaning not genuinely horrified, only sisters-shouldn't-have-functioning-sex-organs horrified. Her friends in Denver had thought it perfectly hilarious. The people in Tumble Creek didn't know what to think. And her parents… Well, Molly preferred not to put too much thought into that. She had the Ben Lawson problem to deal with before she could take on her parents.

An instant-message window opened on her screen, announcing a visitor with tinkling bells. "Holly Summers?" the message read. Simple enough, except she was logged in to her browser as Molly. Fighting off the cold hole of panic that opened inside her chest, Molly closed the message window with a curse.

Brenda was in jail, unable to make bail, and she'd likely be there for a while, but it seemed Molly needed a security system more than ever. Aspen was crawling with security experts, but she didn't want to wait until summer. She'd called around and found that Tumble Creek was isolated enough to add three hundred dollars and a three-week wait to her order, but erotic writing brought a very specific set of risks to a girl's life. She'd have to give in and pay up.

Or she could just get her own personal policeman to move in and keep watch over her sleeping body. Perhaps the extra three hundred dollars could be better spent.

Molly logged on to her favorite lingerie site for a little research and plotted her next big move. Now that Ben had noticed, she could kick it into Phase Two.

THEY ALL THOUGHT they were so smart. Every one in this whole damn town.

That Brenda woman had confessed—to breaking and entering, harassment, vandalism, threat with a deadly weapon—and the investigation stopped there. Everyone, including the heroic police chief, assumed she was guilty of everything, whether she admitted it or not.

But Brenda was harmless and pitiful, a woman crying out for attention, affection...anything but the cruel invisibility that cloaked the lives of women like her. She was unnoticeable, and so she'd made a nuisance of herself and, in the process, helped to shield and camouflage *him*.

He'd even talked to her about it. Commiserated with her about Molly and all the other selfish, immoral women in the world. Women who drew attention to themselves and away from good, steady helpmates like Brenda. Boy, she'd lapped that up like a cat with a bowl of cream. The fervent glow in her eyes had warned she was close to breakdown. He'd simply offered a tiny, extra nudge. Then...

Boom!

Brenda's implosion had cleared all the obstacles from his path. Now Molly was alone. Totally alone. Lawson had abandoned her without a thought. The investigation had stopped. Hell, the chief had never even figured out the secret of the King Mine. With nothing more than a clear night and a telescope, anyone could spend a comfortable few hours watching Molly's house.

He readjusted his position against the mine's fence and watched Molly finish washing her lunch dishes, face bright in the glow of the afternoon sun. God, she was beautiful. He could just sit there and watch her all day, enjoying her loneliness because he knew he'd be the one to end it.

He loved this quiet place where he could be alone with Molly.

And good old, pitiful Brenda had inadvertently led him right to her favorite hiding place. She deserved something nice in return. Hopefully, she'd get a real kick out of hearing that Molly Jennings had finally realized that her place was back in Denver. Maybe he'd even send Brenda a picture to bring her some peace.

CHAPTER SEVENTEEN

"OH, COME ON," BEN muttered under his breath.

Who the hell went grocery shopping in shiny red heels? She was just taunting him now, strolling through the produce department, legs long, back arched, perfectly rounded ass filling out a pair of tight jeans. Molly was torturing him, pulling out every splinter of feeling from the shattered mess of his heart.

That sounded so much like bad poetry bouncing around his head that Ben added an extra six-pack of beer to his cart and spun on a dime to head for the checkout. Unfortunately old Mrs. Lantern was already up there, sorting through coupons as the young checkout girl waited with unveiled impatience. Mrs. Lantern didn't notice or didn't mind. She handed over the coupons and then watched to make sure that each one was entered correctly before she busted out the checkbook. Ben knew from experience that she didn't believe in duplicate checks. He fought hard not to sigh as she turned to the old-fashioned double-sided register and carefully recorded the transaction.

The squeak of an off-balance cart scraped against his left eardrum. Ben counted slowly to five before he turned in that direction.

"Hey there, Chief," Molly drawled, eyes sparkling above a sly smile.

And that was the moment that the first inkling hit him. An idea so wonderful that it scared him down deep in his soul.

Maybe Molly wasn't *dating* dating. Maybe she wasn't looking for someone new to talk dirty to. Maybe she was just trying to make him jealous.

He was staring at her, drinking in the pretty pink of her cheeks, the soft green specks in her hazel eyes, when she began to chuckle. She tilted her head forward, alerting him to the fact that Mrs. Lantern was long gone and the checkout clerk was calling his name.

"Hi," he finally answered before he turned to put his groceries on the counter.

Molly Jennings had some type of power, a perfectly honed force field that disabled any shred of dignity he might try to assume. He was helpless in her presence. Powerless in the face of her knowing smile. And it occurred to him then that he liked it. Really liked it.

Too bad she was dishonest and untrustworthy. Not to mention unrepentant. Scandalous. Wicked. Deliciously cute. Amazingly creative and good at her job.

Ben grabbed his receipt and his bags and got the hell out of the market, terrified by his reaction to her.

Things hadn't gotten better in the week since he'd seen her with Griffin. Things had gotten much worse. Miles was loving the new novella, and so were Molly's fans. Some of the women who'd found the *Tumble Creek Tribune* online had even written to Ben, to flirt with him or tell him how much they'd loved his character. And, of course, some of them just straight-up asked for kinky sex.

He couldn't stand that strangers and friends alike now thought he enjoyed whipping women or tying them up. He hated the looks he got as he moved through his life. It reminded him of his father and those terrible years. And yet... And yet it didn't.

It was ridiculous and embarrassing, but it was also just...starting to wear off. Get old. Roll off his back. He almost didn't care. He wasn't a fucking kid anymore, drowning in the judgments of others.

And he missed Molly.

Which was a good reason to get out of town. He wanted to get out of the public eye and just think. Spend some time *not* staring across the street at The Bar, wondering if she was in there with some other guy.

So he dropped by his house to repack the groceries and stuff some clothes into a bag. The weather was supposed to be decent for a few days. There was no reason to think he couldn't get up the dirt road to his cabin. No memories of Molly awaited him there, thank God, and he could examine this ridiculous temptation to try again with her.

His cell phone wouldn't work in the back country, but he grabbed it anyway, then regretted it when it rang before he made it halfway out the door. Cursing, he tossed his bag in the back of his truck, pushed in the box of groceries and punched the call button on the phone.

"Lawson," he barked.

"Afternoon, Chief," Quinn murmured. "Or should

I call you Sheriff and then take your ass out back for a beating?"

"I swear to you, one more time, that story wasn't about me. What can I say to convince you?"

"Oh, I believe it now. I'm just having a good time torturing you."

Ben closed his eyes. "Well, I'll be out of cell range soon, so knock yourself out."

"You still shunning my sister?"

The tightness was back, pushing from the inside out, blocking his airway. "Have you talked to her?" he muttered, not what he'd meant to say at all.

"Not much, which was why I hoped you'd given up your campaign of silence. She swears she's okay, but I wish I could drop by and see myself."

Was she okay? "She looks good." Surely she was fine.

"My parents..." Quinn started, and Ben winced. This couldn't be good. "My parents called to tell her they still loved her 'despite everything,' and then they took off for a conveniently long road trip. They haven't called her in three weeks."

"Maybe that's for the best. It'll give them time to calm down and respond with diplomacy."

"Yeah. You're probably right." Quinn's voice spoke volumes of doubt and concern, and Ben felt all his protective instincts rise to the fore. Shit.

Sighing, he let his head fall back on the headrest. "I really am on my way out of town, but I'll be back in two days." Two days? Hadn't he meant to take three? "I'll talk to Molly as soon as I get back."

"Thanks, Ben. That would be great. I know she's all grown up—way too grown up, it turns out—but she's still my little sister."

"I know." Yeah, he knew, because despite everything she was still just Molly Jennings to him, too, albeit spiced with new memories of dirty talk and blow jobs.

Ben hung up and backed out of his garage with a shudder of relief. He'd talk to her when he got back, but in the meantime he'd dispose of a couple six-packs and watch the moon slide across the night. The hot springs would've offered a whole different enjoyment with Molly, but he was still looking forward to a soak.

And he'd try his best to get through one whole day before he began debating exactly what he would say to his very naughty ex-lover. The possibilities ranged from "No hard feelings. I'll see you around," to "Please say you can't live without me because I'm miserable and I need you." Neither of those options gave him a happy feeling, so he'd hopefully come up with something better tomorrow.

Any hope of that happy feeling vanished when he hit Main Street and saw a very red, very unwelcome sight rolling toward him. He'd only seen one car like that in town recently, and it belonged to that smarmy, slimy police sergeant, Cameron Kasten.

Slowing as he passed, Ben tipped his head to look down into the low driver's seat. Yep, it was Cameron, cheerfully raising a hand to offer a quick salute that matched his pleased smile.

"What the fuck?" Ben growled. He watched in the mirror as Cameron slowed and turned into the grocery store parking lot. Ben slowed, too, and pulled to the side of the road to spy.

Cameron parked and got out with a long stretch. Then he tipped his head to a passing woman, offering a compliment that made the frumpy woman smile before he passed by her. He disappeared into the market, not hiding or slinking around. In fact, he looked right at home, not that Ben trusted that at all.

He slipped out of his truck and walked the half-block back to the market, reaching Cameron's car just as Cameron sauntered out of the store carrying a small plastic sack and a big bouquet of flowers.

"Chief Lawson! Good to see you!"

Ben ignored the man's hand and crossed his arms. "Why the hell are you in my town, Sergeant?"

"Well, I'd tell you I was invited, but I don't want to hurt your feelings."

"Invited by who?"

"Come on, Chief. Who do you think?"

Ben's jaw began to tic, but he managed not to punch the smug bastard in the nose. "You're trying to tell me that Molly invited you to visit? After she told you never to contact her again?"

Cameron's smile made Ben want to go home and take a shower. "Molly says lots of things. She always has. But she never actually took out that protective order, did she? Why do you think that is?"

"She didn't want to jeopardize your career unless she absolutely had to. And she's been a little busy."

"Yeah, she's been busy realizing I wasn't the one stalking her. And now that she's also realized you're no longer interested, Molly's headed right back to me, just like I always said. Sorry, Chief."

"She called you," Ben ground out.

Cameron nodded his head, sympathy smeared across his face. "Molly's a complicated woman, a little wild, but I'm used to it. I'll take good care of her. Scout's honor."

She's just using him, Ben told himself, but it didn't make him feel better. Molly was either using Cameron to make Ben jealous, or she was truly interested in the creep. Either way, that was far too much drama and stupidity for Ben's life. He simply couldn't love a woman who lived like that, no matter how much he wanted to.

There was only one choice left to him now: No hard feelings; I'll see you around.

"There'd better not be any trouble," he growled to Cameron, then walked away from the whole fucking thing, painfully glad he had somewhere to go to hide.

THE DAMN HEELS were killing her. Oh, four-inch heels had been fun and games at the bar that night when she knew she'd be getting a little some-some later, but today at the market? No immediate gratification. Well, aside from making Ben drool. That had been pretty fun.

But then she'd had to walk home uphill, because driving to the store would have lost her any potential Ben-driving-by-watching-her-ass moments. Now she was beginning to think all this junior-high behavior was better reserved for people with junior-high energy. Maybe she could find some way to entice him with her butt planted on the couch.

Lori's idea was starting to sound good, too, if only she could think of a way to keep him from shooting her. Hmm. Maybe instead of breaking in, she could just pull the old trench-coat trick and knock on the door.

After tossing the last frozen dinner in the freezer, Molly headed for her bedroom closet to look for a coat long enough to cover her modest bits. She could let him stew for a couple more days and then pounce on him like a mercilessly horny cat. Perfect!

She was rifling through the pile of clothes that had somehow ended up on her closet floor when a tiny sound popped behind her. The old house made a lot of noise, so she hardly even raised her eyebrows when she glanced back. The sight of a man's legs raised her eyebrows plenty. Molly gasped and fell onto her ass to scramble farther into the closet.

The man crouched down, and Cameron's amused smile came into view. "Hi there, Molly."

Jesus. She considered the brief thought that he might go away if she just closed the closet door and waited, but he didn't look ready to budge. He looked downright comfortable hunkered there with his forearms resting on his knees. He gestured with a bouquet of flowers.

"Are you coming out or should I come in?"

"What are you doing here?" she demanded, voice shaking. "How did you get in here?"

"You left the door unlocked."

She shook her head. "No. I locked it."

Cameron winked, still grinning like a boy with stolen candy. "I've been reading your books. That was quite a little secret you were keeping, Ms. Summers."

Strange. She'd put her books out there to be read by thousands of people, but his words felt like a violation. "Get out. You're not supposed to come near me."

"What, legally? Because I checked that before I came. No order of protection on record. There never has been and there never will be, because you don't want me to stay away."

Genuine fear started to bubble up in her blood. She gave a half-assed kick with one high heel. "Get out of my house!"

He reached for her leg and Molly kicked again, to no avail. His hands, perfectly manicured but still strong, wrapped around her ankle and tugged her out. "You should have just told me you liked it rough, Molly. I have no problem with that." The words held an edge she'd never heard in his voice before.

He pulled harder, fingers twisting into her skin. Oh, no. Oh, no, no, no. She tried to dig her hands into something, but all she found was wrinkled clothing that slid out with her. "Don't do this, Cameron. Stop!"

"Come on, Molly baby. Let's play."

"No, no, no." Unable to stop the motion, she gave in and let him pull her, getting her knees under her so she could try again. As soon as his hold eased, Molly lunged away, breaking free of his hand. The rush of hope lasted only a moment, and then her ankle was in his grip again. She sobbed.

He tugged her back and then he was over her, pulling her to her feet just so he could drop her into the chair in the corner of her room. She fought and scratched, kicking and clawing, but he wrenched her arms back. The click of handcuffs surprised her before she even realized that he'd caught her arms behind the chair.

"You've lost it!" she screamed. "What the hell do you think you're doing?"

"Tying you up," he said as he yanked one ankle into place and zip-tied it to the chair leg.

"Cameron, listen to me. Listen. Those stories were *not* about me. I am not enjoying this. You will go to prison if you do this." She managed to kick him hard in the shoulder.

"So feisty," he chuckled, as he latched on to her free ankle and fastened the plastic tie around it.

When he stood, Molly bucked and struggled, but her limbs didn't move an inch. She should have fought harder, should have attacked, because now her only hope was talking her way out of this, and he definitely had the advantage there.

"Are they tight enough for your taste?" he asked as he walked toward the door. For a split second she thought he was leaving, but he only grabbed a duffel bag he'd dropped by the door.

The stuff he started pulling out didn't encourage her in the least. In fact she fully considered screaming when she saw the wooden paddle he set on the bed. But if she screamed, he'd cover her mouth, and then she'd be tied *and* silenced. Plus the damned neighbors wouldn't pay any attention. A sex-crazed pornographer screaming like a banshee in her bedroom? Alert the national media!

So Molly switched off the screaming impulse and started talking. "Okay, I know what you're thinking.

You've read my books and you think those stories are about me—"

"No, I'm sure they're about you," he countered.

"They're not about anyone! They're *fiction!*"

Cameron smirked at her, clearly amused as he pulled a black rope from the bag and began coiling it around his hand. "Everyone in town knows *Stolen Kisses* is about you and Lawson, so don't give me that fiction shit."

"How do you know what everyone in town thinks?"

"The *Tribune.* I follow the online issue quite closely. How did you think I was keeping up to date between visits?"

That stopped her tugging against the restraints. "Visits? You only came here once."

"Oh, come on, Molly. You enjoyed the little shows you put on for me. Swaying around town in heels and short skirts. Fucking your new friend in a truck so I could watch. But I've gotten really, *really* tired of just watching."

"Oh, God, you were here," she whispered. "You were here the whole time."

"Not the whole time, no. That Brenda chick really helped my cover. I couldn't believe it when I caught her spying on your house. A stroke of good luck that a real stalker came along, huh?"

"Like you're not a *real* stalker! Oh, my God, Cameron, were you the one who cut my brake lines?"

"Okay, I admit that was over the top. I just wanted you to move back to Denver, Molly. Make you see reason."

"By *killing* me?"

"No, by scaring you. That's why I cut the electrical, too. Duh. I didn't want you driving with faulty brakes."

"Oh, all right. I get it. That's perfectly reasonable *for someone who's a raging lunatic!*"

Rolling his eyes, Cameron shrugged off his coat and aimed an exasperated stare in her direction. "You're clearly ready to be gagged."

Molly choked on outraged horror. *"What?"*

He tugged a length of white material from the bag. "In all seriousness…" The bed creaked beneath him when he sat down hard and put on a somber face. "I've spent a lot of time thinking about you, Molly. When I read about your little hobby in the *Tribune,* I downloaded all your books. I realized how hard it must have been for you."

He was winding that white fabric around and around his fist. Molly watched, transfixed.

"You had all these desires, these needs, that you couldn't tell anyone about. No wonder you're so disconnected. But I see it now. As soon as I read that new story, the one about me, I—"

"Whoa there, buster. What the hell are you talking about?"

"The new book. The one with the tall, merciless lawman who just happens to live on the Western plains."

"Good Lord, you have got to be kidding me. *The Wicked West* is not about you, Cameron. And it's not about me, either. I'm not into that. You have to believe me. You've misinterpreted the—"

"You're cute when you lie," he chuckled.

"I'm not lying! I'm not. This is kidnapping, and…and whatever else this is going to be. Please don't do this."

He nodded in answer, but his eyes sparked with excitement. "Maybe you really haven't done this before. Maybe it's a fantasy you've never acted out. That's even better. I've spent the past few days reading about control and submission. Funny, all those times you called me a control freak, I never suspected just how much control you wanted me to have. But I know now, and it might be embarrassing for you, but I'll let you do all the begging you want. I'm kind of enjoying it, actually. More than I expected."

Oh, God, he was really into this. And she had no doubt that he was planning to take it to the next level soon. "If you have sex with me, it will be rape."

"Oh, come on, Molly. I'd never rape you. We'll go slow. Ease into it with some fun and games. We won't take it to the next level until you're ready." He smiled. "Begging for it, even."

Okay, maybe he wasn't going to attack her. Maybe she could talk her way out of this. She had to get serious if she wanted to get out of this situation. He'd think pleading was part of the act. If she got assertive, he'd probably decide she wanted discipline. There was only one thing to do.

"I've got my period," she blurted and watched his forehead crinkle.

"What?"

He was one of *those* guys, the squeamish kind who secretly wished women would withdraw to a mysterious hut for one week out of every month. "I've got my period," she repeated. "Wanna check?"

"Ew! No, I do not."

"Yeah, you picked the wrong week to kidnap me, Cameron. Sorry. You'd better just go."

He wasn't running out in horror, which was too bad, but he definitely looked troubled as he nibbled on the edge of one thumbnail. "Okay. Not ideal. How many more days?"

"Uh…five!" Duh.

"Shit. I took the whole week off, but *damn*." His shoulders slumped. "Still, there's a lot we can do without involving your…your stuff."

"My *stuff*? Wow. Even if you weren't a crazed stalker who'd broken into my house, this would so be over."

Ignoring her sarcasm, Cameron drew in a deep breath and slapped both hands against his thighs. "Shit, I need a drink. Fun as this is, it's kind of stressful. Can I get you something?"

"Cyanide?" she snapped.

"Oh, for God's sake," he snarled back. "You're the one with her period. This isn't my fault."

Her smart mouth had finally pissed him off, and she wanted to rewind and try that again, but it was too late. His hand snapped out and the white fabric unwound.

She whispered, "Please don't," but he still rose and crossed the room.

"You need a little time to stew, I think. And I need a glass of wine. I brought some good stuff. Not from a box. You sure you don't want a glass?"

She pulled her chin in, tucking it down, clamping her

teeth together so he couldn't get the gag between them. Not that it mattered. This was hopeless. Ben wasn't gonna drop by and—

She threw her head back just as his hands touched her. "Ben will be here in a little while. You don't want to be around. He's—"

"Not likely. I just talked to Ben a few minutes ago. Seems he's still over you."

"You talked to him? He…" Maybe he was coming right now. Maybe the whole police force was crouched outside her front door!

"Don't worry. I shook him off. Last time I saw him, he was driving in the opposite direction, none too pleased with you, Ms. Jennings."

Shit. All her scheming must have backfired on her. "Shit, shit, shit," she cursed, then clamped her lips shut and turned away from the handkerchief coming toward her.

"You've got a lot of spirit, Molly." His lips brushed her temple as the words whispered over her face. "That's what makes it fun for you, isn't it? You're so strong and you want to be weak. Helpless."

"No."

"It's all right, hon. It's no big deal. Everyone has fantasies. Everyone wants to be happy."

"No, Cameron, please just go. Leave now and we'll forget everything, all right? Truce."

The cloth touched her lips and she clenched her jaw, but Cameron held both ends behind her head with one hand and pinched her nose shut with the other. "Open up, babe."

Lights were swimming in front of her eyes before she finally gasped and the cloth slipped in. He tied it quick and tight.

"There we go. That should get your engine purring, and damned if it's not turning me on, too. Don't worry. I'll hurry back."

He strolled out, whistling, while Molly worried that she'd cry and clog up her nose and suffocate on her own snot. Definitely not the way she wanted to go. But truthfully, she could breathe just fine, so her panic faded in a few seconds, and she was left to think about things she'd rather avoid.

Cameron wasn't going to kill her. Hopefully. He'd lost it but seemed to genuinely believe she wanted this. He'd talked to Ben, for Pete's sake, a sure path to conviction if she turned up dead. And he wasn't going to rape her, or wouldn't now anyway. Her menstruation story had been a stroke of genius.

Which left torture. Just torture. And a wooden paddle? Come on, she could handle that. Cameron wasn't exactly an Iraqi prison guard. She'd be okay.

But Molly began to cry, gasping against the tight band of cotton that chafed at her mouth. Her wrists and shoulders hurt and her feet were fucking killing her. Why hadn't he at least taken off the heels before he'd tied her up? He was probably going to make her wear them all day and all night. She'd never seen any S&M pictures of women in slippers and cozy socks. The thought of her bunny slippers sitting just inches away made her cry harder.

Okay, murder was off the table, but she just wasn't

up for torture, either, even the spanking kind. She was weak. Screw bravery and defiance. She'd grovel and beg. She'd sob and moan and bubble with snot.

Just as she was feeling hopeful that her runny nose might put Cameron off completely, Molly heard a faint concussion, a little thud that floated around her consciousness, promising to reveal its meaning if she could just get it together.

Probably just the fridge door closing. She strained her ears, trying to hear something more past the bedroom door and the foot of floor between them. She thought Cameron uttered a curse, and then he confirmed it with a shout.

"Where the hell are your wineglasses?" he yelled, as if she could answer.

Idiot. Watching him drink pricey wine out of a juice glass would be a small revenge, but she'd take it.

He slammed a few more cabinets and grumbled, but his complaints were interrupted by a faint stutter of sound, sharper than the others.

Molly's heartbeat kicked into overdrive. She tried to breathe deeply and slowly, because she couldn't hear a damn thing with her pulse pounding in her ears. Then it came again. *Knock, knock, knock.*

Ohmigod, ohmigod. That hadn't been the fridge closing, it had been a car door slamming. Or a truck door. A big, black police truck door slamming behind a big, strong policeman! Please, please, please let that be true.

Molly sucked in a deep breath and started screaming.

BEN'S FISTS WERE NUMB from clenching the steering wheel, and he felt almost nauseous standing on Molly's porch like a damned fool. He'd been halfway to his cabin, turning off the highway onto the old logging road, when responsibility had finally got the better of his temper.

Cursing himself and Molly and every single one of her ex-boyfriends, Ben had turned his truck around and headed back to town. So he'd lose nearly an hour of his day. At least he'd know he hadn't driven off in a cloud of enraged testosterone and left Molly in danger.

Still, there was every chance that he was about to make a huge fool of himself, the very reason he hadn't just called one of his officers and sent him over. *Hey, Frank, could you run by my ex-girlfriend's place and see if she's willingly entertaining a gentleman caller?*

So here he was.

Just as he raised his fist to knock for the third time, Molly's front door opened, letting free the sound of a loud TV show. At the sight of Cameron, Ben felt a shiver of violence crawl over his skin. The man looked very at home, shirt untucked and sleeves rolled up. He stepped out and closed the door behind him, juice cup of wine in hand.

That should be my cup of wine, Ben thought, then wanted to punch himself almost as much as he wanted to punch Cameron.

"What can I do for you, Chief?"

You can fuck off and die. Ben took a deep breath. "I'd like to speak with Ms. Jennings, please."

Cameron flashed a wide smile. "I'm afraid she's not available at the moment. Is there something I can help you with?"

"Go get Molly, damn it."

Leaning a little closer, Cameron raised the cup like a pointed finger. "I'm trying to be subtle here. She's unavailable." The glass swirled in a slow circle as Cameron raised one eyebrow. "Not decent."

"You," Ben ground out, "got here less than an hour ago."

"Yeah, well." He raised the cup slowly and took a long sip of wine. When he met Ben's gaze, he practically glowed with self-satisfaction. "You know how she is."

Everything—the door, the porch, the smug dickhead—everything went scarlet red for a split second, and then just as suddenly, his eyes were crystal clear, as if this were a movie playing in slow motion.

"All right," Ben said, the words echoing in his ears like ominous drums. "All right. But I'd really like to see her."

"Sorry, Chief. But you know what they say. Easy come, easy go."

"Yeah. Sure." He waited, trying to force Cameron to turn away first, but he looked comfortable leaning against the door, sipping from his wine.

"I'll come by later," Ben said numbly.

"You do that." Cameron gave him a half salute with the glass before he took another sip.

Ben backed up and stepped sideways down the stairs, not wanting to leave, but knowing it was the right thing to do. When he got back to his truck he scanned the windows, hoping to get a look at Molly, but the curtains stayed closed as he backed away.

Nerves shaky and screaming for action, Ben forced himself to drive down Molly's block very slowly. As soon as he reached the shelter of the pine trees, he pulled to a stop, reached to unlock the glove compartment, and withdrew his handgun. Only then did he lift the radio.

"This is Chief Lawson. I need every available officer at twenty-five Pine Road. Code two. Sirens off. We've got a possible two-oh-seven. Suspect is likely to be armed and dangerous."

What had seemed like a normal confrontation between two rival males had shifted as he'd stood there in the doorway. The scene had suddenly cracked into pieces, showing jagged edges that didn't fit together.

Cameron hadn't looked the least bit ruffled, hadn't looked like a man who'd just had a passionate quickie. His shoes had still been on, his shirt not creased or wrinkled, every hair smoothly in place. The downstairs television had been on, blaring some nature program.

And there'd been scratches on Cameron's hand. Deep scratches.

A picture of Molly—Molly fighting, crying, scratching—flashed through Ben's mind, snatching the breath from his throat. He checked his gun, steeled his frantic nerves, and stepped out of his car into the cold, pale sun.

CHAPTER EIGHTEEN

FOOTSTEPS ROSE up the stairs, drawing closer to Molly's bedroom. She waited, eyes wide, breath rasping in her sore throat. She'd screamed as loudly as she could around the gag, but she doubted the visitor had heard anything. Cameron had turned the downstairs TV on to muffle her cries.

Still, maybe it had been Ben and maybe he had magically picked up on her distress and taken Cameron out with a strangely quiet gunshot. Anything was possible. But the footsteps approaching were slow and easy, not stealthy and urgent, and Molly was growing more panicked with each footfall.

"Where the hell are your wineglasses, Molly?" Cameron asked as he opened the door. "You're living like a damned bumpkin up here."

What happened? she screamed inside her head, trying to yell with her eyes, her face, but Cameron ignored her grunts and strolled nonchalantly to the bed.

"I almost forgot this," he said, rooting around in the bag he'd dropped on the mattress. He pulled out a black satin mask with a flourish and wink.

What the hell happened down there? She pushed

both spiked heels into the carpet and tried to hop the chair around.

"Ooo, does that get you excited?" he laughed, raising his glass for a long draw. He licked his lips and looked her up and down. "I don't have much experience with this, but I think I know just where I'd like to start." His eyes lingered on her breasts as Molly tried to hunch over, curling her spine into the hardwood back of the chair.

It's okay. I'll survive.

If she could get through a few hours, he'd relax, pay less attention. He'd have to untie her at some point, if only to get her clothes off. She just had to play along. No problem-o.

Then Cameron toed off his shoes and started unbuttoning his shirt, and Molly lost all sense of calm. She was hyperventilating, couldn't get enough air, wanted out of there *right this minute*. He didn't even notice.

The shirt parted and he shrugged it off to reveal a slim, muscled chest and tight shoulders. He wasn't as big as Ben, but he was strong and, more importantly, completely insane. He smiled serenely as he pulled a wine bottle from the bag and popped out the cork to refill his cup.

"Don't worry, I'm just getting comfortable." He sipped his wine and stared at her legs for a few long seconds, lost in thought. "I know I seem like a pretty confident guy, but it really tore me up when you left. Everything was so great between us at first. I couldn't figure out why you got so distant, why you broke it off. But now I see it didn't really have anything to do with me. It's about you and your inability to open up. To tell your secrets."

A faint smile overtaking the thoughtful frown, he shook his head as if she were an exasperating and adorable child. "You'll share your most secret thoughts with strangers but not with the person who loves you. That's just sad." Cameron finished off his wine and shrugged. "But that's done now. We're working it out. How about we start with pictures?"

"Ghan?" Molly groaned against the fabric.

"Pictures. When I was planning this trip, I thought maybe Lawson might still be hanging around. What better way to get rid of him than to show him exactly how involved we still are?"

He crossed to the bag and triumphantly drew out a camera. It was a big thing, silver with a professional-looking lens.

Molly groaned. Oh, God. This was just what she needed to add to the disaster of her life. He'd probably send them to her family, pass them around the station, post them on the Internet. *See, I told you she was still hot for me!*

But what really made her heart lurch was the fact that she'd been asking for dirty pictures just a few weeks ago. But she'd wanted them with Ben, not Cameron! Not anyone else. Just Ben.

And in return, Ben had given her something beautiful.

The tears started again. When she sniffed, Cameron seemed to finally realize the state of her face. His smile froze.

"Jeez, Molly, you're a mess! All blotchy and slimy."
He shuddered. "Is this part of the game? Because I don't
like it at all, and it is *not* going to photograph well."

She tried to call up a storm of more tears, but her
ducts petered out in the excitement. Cameron hurried
away to get a wad of tissue from the bathroom, looking
as if he wanted to thrust the paper into her hand when he
returned, but of course she was cuffed. Forced to clean
her up, he dabbed at her nose until he was satisfied, then
retreated to pour another glass of wine.

"Not," he continued as if the interruption hadn't happened, "that I wouldn't want to take pictures regardless
of Ben and his persistence. In fact, I can't believe we
never did this before. Maybe if I'd had pictures of you,
I wouldn't have been so damned lonely these past few
months. I really missed you."

Molly watched him, growing wearier as the seconds
ticked past. Her toes were throbbing in the pointy heels,
her hands had ceased tingling and were now officially
numb, but the tightness in her shoulders had crept up
her neck and set off a wicked headache that wrapped
around her head. Oh, yeah. This bondage stuff was hot.

Then again, maybe it was working. She'd almost
rather have sex with him than be tied up in this chair
for another hour. Boy, she would make a terrible pris-
oner of war. She'd be in front of a camera filming pro-
paganda pieces within two and a half hours of capture.

"All right," Cameron said loudly, startling her into a
jump. He clapped the glass down onto the bedside table.
"Let's get this party started, shall we?" Mouth pursed
in thought, he grabbed the bag off the bed and walked

closer, cradling the camera in one hand as he studied her. "This might be a good place to start."

Molly squinched her eyes into a glare as he dropped the bag and started snapping pictures. Her fear was almost gone now, replaced by anger and disgust.

Ben knew what lust looked like in her eyes. If he did see these pictures, he'd see the truth. Maybe Cameron was planning to e-mail them right away. She tried to cross her fingers, but was pretty sure that nothing actually happened below the cuffs. She glared daggers at Cameron.

"All right," he murmured. "All right, we've got the preliminaries. Now…" Aiming a Cheshire grin at her, he set down the camera and reached into the bag. When he slowly drew his hand out, Molly was not happy to see a big pair of shiny scissors.

"First things first. Let's see those beautiful breasts."

The blades grew longer and more menacing the closer he came. Molly's fear popped back in full force. She tried to shrink into the chair, but the wood refused to absorb her, and she could only pray over and over again that the scissors were not as sharp as they looked.

Cameron crouched beside her and, ignoring her alarmed squeals, began to cut through her brand-new sweater. Waiting to see the white cashmere begin to soak through with red, she was so absorbed in holding her breath and sucking in her stomach that she didn't register the staccato sound drifting up the stairs.

"Oh, for fuck's sake," Cameron sighed. He took two more clips with the scissors and let her sweater fall open. "If that's Lawson again, I'm gonna sue his ass for harassment. Unbelievable."

Ben! It had been Ben downstairs!

Cameron's thumb grazed the top of her right breast, then slid across her cleavage with a more deliberate pressure. "He'll go away," he murmured, seemingly transfixed by the sight of her bra, the ivory lace she'd picked out for Ben. "God, you're beautiful. I've always loved your breasts. I almost hate to share this pretty image, but I'll do anything to keep you, Molly."

The doorbell rang as he was sliding one cold blade of the scissors beneath the little bow between her breasts. *Snip.*

Molly cringed. Her pulse leapt to furious panic. But when she opened her clenched eyes and looked down, her bra was still intact, or nearly so. It wasn't some Wal-Mart special. This baby was reinforced.

"Shit!" Cameron shouted, throwing the scissors at the nearest wall. They gouged out the plaster and fell with a clatter to the oak flooring. "I'll be right back. That racket's gonna drive me fucking mad."

As if that was a long road trip.

Cameron wrenched his shirt on before he tucked something into his waistband and raced out.

The knocking had turned to pounding below, and Molly felt certain to the bottom of her soul that it was Ben. Maybe she hadn't pushed him too far, maybe he didn't believe that she'd invite a smarmy stalker into her bed. Oh, God, if Ben was here to rescue her, she was going to love him for the rest of her life. He'd get his very own personal stalker, complete with unlimited booty calls any time, day or night.

Molly crossed her fingers—or tried to—and closed her eyes to wait for some promising sound to emerge from the silence below.

BEN KEPT HIS PALM low and open, signaling his men to stay hidden. If Cameron had a gun on him as Ben suspected, he didn't want to give the guy any warning that he was about to be arrested. But now panic was beginning to worm through his veins, screaming that something was terribly wrong. He'd been pounding on the door for nearly a full minute, and he wanted to simply kick it down, but if Cameron was upstairs with Molly and he had a weapon...

Jesus, he should have grabbed him when he'd had him alone at the door. But Ben hadn't had his gun, hadn't put a call in to the station, and hadn't known what Cameron had up his sleeve. Hell, all he had to go on right now was a creeping feeling along the sides of his spine; he didn't even have probable cause.

He'd almost given in to the twisting-tight impulse to kick down the door when he heard a thud from inside the house, followed closely by a shouted curse. Hard footsteps actually shook the wood floor of the porch just before the doorknob twisted and the door swung open.

"What the hell do you want?" Cameron yelled.

"I'd like you to step outside for a moment."

"No!" He started to slam the door, but Ben caught it with the palm of his left hand and rested his right hand deliberately on his gun.

"That wasn't a request, Sergeant, that was an order."

Cameron's face mottled red with rage. Even his hair slipped slightly out of place. "Fuck! You!" the man shouted straight at Ben. "I'm busy fucking your girl-friend, *Chief*."

It suddenly all seemed very simple. Ben reached past the threshold, wrapped his fingers around Cameron's throat, and pulled him out the door at the same time he drew his weapon from its holster. He had Cameron against the wall, the gun tucked under his chin, before he'd even stopped shouting.

"Do you have a weapon on you, Sergeant?"

"I'm gonna sue your ass three ways to Sunday!" He didn't look the least bit frightened, which made Ben want to slam the butt of the gun into his straight nose, but there were witnesses, unfortunately.

"Your weapon," he ground out instead.

"The one I use on the job or the one I just used on Molly?"

Ben supposed he should have been glad when Frank said, "Chief," from just behind his back, but he was exceedingly resentful of the warning.

"Pat him down," Ben said instead of "Hold my gun while I kick him into mush against the wall."

Cameron sneered as Ben pressed the muzzle harder and Frank began to pat him down. "You're pitiful," the bastard growled. "She wants a real man. Just accept it."

"Gun," Frank called, confirming what Ben had suspected. As the officer was removing the magazine and ejecting the cartridge, Ben spun Cameron around and slapped him into cuffs before the first curse had left his lips.

"That's my service pistol, asshole. I have a perfect right to carry it."

"And you're legally obligated to reveal its presence to a police officer. I'll read you your rights in a few minutes, Sergeant. Frank, stick him in your truck. Andrew, come with me."

"Chief," Andrew said softly as they stepped into the house. "We're gonna be in a world of hurt if there's nothing going down."

"I know," Ben breathed, not caring in the least. He knew something was wrong with every ounce of instinct he'd developed over his career.

He strained his ears, hearing nothing, wanting to rush through the house and not daring to. For all he knew, Cameron had brought his whole gang with him. It seemed unlikely and unthinkable, but his job was to suspect the worse.

"I'll take upstairs," he said. She was up there. He could feel her as he took the stairs in a slow rush. Her door was second, just after the bathroom. He had the bathroom cleared within a few quick moments and then he was turning, sliding up to the closed door of Molly's room, and there was no sound, none at all, and what did that mean?

Twisting the knob, he breathed deep and slow before he flung it open and entered on a crouch, gun drawn, eyes flying over every inch of the big room.

His gaze caught her even before he heard her muffled squeal. "Oh, Jesus," he croaked. He hadn't known what to expect, but it hadn't been this. Molly tied up and half-naked, eyes pleading and terrified over a white gag.

"Molly, is there anyone in the house besides Cameron?"

She shook her head, and that was the only signal he needed to sprint across the room and kneel at her feet.

"Oh, Molly. Oh, God." He fumbled at the knot of the gag while her eyes filled with bright tears. "I'm sorry," he choked. "I'm so sorry."

He finally got his useless fingers into a crease of the knot and managed to tug it loose. She gasped when he pulled it free, pressed her swollen lips together as she tried to swallow.

"Molly." Framing her face, he met her wild gaze with his own. "We've got him. You're okay. You're safe."

"Take..." She shook her head and tried again to make her broken voice work. "Take these damn shoes off."

Ben shook his head and swallowed the growing lump from his throat. She'd gone over the edge, didn't know what was real. "Shh. It's okay, Molly. I'm here."

"Take these goddamn heels off me, please! *Please!*"

"Okay." There was no point arguing with her in this state, so he reached down and slipped off one red heel and then the other.

"Oh, thank you, Ben. Thank you. Oh, my God, I can't believe you're here. Thank you. I love you. I do. I really do. I'm not saying that because—"

"Just doing my job, ma'am," he said, just to stop all those arrows piercing his heart. He managed to cut through the plastic restraints quickly, but the cuffs were going to be a problem. "I've got to find the keys, Moll.

I'm just going across the room to look. I'll be right back."

He radioed his officers as she nodded, to let them know that he'd found Ms. Jennings and the house was likely clear. "Give me a minute up here," he added, wanting to spare Molly the embarrassment of an audience until he could get her uncuffed and covered up.

Almost calm now—she wasn't dead or unconscious—Ben turned toward the bed to search through the mess there for the tiny key. But when he registered the individual items laid out on the comforter, his gut jumped so hard he thought he might actually puke. Hand shaking, he pressed a palm to his eyes until he felt steady enough to open them again.

A whip, a paddle, a blindfold. Another pair of handcuffs, a black length of tightly woven rope. And that very shiny, very sharp pair of scissors on the floor by her chair.

His gaze touched on each object and then started over again, spinning his brain into a dizzy circle.

"Ben," Molly whispered behind him. That small word snapped him from his daze and he nodded. There. On the bedside table, the handcuff key glinted beneath the lamp.

"It's okay," she was saying as he retrieved the key and returned to her side.

"I'm so sorry. I should never have…" He had to stop talking in order to calm his breath enough to fit the key into the lock. "I'm sorry, Molly. I let him hurt you."

The lock freed with a snick and her arms fell free,

the cuffs still jangling from one wrist. "Oh, shit," she gasped. "That *hurts*."

Ben carefully rubbed each shoulder, kneading his way over the muscles of her back and down her arms until she sighed. As soon as she was able to move her hands to her lap, he stood and grabbed a blanket from the bed to gather her into his shaking arms.

"We need to get you to the doctor."

"No, I'm fine." She pressed her face to his chest, eyes squeezed shut.

"Molly… You're not… He didn't hurt you?"

"Nope. You got here in the nick of time, Chief."

"Oh." He shifted a little closer to the bed. "Oh, thank God." When his knees gave way, he sat hard on the paddle and the other pair of cuffs, and didn't care in the least. All the blood in his body had drawn in, filling up his heart until it felt five times its normal size, beating a giant, broken pulse in his chest.

"Is this all I have to do to get you back in my bed?" Molly whispered. "Get kidnapped and tortured?"

He groaned, "Shut up," and held her tighter, thinking if he got her close enough the fear would retreat.

"Chief," his radio squawked. He just wanted the world to go away, leave them alone, but he was supposed to be a professional, and he'd be damned if was going to screw this case up.

He gave the men the go ahead to come upstairs, then kissed Molly a dozen times on her hair, her forehead. "Sorry, but they're gonna need to process the evidence. Interview you."

"It's fine, as long as I can do it without heels or handcuffs."

"I think that can be arranged."

Despite her jokes, she suddenly started to cry, weeping quietly into his chest while Ben rocked her back and forth.

He'd let this happen to her. His jealousy and anger had caused this as much as anything else. Instead of believing in Molly—bright, warm, joyful Molly—he'd trusted in his fears and the words of a psychotic asshole. He'd never forgive himself for that. Maybe she wouldn't, either.

He could hear his men moving around downstairs, making their way up to the second floor.

It'd be easy to avoid this right now, but he needed to give her the truth. "Molly, I saw Cameron in town, and I didn't stop him."

"I know."

"I listened to his lies, and I bought them."

"Only because of the game I'd been playing, Ben. Pushing you. Trying to make you jealous."

"That's not an excuse," he insisted, but Andrew came through the door then, flinching at the sight of the paraphernalia on the bed, and their conversation was over. Or so he thought.

Molly didn't seem to mind the audience. "You came for me." She pulled slightly away so she could meet his eyes. "Despite everything, you came here and you weren't fooled."

"Almost too late." He lifted her off the bed and carried her out to the second bedroom so that Andrew could begin taking notes and pictures.

"I'm totally going to use this to get you back. What's the point of being tied and gagged if you can't use it for sympathy?"

"Stop it."

"Seriously. I'm gonna have nightmares. Anxiety. I'll need you here to take care of me."

"Molly—"

"Okay, I don't really want your sympathy lovin'. Or maybe I do. I don't know. But please stop being mad at me. I didn't mean to hurt you and, Ben, I need you—"

"Hush. You're being ridiculous."

"Oh. Oh, sorry. I just… Crap." She slumped into him, her body melting into his chest, his lap. She was warm and so fucking alive, and he couldn't imagine that he'd ever given a thought to letting her go.

"I gave up being mad at you a while ago, Molly."

Her hand skittered nervously over his chest, tracing an increasingly smaller oval. "You did? So what, you're just over me now?"

"No."

Her hand stopped.

Ben folded his fingers over hers, noticing the fine texture of her skin, the jagged edges of a broken fingernail. He felt he could spend days touching her, reacquainting his body with hers.

"I can't pretend I wasn't hurt by all this," he started. "We don't have enough time to talk right now, and there's a lot to talk about. A lot. But please say you can't live without me, because…because I'm miserable and I need you."

There. That hadn't been so bad. His voice had barely even squeaked there at the end. No, saying it out loud hadn't been bad.

But when she screamed and pounced on him and slipped her tongue into his mouth just as his men ran into the room with guns drawn? That was pretty bad.

CHAPTER NINETEEN

BEN WATCHED MOLLY bounce up and down in the seat of her brand-new, cherry-red hybrid SUV. "You enjoying yourself there?"

"Yes!" she squealed, hands flexing on the wheel.

"You still want to go up to the cabin? Because you look pretty excited about trying out all those new buttons."

"Mmm," she purred. "Just give me a few minutes. I didn't expect it to be delivered today."

"All right," Ben agreed. "I'll give you some privacy. See you in about half an hour." She was too busy laying her cheek against the steering wheel to respond, so Ben hopped into his own truck and drove toward Main. He had a couple things to do before leaving town.

The first errand was easy enough. A quick check of his office computer confirmed that Cameron had been placed on administrative leave from the Denver PD and his bail hearing set for Tuesday. The charges—home invasion, assault, false imprisonment, menacing—were serious enough that Kasten would never work in law enforcement again, even if he pled them down to more minor offenses.

Molly had confessed that she'd be okay with Cameron getting probation as long as it was accompanied by some serious court-ordered therapy. Ben wasn't feeling quite so generous. In fact, he'd been dreaming of the days when Australia was a penal colony. A few thousand miles seemed a safe distance between Molly and her attacker. But Australia no longer accepted prisoners, at least according to their official Web site, so Ben would have to be satisfied with the few months in jail that Cameron would likely serve. He was also going to do his damnedest to ensure that any probation was served under house arrest, complete with an ankle bracelet locator.

Still, there was nothing to be done this weekend, and Ben was desperate for time alone with Molly. Just one more stop, and then they'd have two days of privacy to renegotiate their relationship. Or just have lots and lots of sex. Either way, he was looking forward to it.

While the computer took its time shutting down, Ben braced himself for his last errand. When he felt in control of his blood pressure, he grabbed a sheet of paper from his desk and headed out the door. A quick walk down Main Street and he was standing in front of the icy steps of Miles Webster's small blue house.

The enclosed front porch served as the offices of the *Tribune,* so Ben didn't bother to knock before entering. Miles's face froze with shock when he looked up at the little bell that chimed, and Ben felt immature satisfaction at the brief flash of nervousness that glinted behind Miles's glasses.

"I already paid that ticket, Ben. The new stickers are on the truck."

"I saw that."

"What do you want then? I had every right to interview Kasten, so I hope you're not here to try to talk me out of printing the story."

Though he felt a vein in his temple begin to throb, Ben gritted his teeth and shook his head. He was done with worrying about Miles and his stories. Done with worrying about gossip. He was done with everything except convincing Molly that her messy life would fit perfectly into his careful world.

"I'm here to take out an ad."

Miles's eyebrows fell so low they must have obscured his vision. "An ad?"

"Yes." Ben handed over the paper with only a twinge of discomfort. "I want this in your next edition. Only the paper copy, not online."

The paper shook a little in Miles's hands, and Ben was surprised to notice how old he was getting. Close to eighty now, but still working hard at the paper, not to mention watching his granddaughter three days a week.

"You're throwing a party?" Miles finally said, disbelief clear in his voice.

"That's right. Molly just landed a huge contract with a new publisher and we're going to celebrate. Party at The Bar. Everyone's invited."

Miles smirked. "These new stories going to be about you, Ben?"

Ben didn't even blink. No, the stories wouldn't be about him. Molly had already promised to keep their private life private. But people would think what they wanted. He couldn't control that, so he wasn't even going to try. "Just be sure you get that in Monday's paper, Miles. I'll see you at the party."

He'd expected to feel slightly sick walking out of there, but instead he felt almost faint with relief. Light. Free.

And totally ready for a date with Holly Summers.

MOLLY HEARD THE booted footsteps approaching down the short hall of the cabin and scooted higher on the bed, squealing just a tiny bit under her breath. Oh, boy. Hoo doggie. Her week was finally about to take a very good turn.

She tugged her short skirt down to an almost-decent length. Not to be decent, of course, but just to hide the fact that she wasn't wearing any panties. *That* was supposed to be a surprise.

Eyes glued to the doorway, Molly waited.

When Ben walked through, she was happy to see that he hadn't obeyed her directions to the letter. He wasn't naked. Instead he wore boots, jeans, and no shirt. And, most importantly, the black hat.

"Ma'am," he said, tipping his hat. Molly almost swooned. Those muscled shoulders, that flat, hair-dusted belly. All of it framed against the rough wood logs of the bedroom wall. He should have been the cover model for *The Wicked West*.

Mouth dry, she had to swallow before she could speak. "You're sure you're not doing this out of guilt?" Not that it mattered, really.

"Guilt?" Chocolate eyes swept down her legs, pushing heat along her skin. "If so, this is the first time I've ever had a guilt hard-on."

"Your first? Ooo, I'll take it!"

He touched two fingers to his hat in a little salute. "At your service, ma'am."

She hoped he didn't hear the way her breath hitched in her throat. Really, it was almost embarrassing how much this was turning her on.

The air in the room flashed hot when he toed off his boots and reached for the button of his jeans. She almost told him to tamp down the fire before she realized he'd never lit the fireplace.

Urging him on with her eyes, she licked her dry lips, clenching her hands in the covers. Ben smiled.

"I've been thinking," he drawled.

No! No thinking. "Zipper," she rasped. She wanted him totally naked, totally aroused, wearing nothing but a wicked look and that hat.

"You know, Brenda was stalking you, but she wasn't the only stalker."

"Uh-huh." The outline of his amazing erection pressed against the rough denim, teasing her.

"So, actually, we were both right."

What was with all the talking? Hadn't she suffered enough this week? "Sure. Whatever. Drop the jeans, Sheriff. I mean, uh, Chief."

His smiled widened, but not to happiness. No, it widened to something wicked and depraved. "So I've been thinking… We both lost that bet. Or, actually, we both won. Ma'am."

She finally managed to swim up from her stupor long

enough to get what he was saying. "Oh? You mean… ohhhh…"

He stalked closer, like a big cougar, and stopped in front of the duffel bag that sat on the bed. After tugging the zipper open, he cut his eyes toward her in a silent order, and Molly thought she might shiver to an orgasm right there.

"Not meaning to be disrespectful, ma'am," he drawled. "But you owe me a show."

Her thighs tightened in a pleasurable spasm, and she could feel how wet she was, how slick and hot. She'd do anything for him. Anything. "And what if I refuse?"

"Well, then." When he hooked his thumbs into the pockets of his jeans, his pecs flexed and bunched, and the denim stretched tighter across his cock. "We've got ways of dealing with cheats in this town, ma'am."

There was really no point in playing coy when he could clearly hear her panting, so Molly reached into the bag and pulled out her toy. "Is this what you're looking for, cowboy?"

"Yes, ma'am. I believe it is."

"And this?" Fighting a smile of anticipation, Molly pulled one knee up, knowing he'd get a tiny glimpse of what he wanted.

He swallowed hard, losing a bit of his cool. "Yes, ma'am."

"Then take off those jeans and give me some inspiration to work with."

For a cocky cowboy sheriff, he followed directions well. He unzipped his jeans and slipped the rest of his clothing off, revealing the hard, thick erection she'd missed for what seemed like months. Then he pulled the brim of the hat a little lower, so all she could see was the glitter of his eyes and that promising smile. And the impossibly wide chest and trim hips and defined thighs. And that cock. Her mouth watered. But she'd have to wait for that.

Molly shimmied lower on the bed, parting her thighs to push her skirt higher, not missing the way his dick jumped at the sight.

She meant to honor the spirit of the bet, she really did, but at this point things were totally out of her control. Ben told her exactly what he wanted her to do with Little Blue, and his harsh, dirty words proved her undoing. Her show reached its big finale in a grand total of forty-five seconds.

Lucky for her, Ben's part of the performance went on for at least half an hour. And he promised to reprise it for her every day for as many years as she wanted.

And Molly definitely wanted.

* * * * *

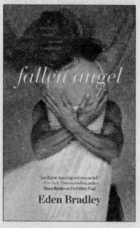

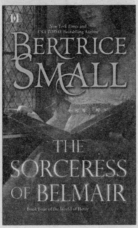

An angel poised on the brink of destruction.

New York Times bestselling author

GENA SHOWALTER

is back with a dark, seductive new series....

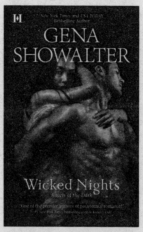

Leader of the most powerful army in the heavens, Zacharel has been deemed nearly too dangerous, too ruthless—and if he isn't careful, he'll lose his wings. But this warrior with a heart of ice will not be deterred from his missions at any cost…until a vulnerable human tempts him with a carnal pleasure he's never known before.

Wicked Nights

Available now.

www.Harlequin.com

A heartfelt and classic collection from
#1 *New York Times* bestselling author

NORA ROBERTS

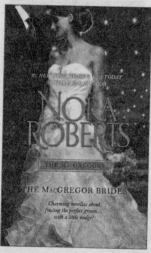

Meet the next generation of the beloved MacGregor family,
as cousins Laura, Gwendolyn and Julia discover that their
busybody grandfather has an unerring instinct for love!

THE MACGREGOR BRIDES

Available now.

REQUEST YOUR FREE BOOKS!

2 FREE NOVELS
FROM THE ROMANCE COLLECTION
PLUS 2 FREE GIFTS!

YES! Please send me 2 FREE novels from the Romance Collection and my 2 FREE gifts (gifts are worth about $10). After receiving them, if I don't wish to receive any more books, I can return the shipping statement marked "cancel." If I don't cancel, I will receive 4 brand-new novels every month and be billed just $5.99 per book in the U.S. or $6.49 per book in Canada. That's a saving of at least 25% off the cover price. It's quite a bargain! Shipping and handling is just 50¢ per book in the U.S. and 75¢ per book in Canada.* I understand that accepting the 2 free books and gifts places me under no obligation to buy anything. I can always return a shipment and cancel at any time. Even if I never buy another book, the two free books and gifts are mine to keep forever.

194/394 MDN FELQ

Name _____ (PLEASE PRINT) _____

Address _____ Apt. #

City _____ State/Prov. _____ Zip/Postal Code

Signature (if under 18, a parent or guardian must sign)

Mail to the **Reader Service:**
IN U.S.A.: P.O. Box 1867, Buffalo, NY 14240-1867
IN CANADA: P.O. Box 609, Fort Erie, Ontario L2A 5X3

Not valid for current subscribers to the Romance Collection
or the Romance/Suspense Collection.

**Want to try two free books from another line?
Call 1-800-873-8635 or visit www.ReaderService.com.**

* Terms and prices subject to change without notice. Prices do not include applicable taxes. Sales tax applicable in N.Y. Canadian residents will be charged applicable taxes. Offer not valid in Quebec. This offer is limited to one order per household. All orders subject to credit approval. Credit or debit balances in a customer's account(s) may be offset by any other outstanding balance owed by or to the customer. Please allow 4 to 6 weeks for delivery. Offer available while quantities last.

Your Privacy—The Reader Service is committed to protecting your privacy. Our Privacy Policy is available online at www.ReaderService.com or upon request from the Reader Service.

We make a portion of our mailing list available to reputable third parties that offer products we believe may interest you. If you prefer that we not exchange your name with third parties, or if you wish to clarify or modify your communication preferences, please visit us at www.ReaderService.com/consumerschoice or write to us at Reader Service Preference Service, P.O. Box 9062, Buffalo, NY 14269. Include your complete name and address.

ROM11

VICTORIA DAHL

77609 REAL MEN WILL	__$7.99 U.S.	__$9.99 CAN.
77602 BAD BOYS DO	__$7.99 U.S.	__$9.99 CAN.
77595 GOOD GIRLS DON'T	__$7.99 U.S.	__$9.99 CAN.

(limited quantities available)

TOTAL AMOUNT	$ _____
POSTAGE & HANDLING	$ _____
($1.00 FOR 1 BOOK, 50¢ for each additional)	
APPLICABLE TAXES*	$ _____
TOTAL PAYABLE	$ _____

(check or money order—please do not send cash)

To order, complete this form and send it, along with a check or money order for the total above, payable to HQN Books, to: **In the U.S.:** 3010 Walden Avenue, P.O. Box 9077, Buffalo, NY 14269-9077; **In Canada:** P.O. Box 636, Fort Erie, Ontario, L2A 5X3.

Name: _____

Address: _____ City: _____

State/Prov.: _____ Zip/Postal Code: _____

Account Number (if applicable): _____

075 CSAS

*New York residents remit applicable sales taxes.
*Canadian residents remit applicable GST and provincial taxes.

HARLEQUIN® HQN™
www.Harlequin.com

PHVD0712BL